the Archie® DIGEST LIBRARY

Archie®

– in –

Jet-Ski Scandal

Spotlight

visit us at
www.abdopublishing.com

Exclusive Spotlight library bound edition published in 2007 by Spotlight, a division of ABDO Publishing Group, Edina, Minnesota. Spotlight produces high quality reinforced library bound editions for schools and libraries. Published by agreement with Archie Comic Publications, Inc.

Library of Congress Cataloging-in-Publication Data

Archie in Jet-ski scandal / edited by Nelson Ribeiro & Victor Gorelick.
    p. cm. -- (The Archie digest library)
   Revision of issue no. 182 (Sept. 2001) of Archie digest magazine.
   ISBN-13: 978-1-59961-259-1
   ISBN-10: 1-59961-259-3
   1. Comic books, strips, etc. I. Ribeiro, Nelson. II. Gorelick, Victor. III. Archie digest magazine. 182. IV. Title: Jet-ski scandal.

PN6728.A 72A69 2007
741.5'973--dc22

               2006050553

All Spotlight books are reinforced library binding and manufactured in the United States of America.

Contents

Archie

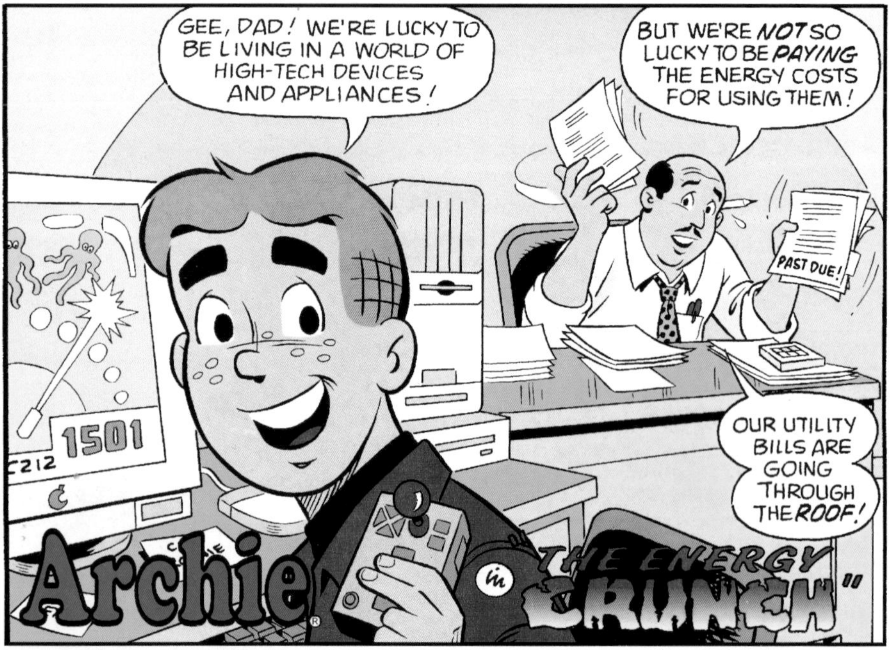
GEE, DAD! WE'RE LUCKY TO BE LIVING IN A WORLD OF HIGH-TECH DEVICES AND APPLIANCES!
BUT WE'RE *NOT* SO LUCKY TO BE *PAYING* THE ENERGY COSTS FOR USING THEM!
PAST DUE!
1501
C212
OUR UTILITY BILLS ARE GOING THROUGH THE *ROOF*!
Archie in "THE ENERGY CRUNCH"

SCRIPT: GEROGE GLADIR PENCILS: ERNIE COLON INKS: JON D'AGOSTINO
COLORS: BARRY GROSSMAN LETTERS: BILL YOSHIDA
EDITORS: NELSON RIBEIRO & VICTOR GORELICK EDITOR-IN-CHIEF: RICHARD GOLDWATER

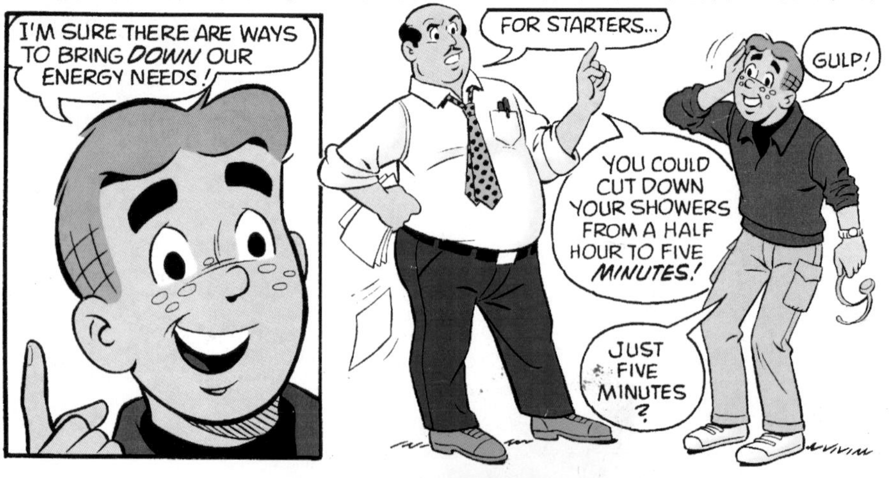
I'M SURE THERE ARE WAYS TO BRING *DOWN* OUR ENERGY NEEDS!
FOR STARTERS...
GULP!
YOU COULD CUT DOWN YOUR SHOWERS FROM A HALF HOUR TO FIVE *MINUTES*!
JUST FIVE MINUTES?

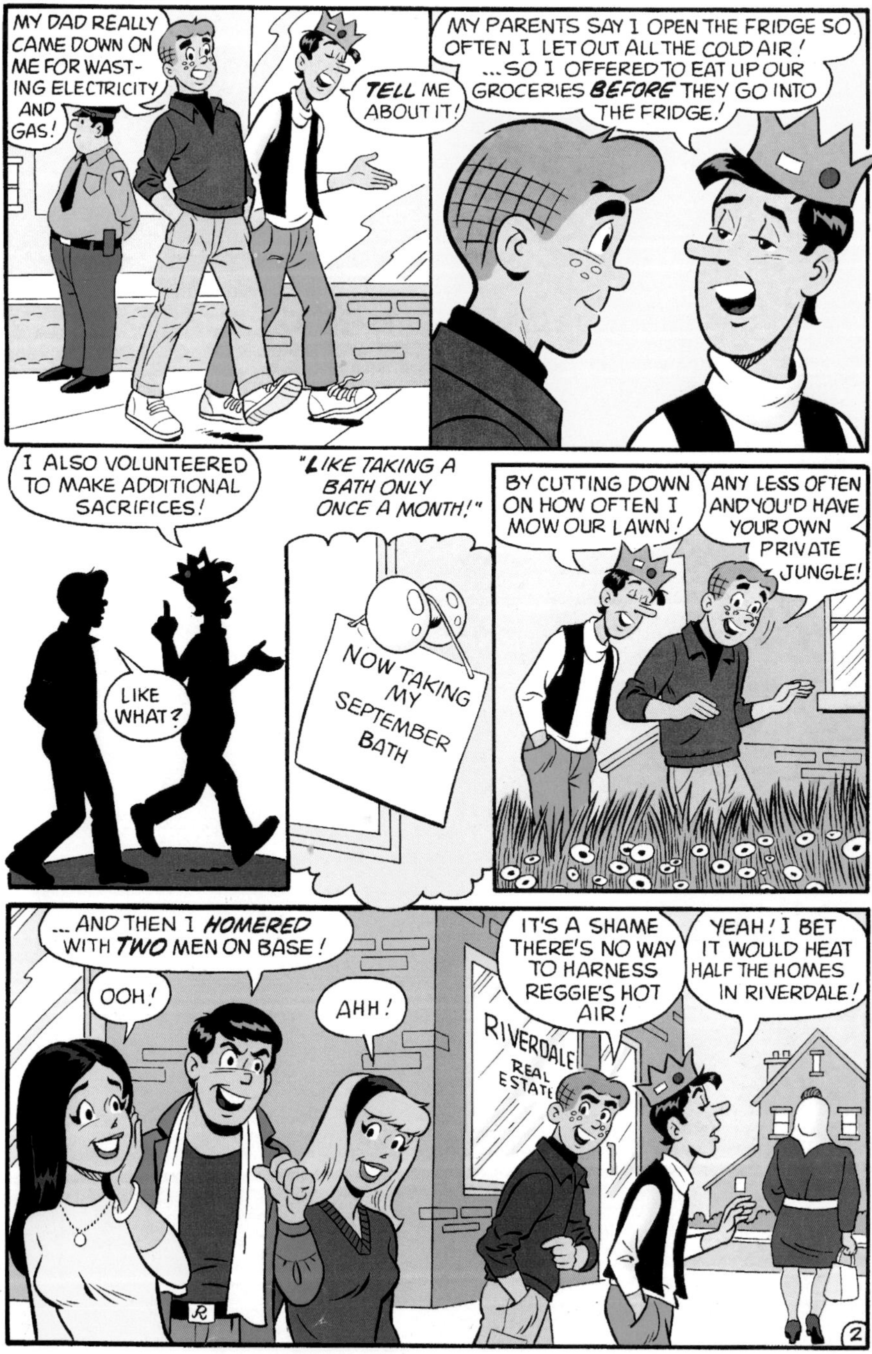
MY DAD REALLY CAME DOWN ON ME FOR WASTING ELECTRICITY AND GAS!
TELL ME ABOUT IT!
MY PARENTS SAY I OPEN THE FRIDGE SO OFTEN I LET OUT ALL THE COLD AIR! ...SO I OFFERED TO EAT UP OUR GROCERIES BEFORE THEY GO INTO THE FRIDGE!
I ALSO VOLUNTEERED TO MAKE ADDITIONAL SACRIFICES!
LIKE WHAT?
"LIKE TAKING A BATH ONLY ONCE A MONTH!"
NOW TAKING MY SEPTEMBER BATH
BY CUTTING DOWN ON HOW OFTEN I MOW OUR LAWN!
ANY LESS OFTEN AND YOU'D HAVE YOUR OWN PRIVATE JUNGLE!
... AND THEN I HOMERED WITH TWO MEN ON BASE!
OOH!
AHH!
IT'S A SHAME THERE'S NO WAY TO HARNESS REGGIE'S HOT AIR!
YEAH! I BET IT WOULD HEAT HALF THE HOMES IN RIVERDALE!
RIVERDALE REAL ESTATE
2

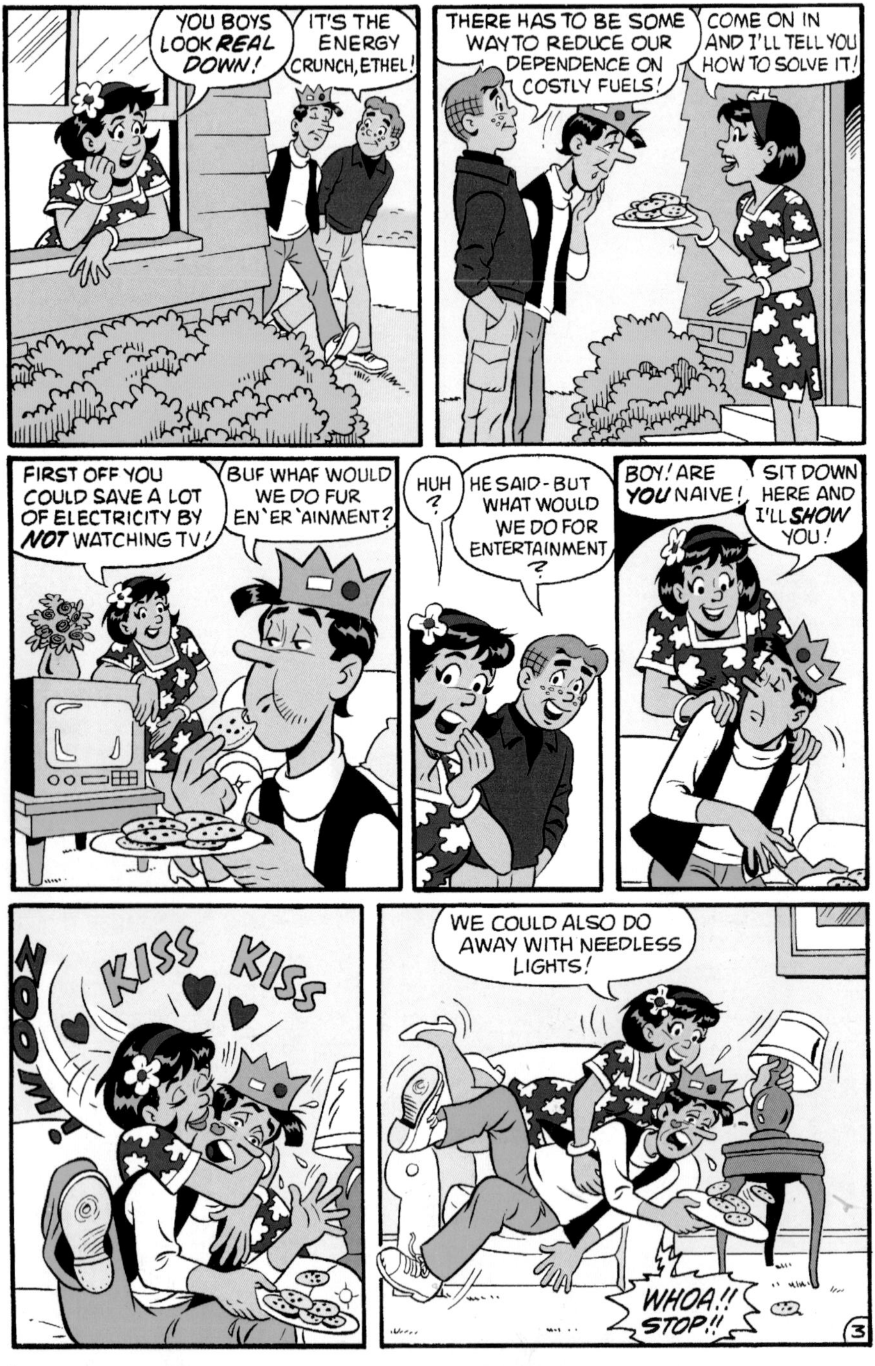

YOU BOYS LOOK REAL DOWN!
IT'S THE ENERGY CRUNCH, ETHEL!
THERE HAS TO BE SOME WAY TO REDUCE OUR DEPENDENCE ON COSTLY FUELS!
COME ON IN AND I'LL TELL YOU HOW TO SOLVE IT!
FIRST OFF YOU COULD SAVE A LOT OF ELECTRICITY BY NOT WATCHING TV!
BUF WHAF WOULD WE DO FUR EN`ER`AINMENT?
HUH?
HE SAID-BUT WHAT WOULD WE DO FOR ENTERTAINMENT?
BOY! ARE YOU NAIVE!
SIT DOWN HERE AND I'LL SHOW YOU!
ZOOM!
KISS KISS
WE COULD ALSO DO AWAY WITH NEEDLESS LIGHTS!
WHOA!! STOP!!
3

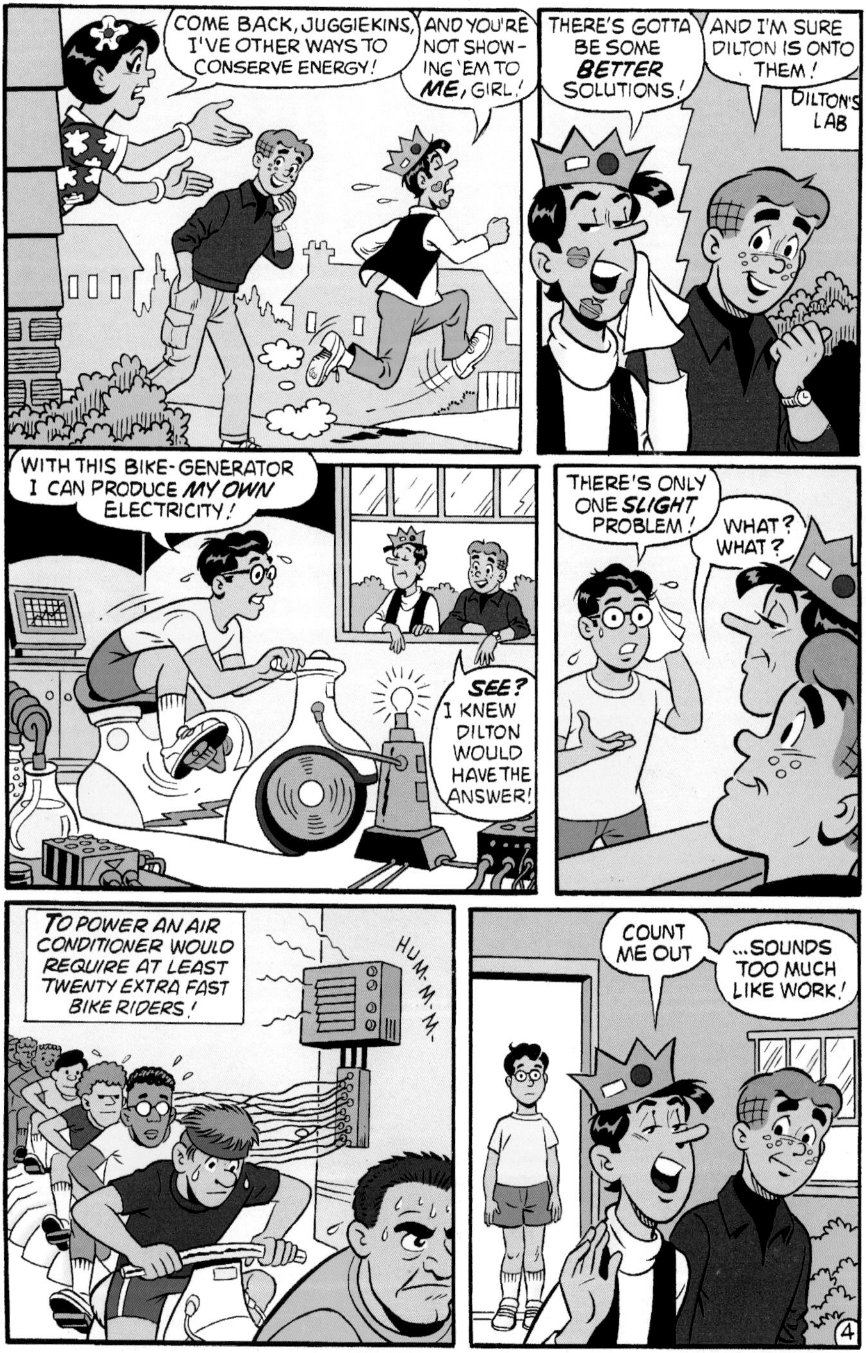
COME BACK, JUGGIEKINS, I'VE OTHER WAYS TO CONSERVE ENERGY!
AND YOU'RE NOT SHOWING 'EM TO ME, GIRL!
THERE'S GOTTA BE SOME BETTER SOLUTIONS!
AND I'M SURE DILTON IS ONTO THEM!
DILTON'S LAB
WITH THIS BIKE-GENERATOR I CAN PRODUCE MY OWN ELECTRICITY!
SEE? I KNEW DILTON WOULD HAVE THE ANSWER!
THERE'S ONLY ONE SLIGHT PROBLEM!
WHAT? WHAT?
TO POWER AN AIR CONDITIONER WOULD REQUIRE AT LEAST TWENTY EXTRA FAST BIKE RIDERS!
HUM-M-M
COUNT ME OUT
...SOUNDS TOO MUCH LIKE WORK!
4

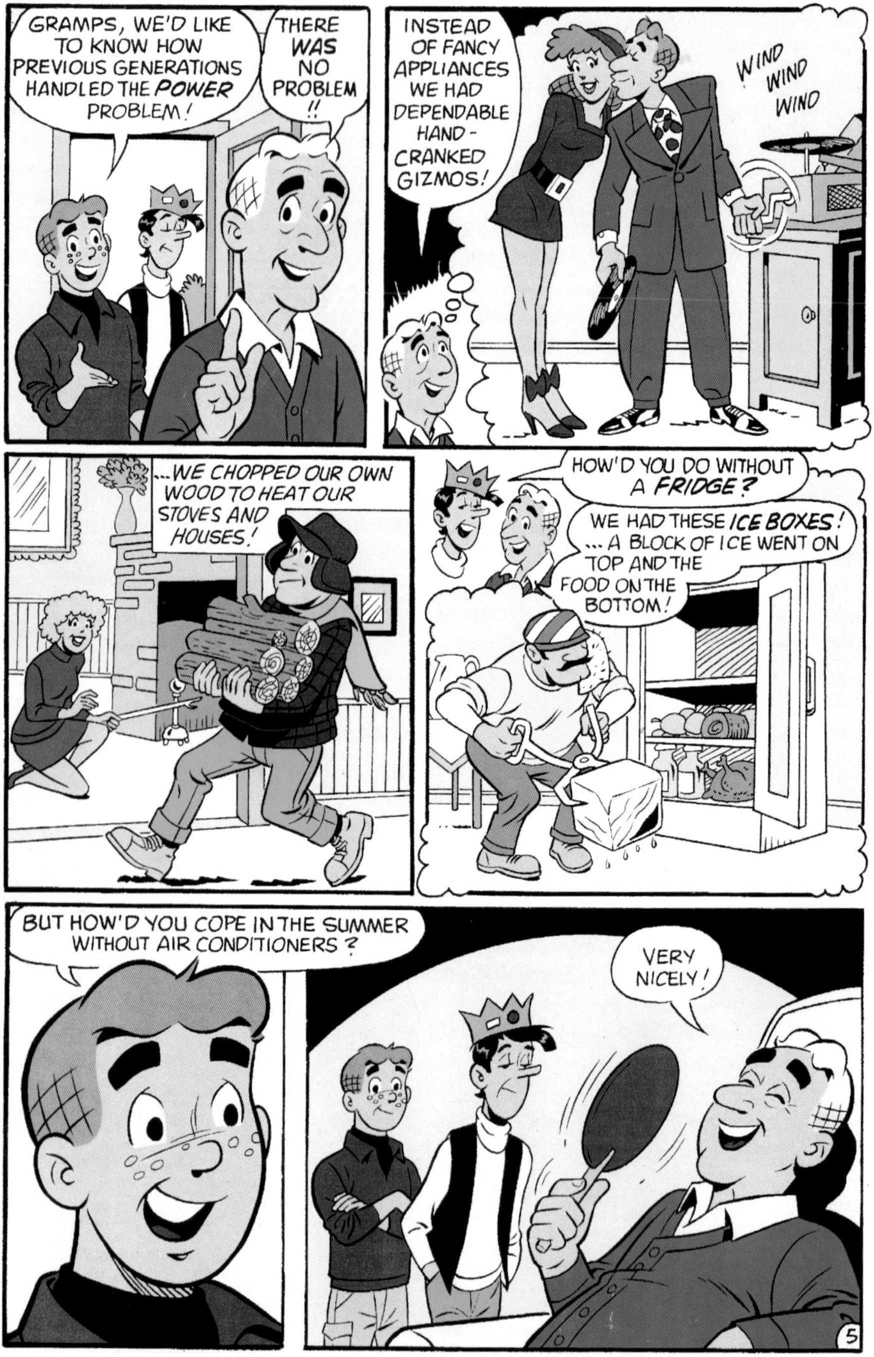
GRAMPS, WE'D LIKE TO KNOW HOW PREVIOUS GENERATIONS HANDLED THE POWER PROBLEM!
THERE WAS NO PROBLEM !!
INSTEAD OF FANCY APPLIANCES WE HAD DEPENDABLE HAND-CRANKED GIZMOS!
WIND WIND WIND
...WE CHOPPED OUR OWN WOOD TO HEAT OUR STOVES AND HOUSES!
HOW'D YOU DO WITHOUT A FRIDGE?
WE HAD THESE ICE BOXES! ... A BLOCK OF ICE WENT ON TOP AND THE FOOD ON THE BOTTOM!
BUT HOW'D YOU COPE IN THE SUMMER WITHOUT AIR CONDITIONERS?
VERY NICELY!
5

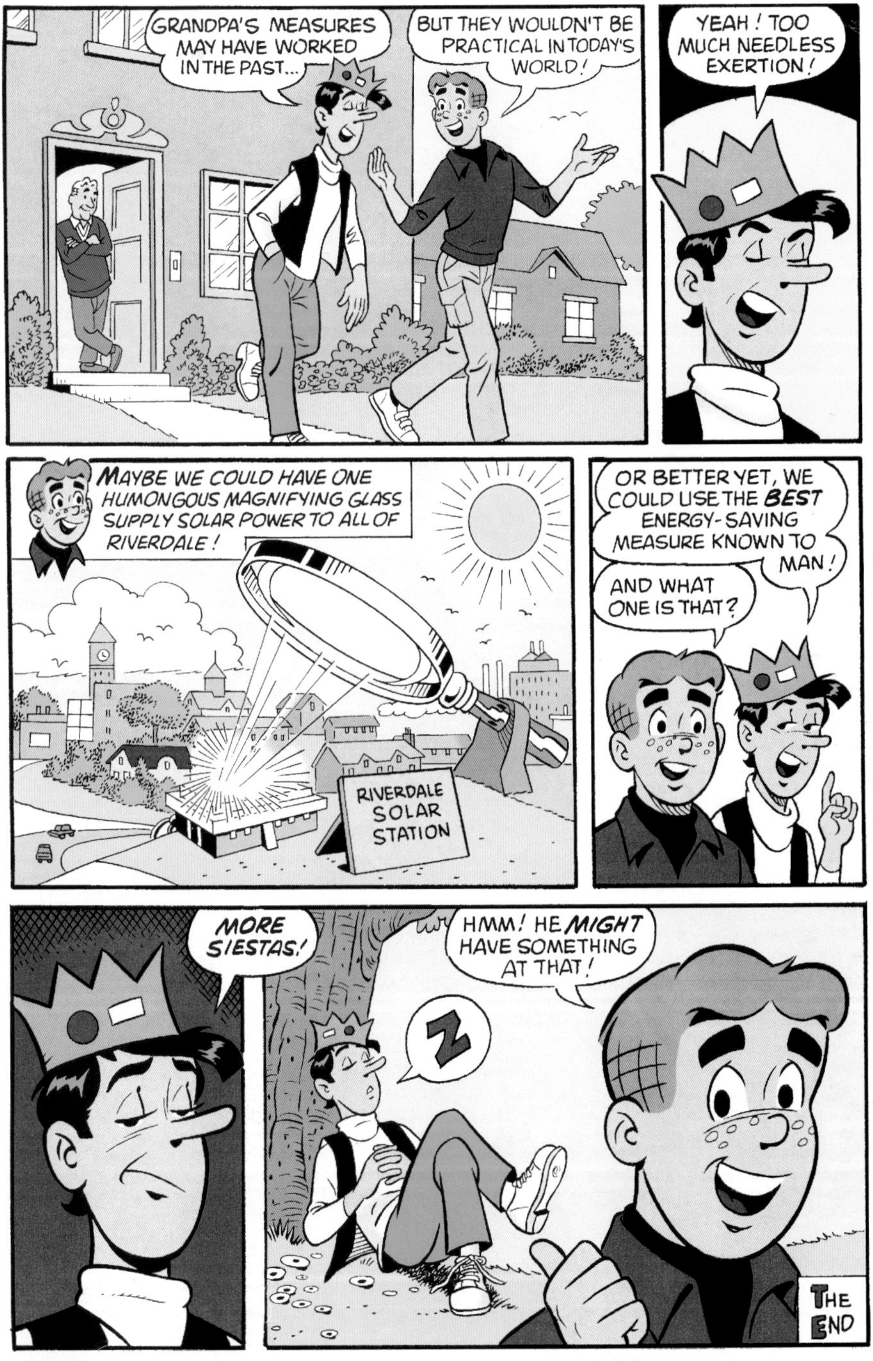
GRANDPA'S MEASURES MAY HAVE WORKED IN THE PAST...
BUT THEY WOULDN'T BE PRACTICAL IN TODAY'S WORLD!
YEAH! TOO MUCH NEEDLESS EXERTION!
MAYBE WE COULD HAVE ONE HUMONGOUS MAGNIFYING GLASS SUPPLY SOLAR POWER TO ALL OF RIVERDALE!
RIVERDALE SOLAR STATION
OR BETTER YET, WE COULD USE THE BEST ENERGY-SAVING MEASURE KNOWN TO MAN!
AND WHAT ONE IS THAT?
MORE SIESTAS!
HMM! HE MIGHT HAVE SOMETHING AT THAT!
Z
THE END

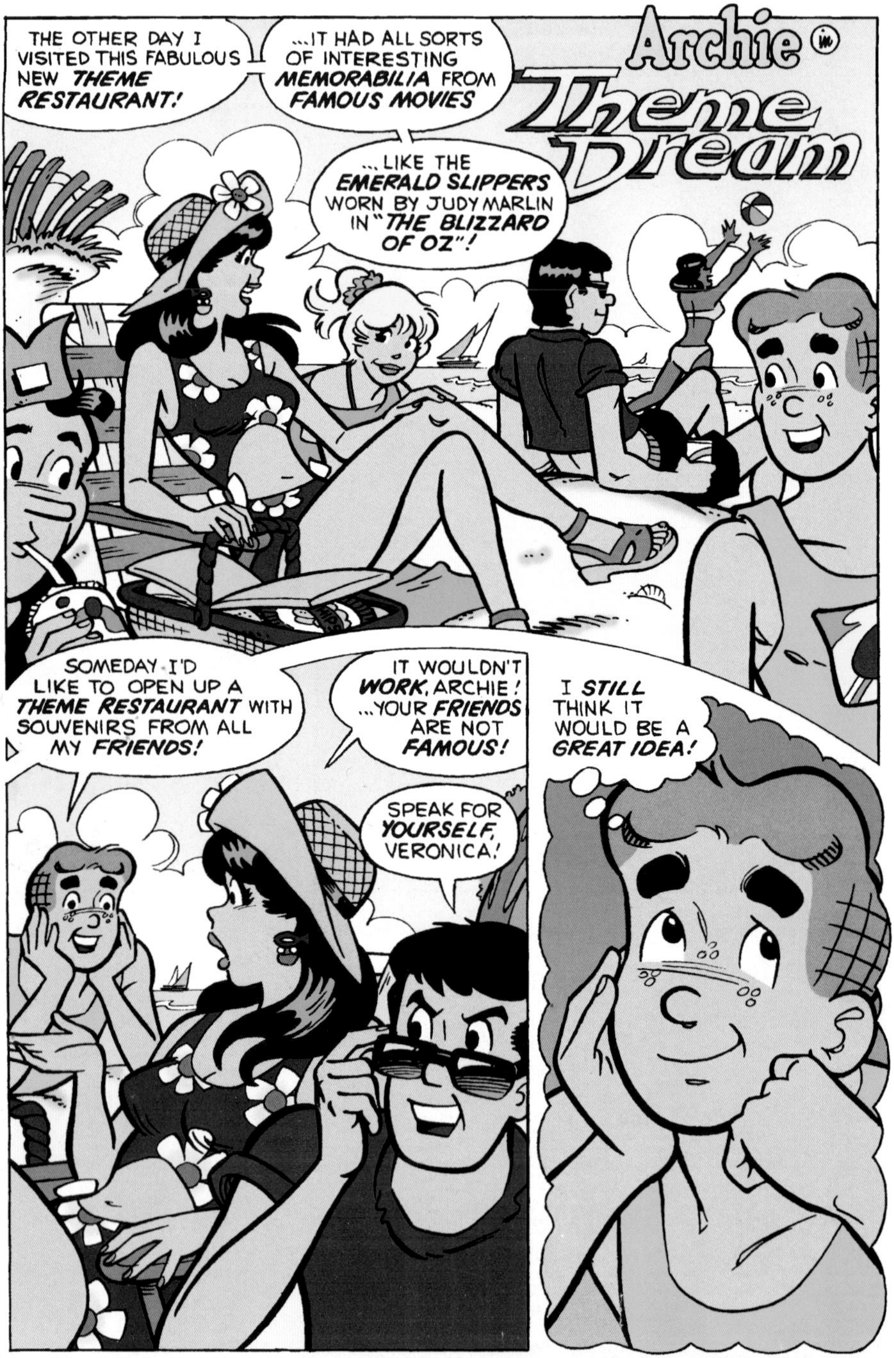
Archie in
Theme Dream
THE OTHER DAY I VISITED THIS FABULOUS NEW THEME RESTAURANT!
...IT HAD ALL SORTS OF INTERESTING MEMORABILIA FROM FAMOUS MOVIES
...LIKE THE EMERALD SLIPPERS WORN BY JUDY MARLIN IN "THE BLIZZARD OF OZ"!
SOMEDAY I'D LIKE TO OPEN UP A THEME RESTAURANT WITH SOUVENIRS FROM ALL MY FRIENDS!
IT WOULDN'T WORK, ARCHIE! ...YOUR FRIENDS ARE NOT FAMOUS!
SPEAK FOR YOURSELF, VERONICA!
I STILL THINK IT WOULD BE A GREAT IDEA!

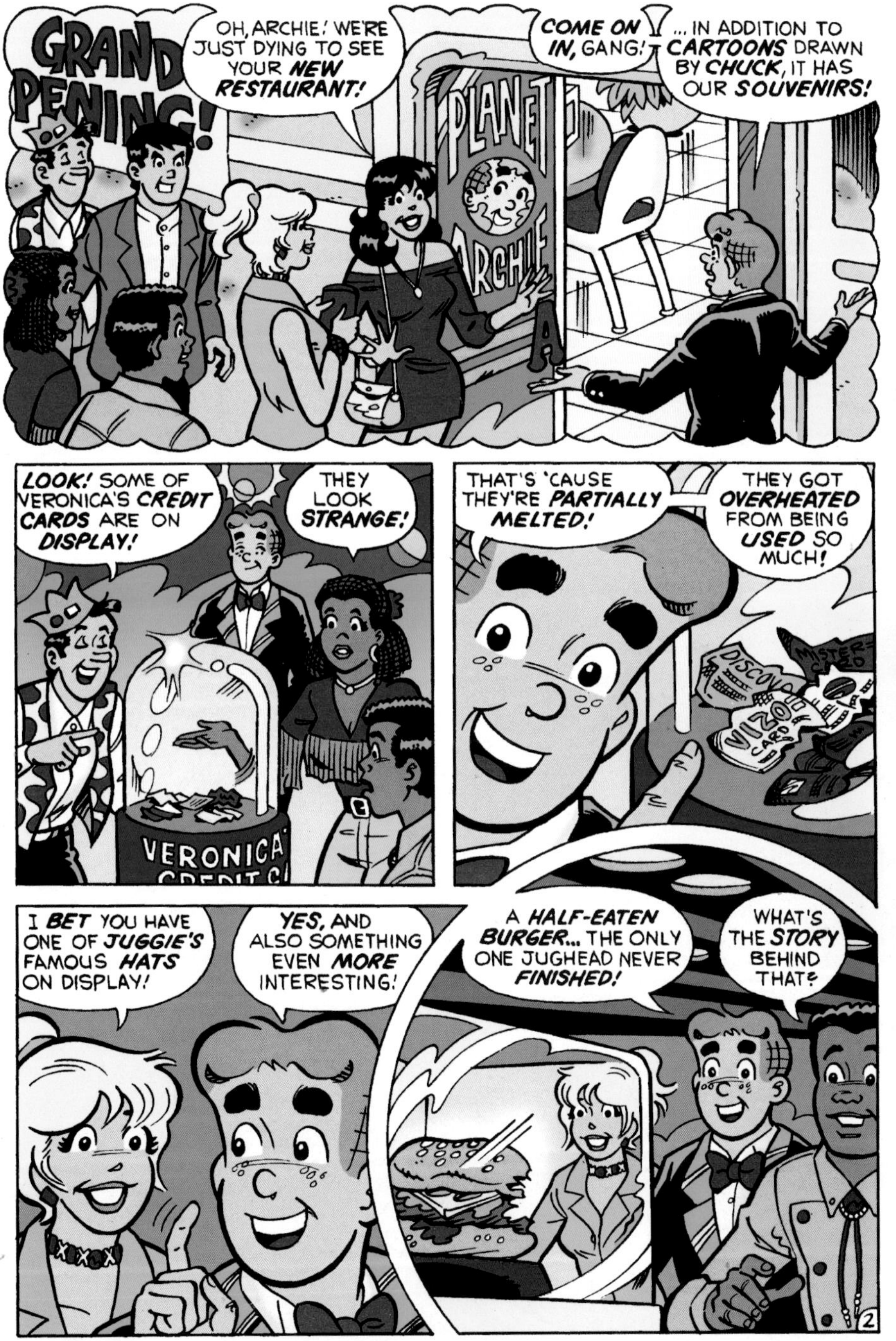
GRAND OPENING!
OH, ARCHIE! WE'RE JUST DYING TO SEE YOUR NEW RESTAURANT!
PLANET ARCHIE
COME ON IN, GANG!
... IN ADDITION TO CARTOONS DRAWN BY CHUCK, IT HAS OUR SOUVENIRS!
LOOK! SOME OF VERONICA'S CREDIT CARDS ARE ON DISPLAY!
THEY LOOK STRANGE!
VERONICA'
THAT'S 'CAUSE THEY'RE PARTIALLY MELTED!
THEY GOT OVERHEATED FROM BEING USED SO MUCH!
I BET YOU HAVE ONE OF JUGGIE'S FAMOUS HATS ON DISPLAY!
YES, AND ALSO SOMETHING EVEN MORE INTERESTING!
A HALF-EATEN BURGER... THE ONLY ONE JUGHEAD NEVER FINISHED!
WHAT'S THE STORY BEHIND THAT?
2

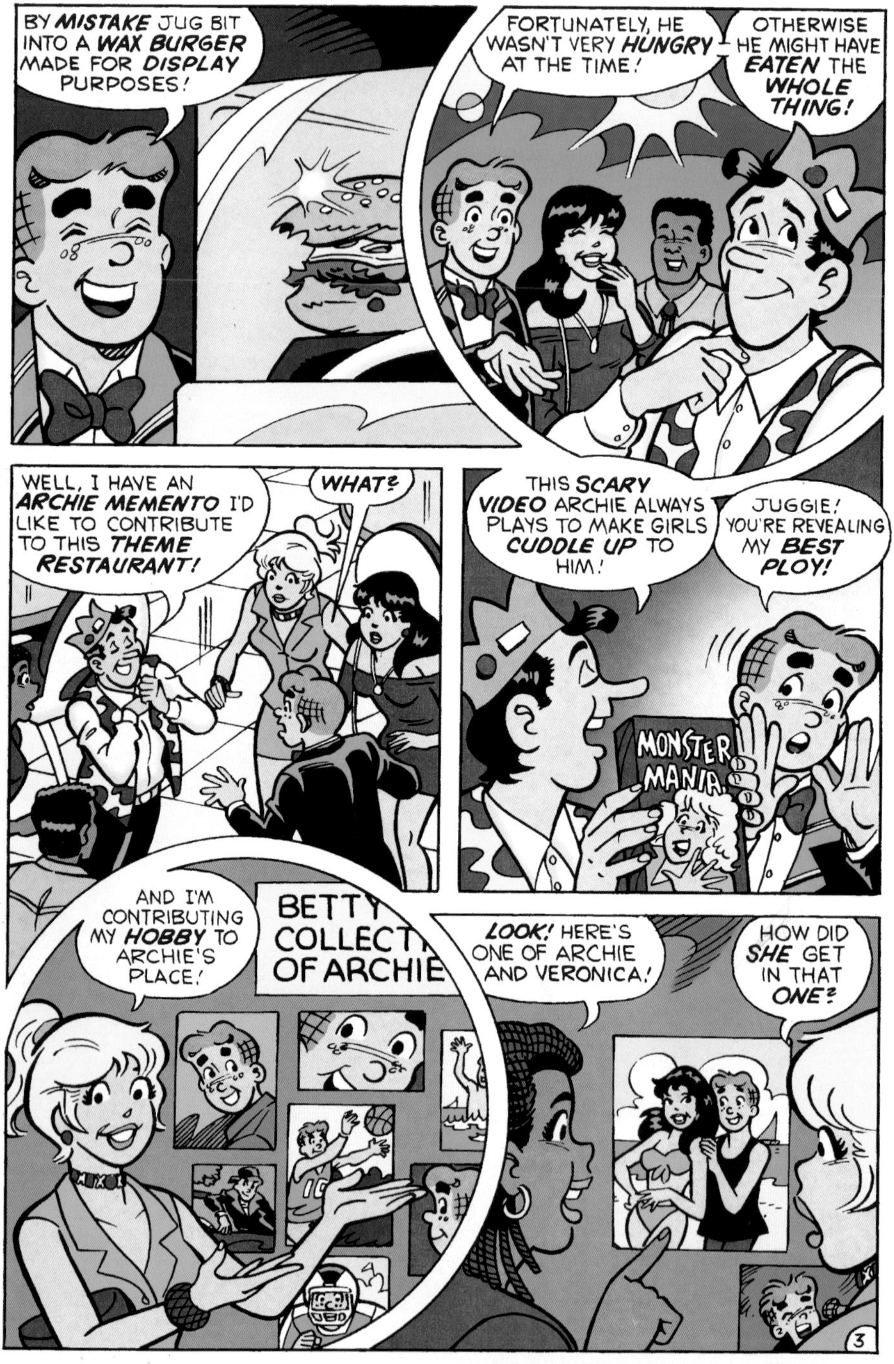
BY MISTAKE JUG BIT INTO A WAX BURGER MADE FOR DISPLAY PURPOSES!
FORTUNATELY, HE WASN'T VERY HUNGRY AT THE TIME!
OTHERWISE HE MIGHT HAVE EATEN THE WHOLE THING!
WELL, I HAVE AN ARCHIE MEMENTO I'D LIKE TO CONTRIBUTE TO THIS THEME RESTAURANT!
WHAT?
THIS SCARY VIDEO ARCHIE ALWAYS PLAYS TO MAKE GIRLS CUDDLE UP TO HIM!
JUGGIE! YOU'RE REVEALING MY BEST PLOY!
MONSTER MANIA
AND I'M CONTRIBUTING MY HOBBY TO ARCHIE'S PLACE!
BETTY COLLECT OF ARCHIE
LOOK! HERE'S ONE OF ARCHIE AND VERONICA!
HOW DID SHE GET IN THAT ONE?
3

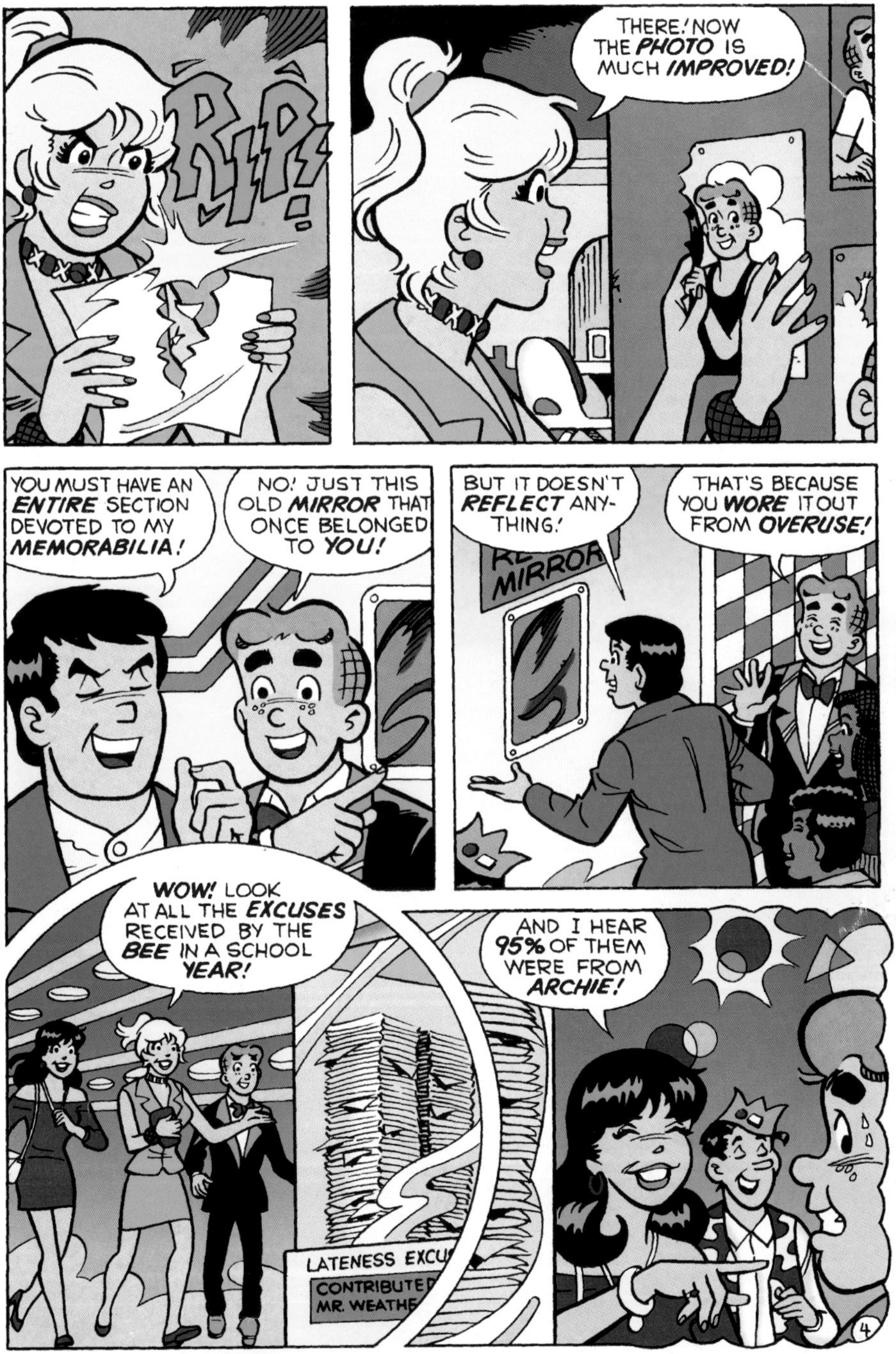
RIP!
THERE! NOW THE PHOTO IS MUCH IMPROVED!
YOU MUST HAVE AN ENTIRE SECTION DEVOTED TO MY MEMORABILIA!
NO! JUST THIS OLD MIRROR THAT ONCE BELONGED TO YOU!
BUT IT DOESN'T REFLECT ANYTHING!
MIRROR
THAT'S BECAUSE YOU WORE IT OUT FROM OVERUSE!
WOW! LOOK AT ALL THE EXCUSES RECEIVED BY THE BEE IN A SCHOOL YEAR!
LATENESS EXCU
CONTRIBUTED
MR. WEATHE
AND I HEAR 95% OF THEM WERE FROM ARCHIE!
4

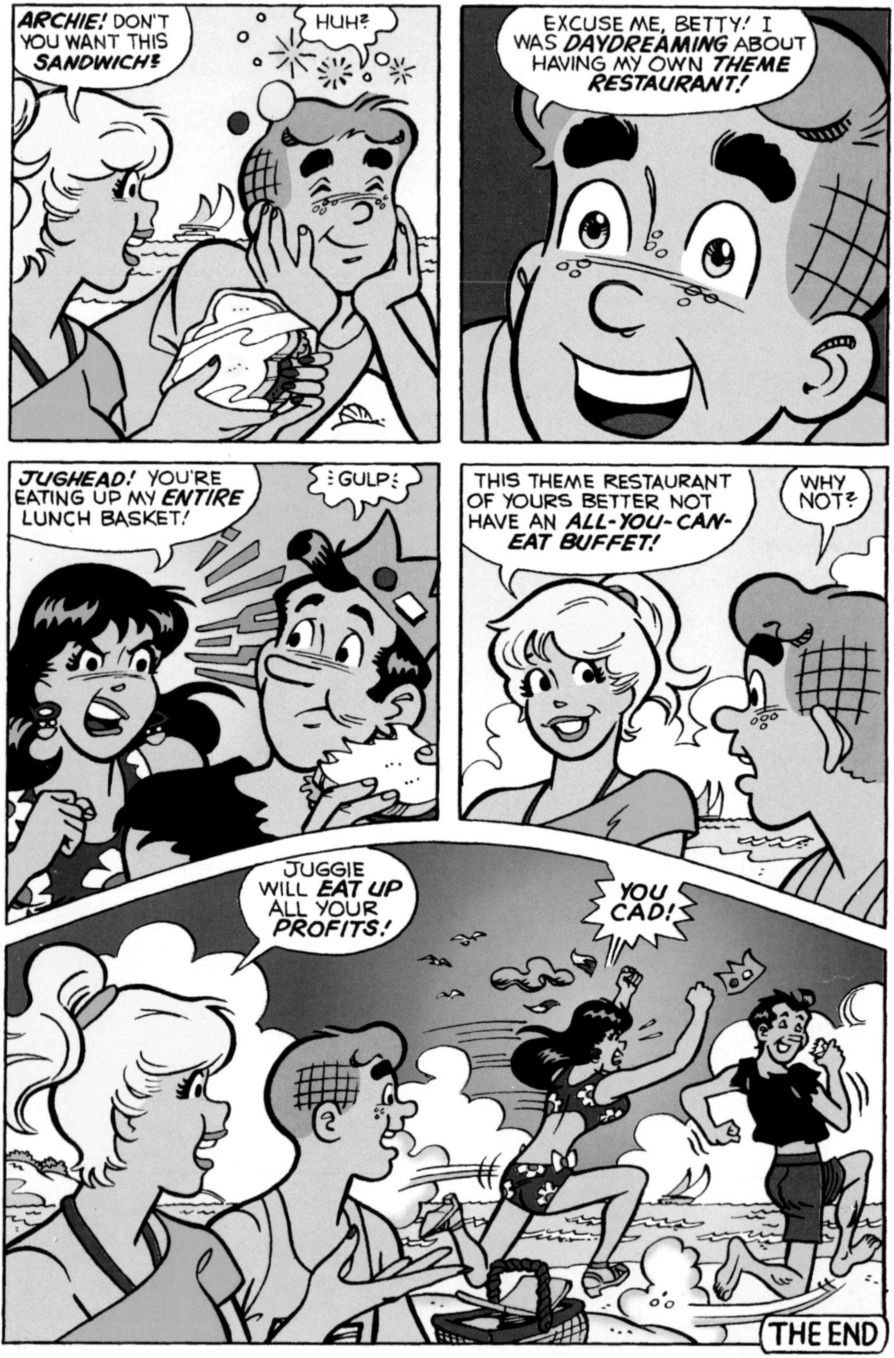
ARCHIE! DON'T YOU WANT THIS SANDWICH?
HUH?
EXCUSE ME, BETTY! I WAS DAYDREAMING ABOUT HAVING MY OWN THEME RESTAURANT!
JUGHEAD! YOU'RE EATING UP MY ENTIRE LUNCH BASKET!
GULP
THIS THEME RESTAURANT OF YOURS BETTER NOT HAVE AN ALL-YOU-CAN-EAT BUFFET!
WHY NOT?
JUGGIE WILL EAT UP ALL YOUR PROFITS!
YOU CAD!
THE END

Archie in "Mr. Softie"

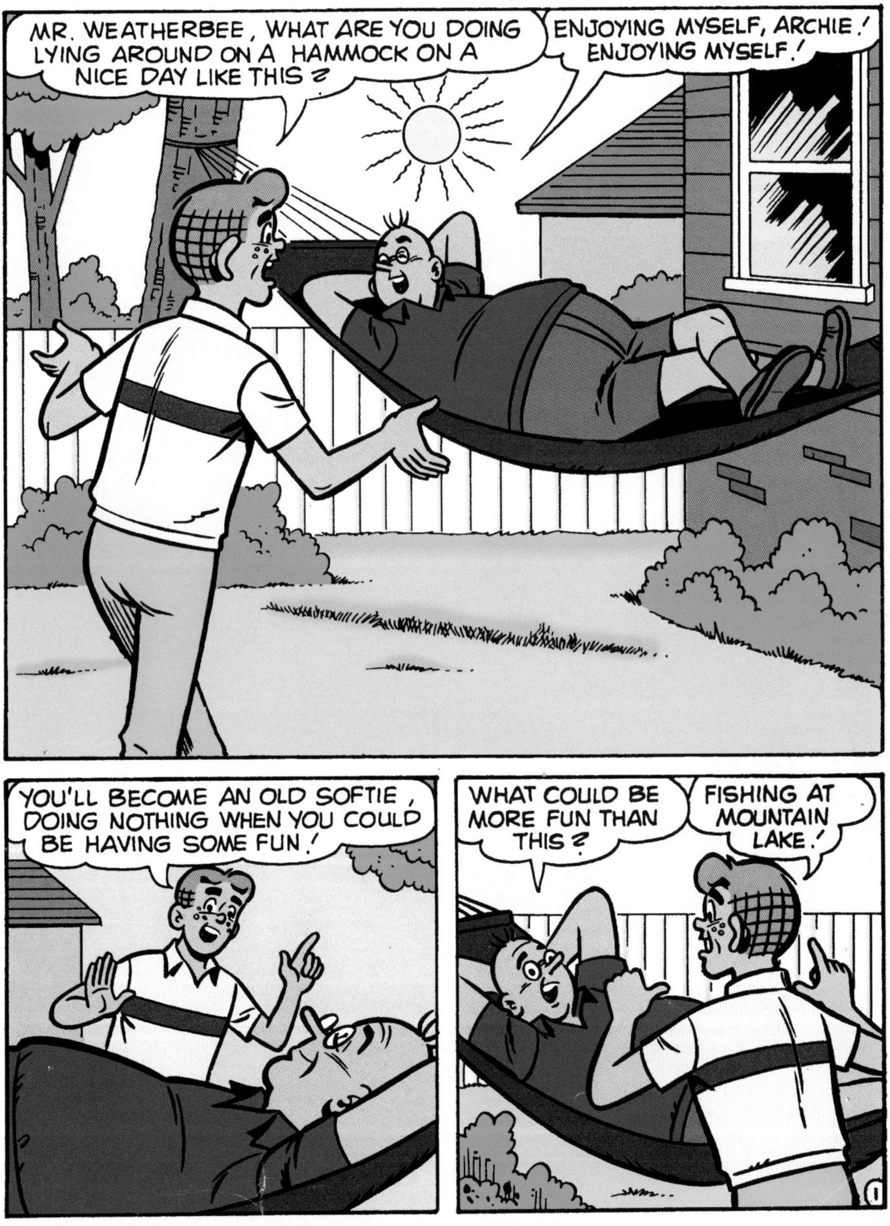
MR. WEATHERBEE, WHAT ARE YOU DOING LYING AROUND ON A HAMMOCK ON A NICE DAY LIKE THIS?
ENJOYING MYSELF, ARCHIE! ENJOYING MYSELF!
YOU'LL BECOME AN OLD SOFTIE, DOING NOTHING WHEN YOU COULD BE HAVING SOME FUN!
WHAT COULD BE MORE FUN THAN THIS?
FISHING AT MOUNTAIN LAKE!
1

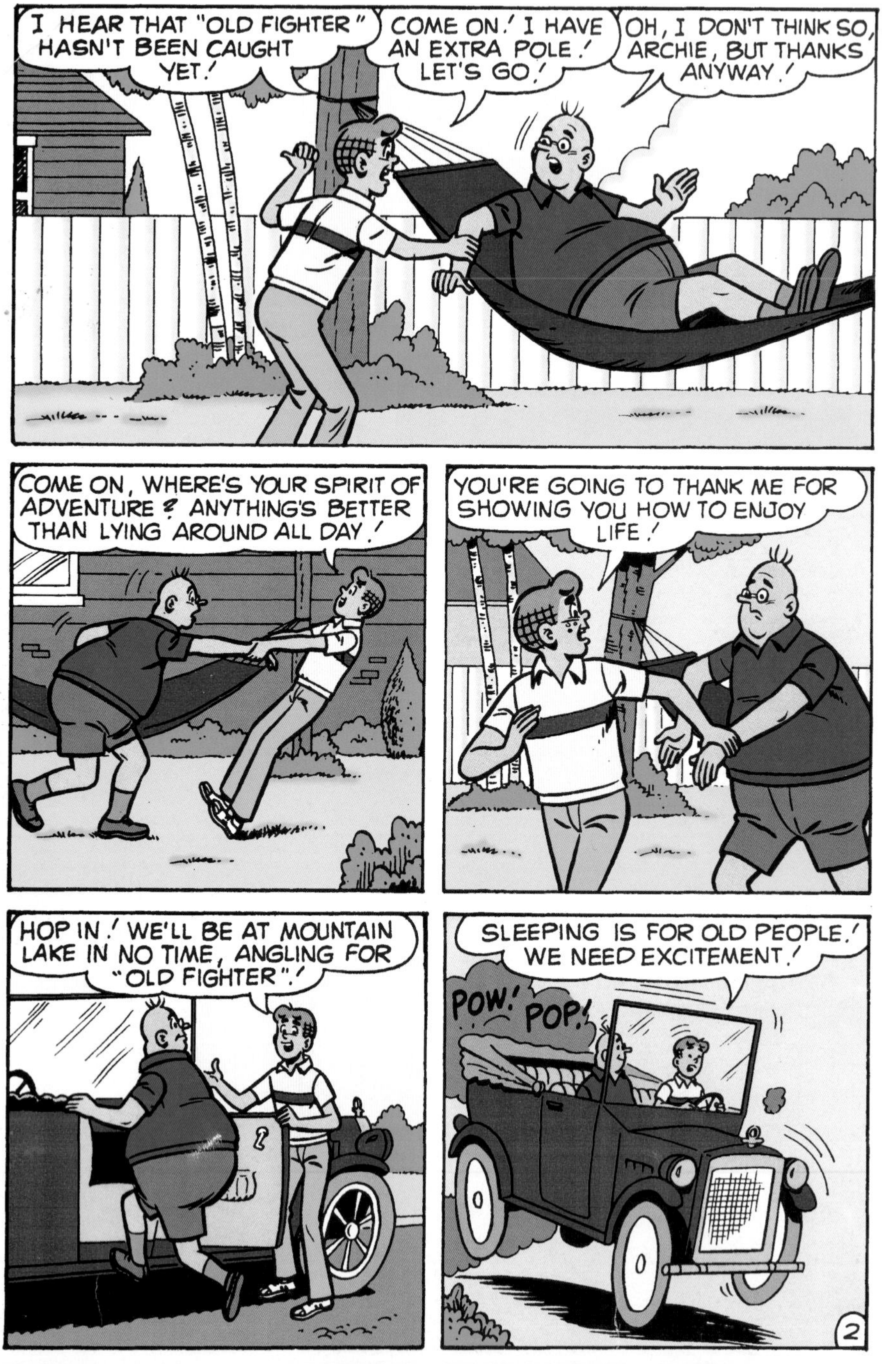
I HEAR THAT "OLD FIGHTER" HASN'T BEEN CAUGHT YET!
COME ON! I HAVE AN EXTRA POLE! LET'S GO!
OH, I DON'T THINK SO, ARCHIE, BUT THANKS ANYWAY!
COME ON, WHERE'S YOUR SPIRIT OF ADVENTURE? ANYTHING'S BETTER THAN LYING AROUND ALL DAY!
YOU'RE GOING TO THANK ME FOR SHOWING YOU HOW TO ENJOY LIFE!
HOP IN! WE'LL BE AT MOUNTAIN LAKE IN NO TIME, ANGLING FOR "OLD FIGHTER"!
SLEEPING IS FOR OLD PEOPLE! WE NEED EXCITEMENT!
POW! POP!
2

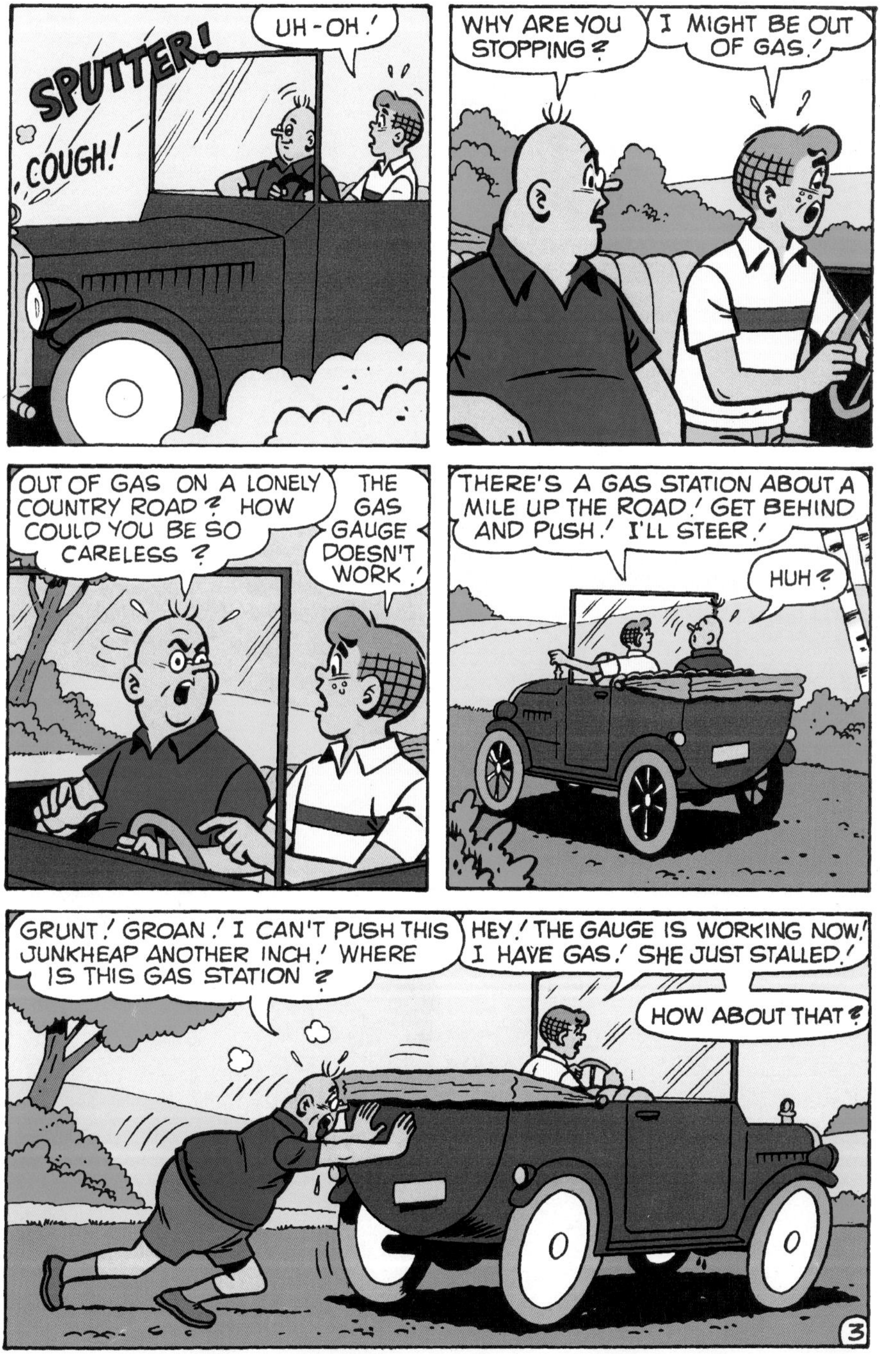
UH-OH!
SPUTTER!
COUGH!
WHY ARE YOU STOPPING?
I MIGHT BE OUT OF GAS!
OUT OF GAS ON A LONELY COUNTRY ROAD? HOW COULD YOU BE SO CARELESS?
THE GAS GAUGE DOESN'T WORK!
THERE'S A GAS STATION ABOUT A MILE UP THE ROAD! GET BEHIND AND PUSH! I'LL STEER!
HUH?
GRUNT! GROAN! I CAN'T PUSH THIS JUNKHEAP ANOTHER INCH! WHERE IS THIS GAS STATION?
HEY! THE GAUGE IS WORKING NOW! I HAVE GAS! SHE JUST STALLED!
HOW ABOUT THAT?
3

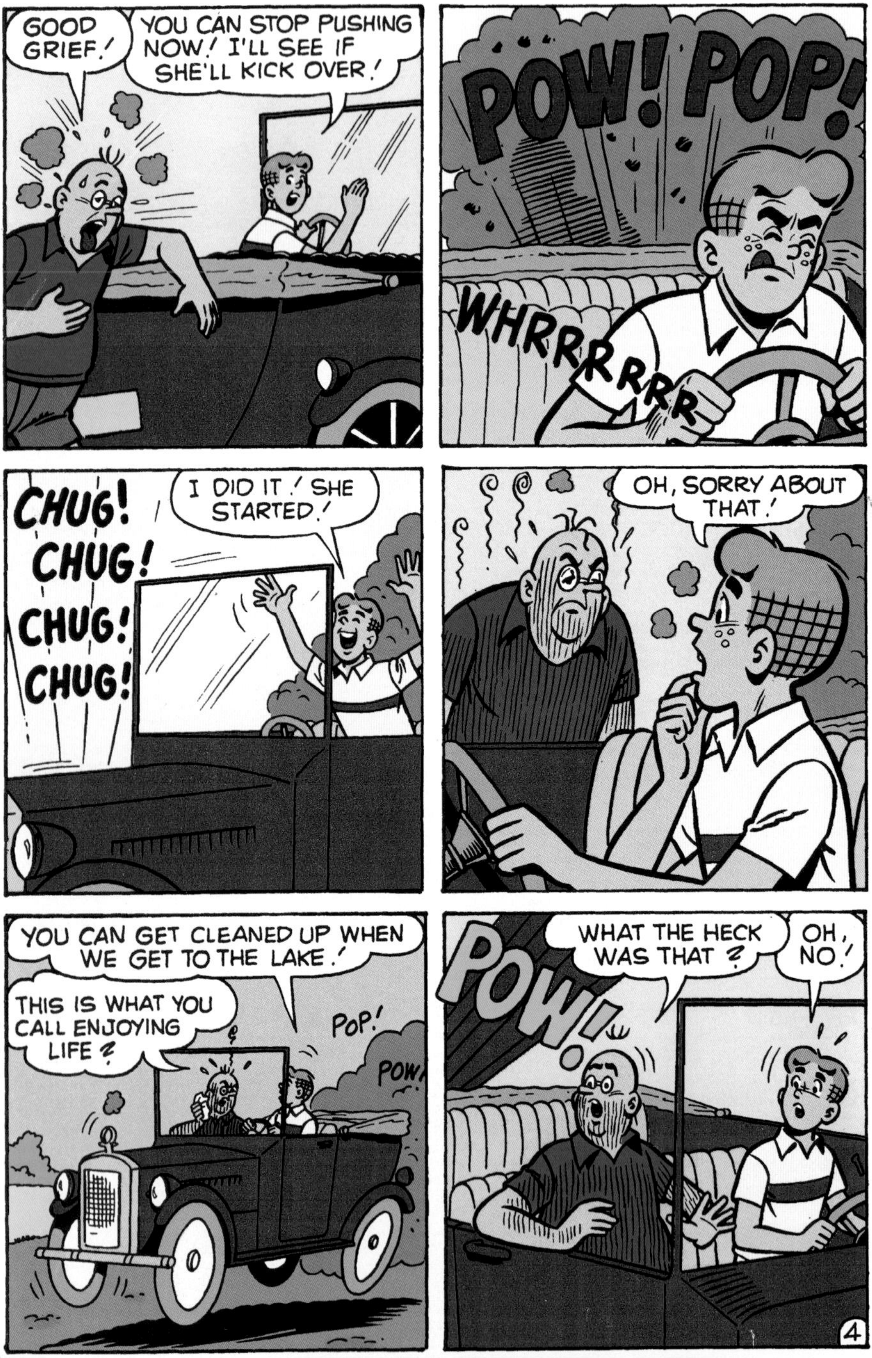
GOOD GRIEF!
YOU CAN STOP PUSHING NOW! I'LL SEE IF SHE'LL KICK OVER!
POW! POP!
WHRRRRRRR
CHUG! CHUG! CHUG! CHUG!
I DID IT! SHE STARTED!
OH, SORRY ABOUT THAT!
YOU CAN GET CLEANED UP WHEN WE GET TO THE LAKE!
THIS IS WHAT YOU CALL ENJOYING LIFE?
POP!
POW!
POW!
WHAT THE HECK WAS THAT?
OH, NO!
4

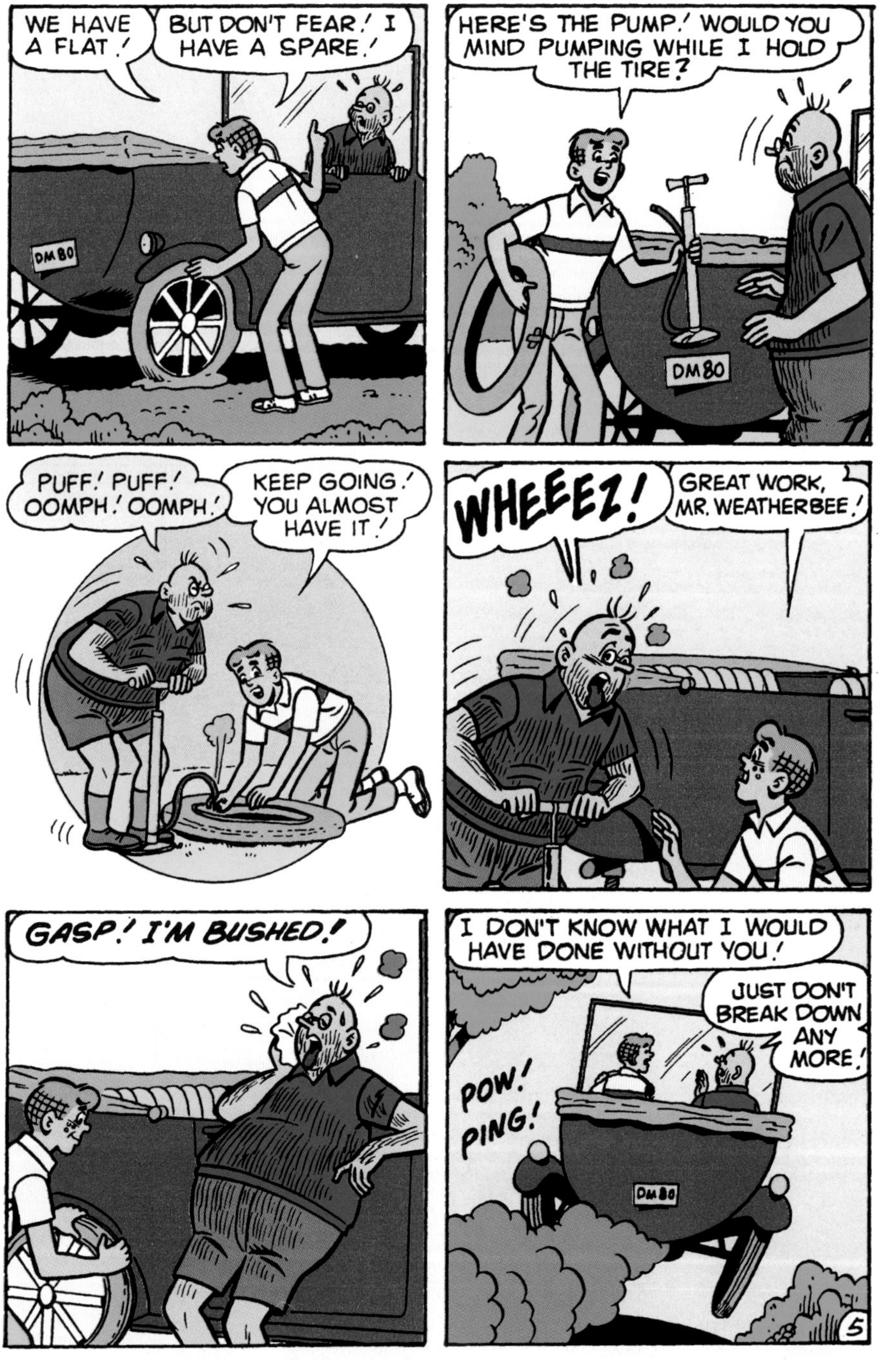
WE HAVE A FLAT!
BUT DON'T FEAR! I HAVE A SPARE!
DM 80
HERE'S THE PUMP! WOULD YOU MIND PUMPING WHILE I HOLD THE TIRE?
DM 80
PUFF! PUFF! OOMPH! OOMPH!
KEEP GOING! YOU ALMOST HAVE IT!
WHEEEZ!
GREAT WORK, MR. WEATHERBEE!
GASP! I'M BUSHED!
I DON'T KNOW WHAT I WOULD HAVE DONE WITHOUT YOU!
JUST DON'T BREAK DOWN ANY MORE!
POW!
PING!
DM 80
5

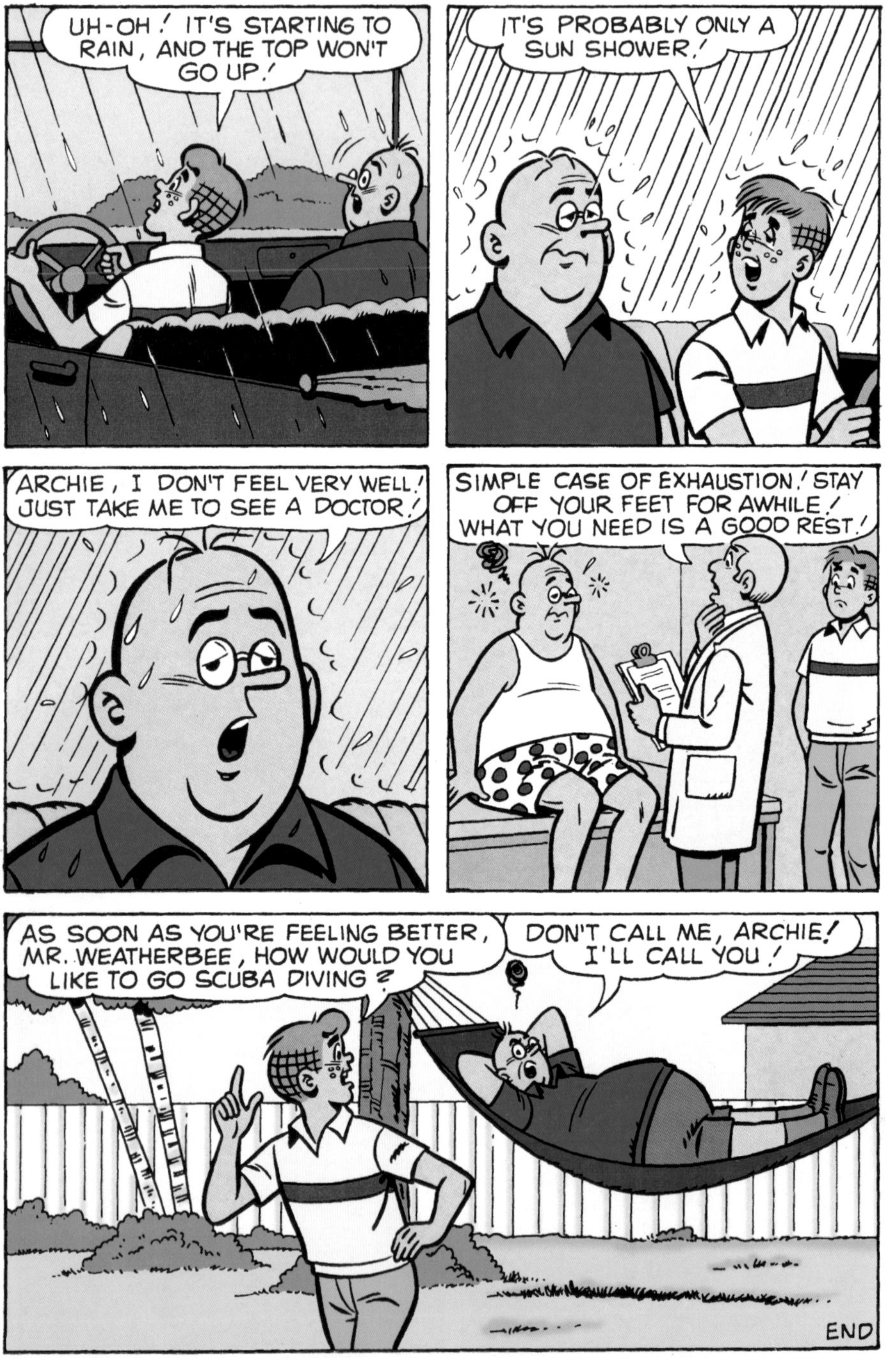
UH-OH! IT'S STARTING TO RAIN, AND THE TOP WON'T GO UP!
IT'S PROBABLY ONLY A SUN SHOWER!
ARCHIE, I DON'T FEEL VERY WELL! JUST TAKE ME TO SEE A DOCTOR!
SIMPLE CASE OF EXHAUSTION! STAY OFF YOUR FEET FOR AWHILE! WHAT YOU NEED IS A GOOD REST!
AS SOON AS YOU'RE FEELING BETTER, MR. WEATHERBEE, HOW WOULD YOU LIKE TO GO SCUBA DIVING?
DON'T CALL ME, ARCHIE! I'LL CALL YOU!
END

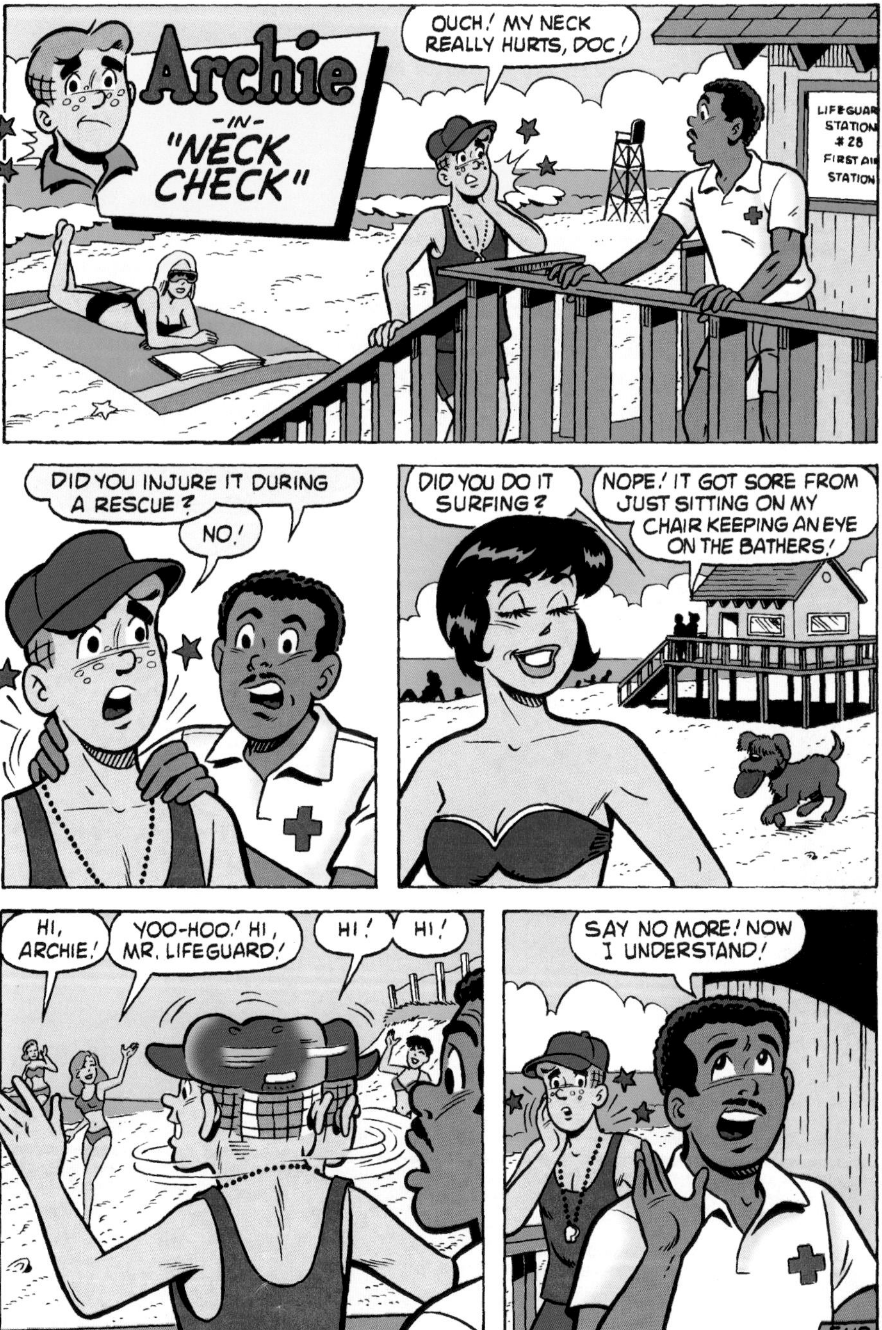
Archie
-IN-
"NECK CHECK"
OUCH! MY NECK REALLY HURTS, DOC!
LIFEGUARD STATION #28 FIRST AID STATION
DID YOU INJURE IT DURING A RESCUE?
NO!
DID YOU DO IT SURFING?
NOPE! IT GOT SORE FROM JUST SITTING ON MY CHAIR KEEPING AN EYE ON THE BATHERS!
HI, ARCHIE!
YOO-HOO! HI, MR. LIFEGUARD!
HI!
HI!
SAY NO MORE! NOW I UNDERSTAND!
END

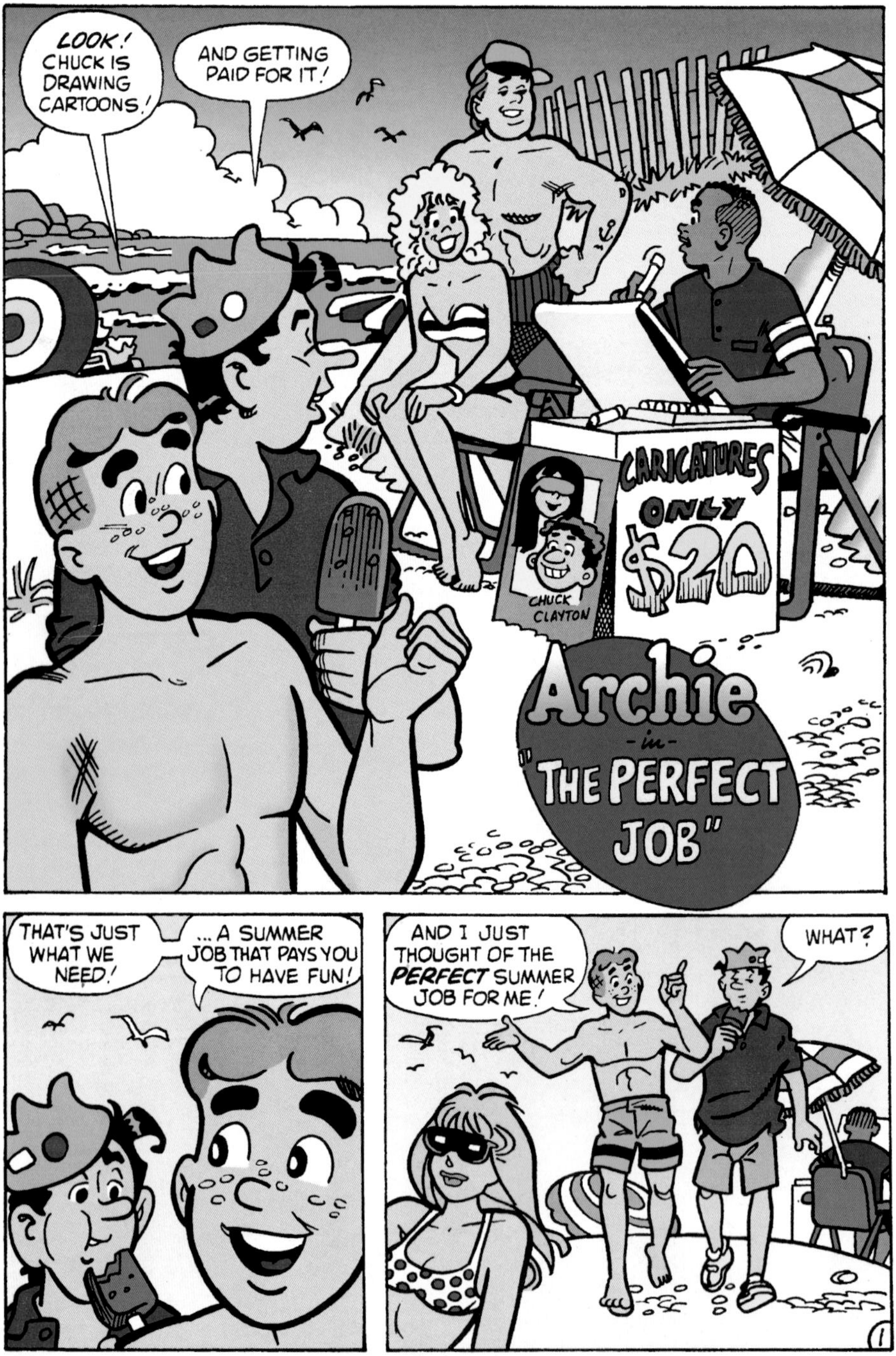
LOOK! CHUCK IS DRAWING CARTOONS!
AND GETTING PAID FOR IT!
CARICATURES ONLY $20
CHUCK CLAYTON
Archie -in- "THE PERFECT JOB"
THAT'S JUST WHAT WE NEED!
...A SUMMER JOB THAT PAYS YOU TO HAVE FUN!
AND I JUST THOUGHT OF THE PERFECT SUMMER JOB FOR ME!
WHAT?
1

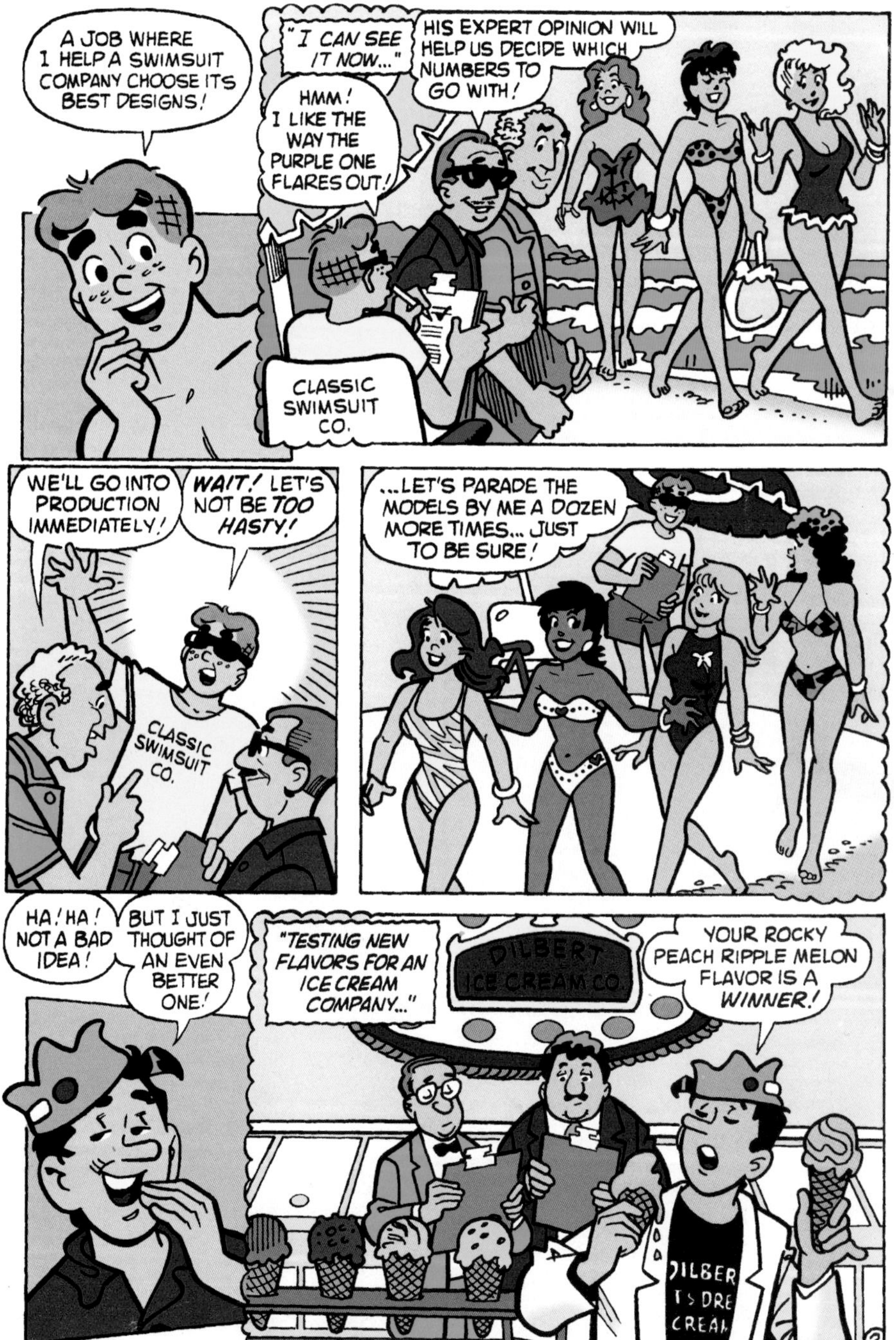
A JOB WHERE I HELP A SWIMSUIT COMPANY CHOOSE ITS BEST DESIGNS!
"I CAN SEE IT NOW..."
HIS EXPERT OPINION WILL HELP US DECIDE WHICH NUMBERS TO GO WITH!
HMM! I LIKE THE WAY THE PURPLE ONE FLARES OUT!
CLASSIC SWIMSUIT CO.
WE'LL GO INTO PRODUCTION IMMEDIATELY!
WAIT! LET'S NOT BE TOO HASTY!
CLASSIC SWIMSUIT CO.
...LET'S PARADE THE MODELS BY ME A DOZEN MORE TIMES... JUST TO BE SURE!
HA! HA! NOT A BAD IDEA!
BUT I JUST THOUGHT OF AN EVEN BETTER ONE!
"TESTING NEW FLAVORS FOR AN ICE CREAM COMPANY..."
DILBERT ICE CREAM CO.
YOUR ROCKY PEACH RIPPLE MELON FLAVOR IS A WINNER!

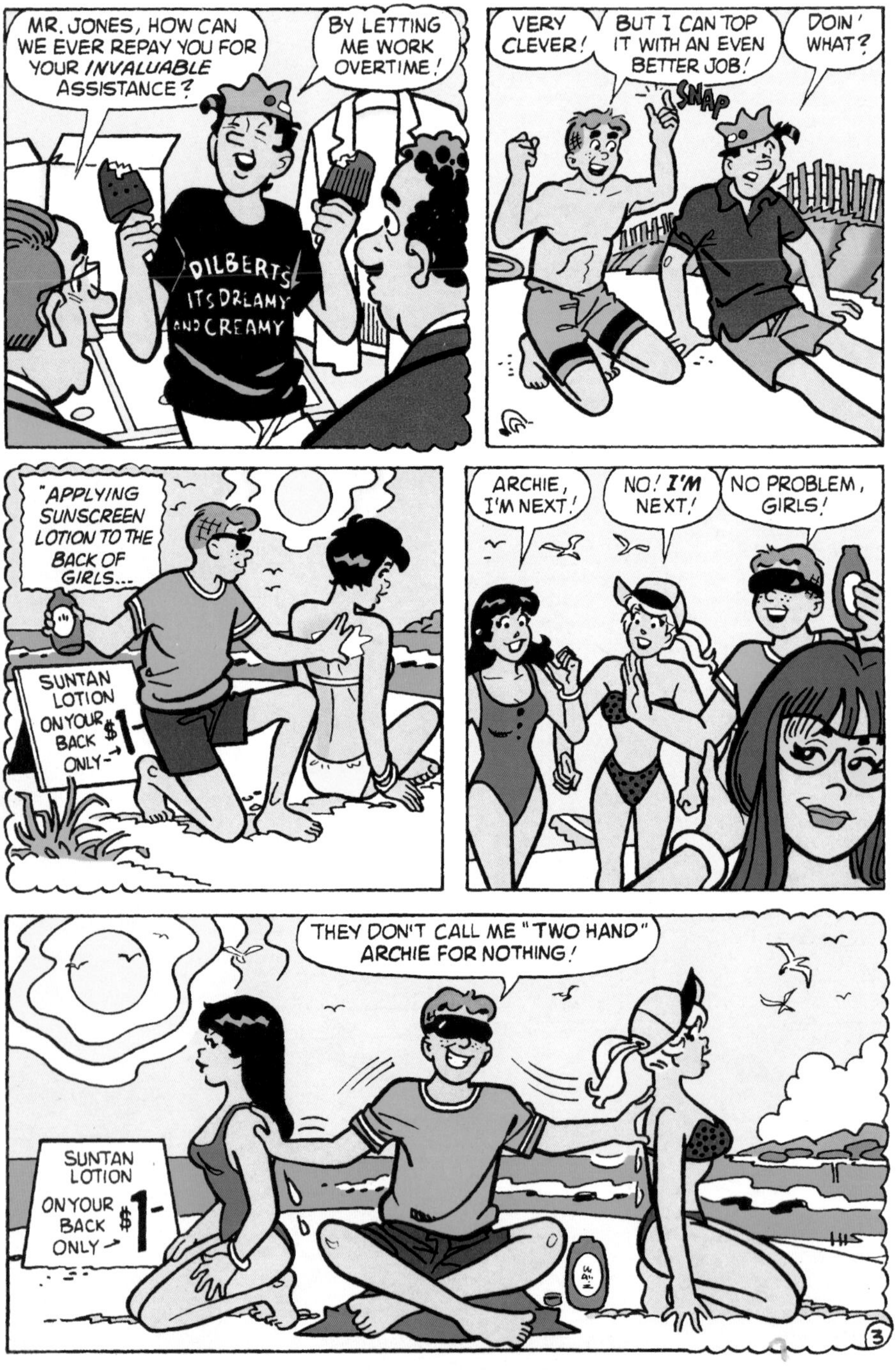
MR. JONES, HOW CAN WE EVER REPAY YOU FOR YOUR INVALUABLE ASSISTANCE?
BY LETTING ME WORK OVERTIME!
DILBERT'S ITS DREAMY AND CREAMY
VERY CLEVER!
BUT I CAN TOP IT WITH AN EVEN BETTER JOB!
SNAP
DOIN' WHAT?
"APPLYING SUNSCREEN LOTION TO THE BACK OF GIRLS...
SUNTAN LOTION ON YOUR BACK ONLY → $1-
ARCHIE, I'M NEXT!
NO! I'M NEXT!
NO PROBLEM, GIRLS!
THEY DON'T CALL ME "TWO HAND" ARCHIE FOR NOTHING!
SUNTAN LOTION ON YOUR BACK ONLY → $1-
3

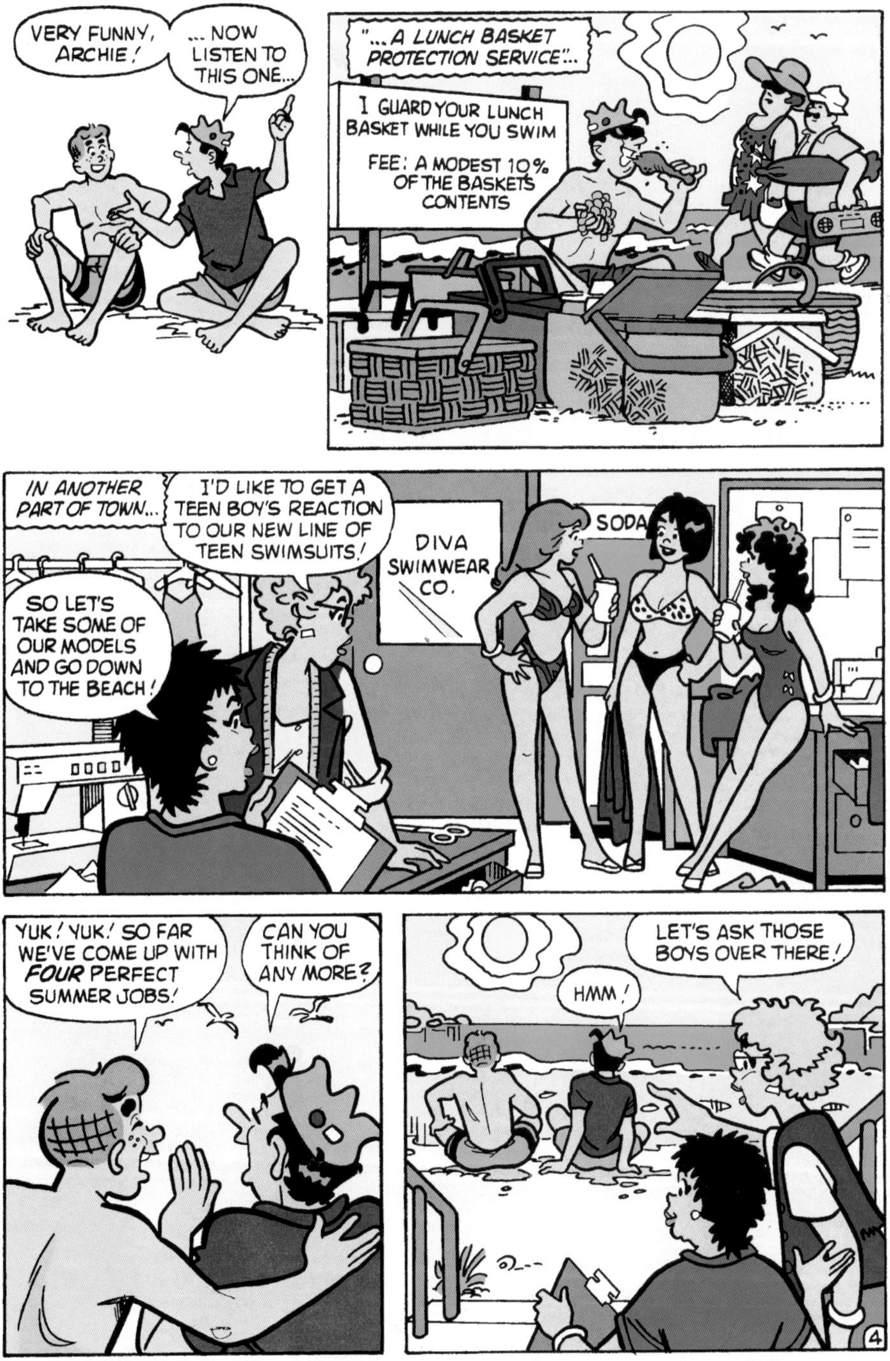
VERY FUNNY, ARCHIE!
... NOW LISTEN TO THIS ONE...
"... A LUNCH BASKET PROTECTION SERVICE"...
I GUARD YOUR LUNCH BASKET WHILE YOU SWIM
FEE: A MODEST 10% OF THE BASKETS CONTENTS
IN ANOTHER PART OF TOWN...
I'D LIKE TO GET A TEEN BOY'S REACTION TO OUR NEW LINE OF TEEN SWIMSUITS!
SO LET'S TAKE SOME OF OUR MODELS AND GO DOWN TO THE BEACH!
DIVA SWIMWEAR CO.
SODA
YUK! YUK! SO FAR WE'VE COME UP WITH FOUR PERFECT SUMMER JOBS!
CAN YOU THINK OF ANY MORE?
LET'S ASK THOSE BOYS OVER THERE!
HMM!
4

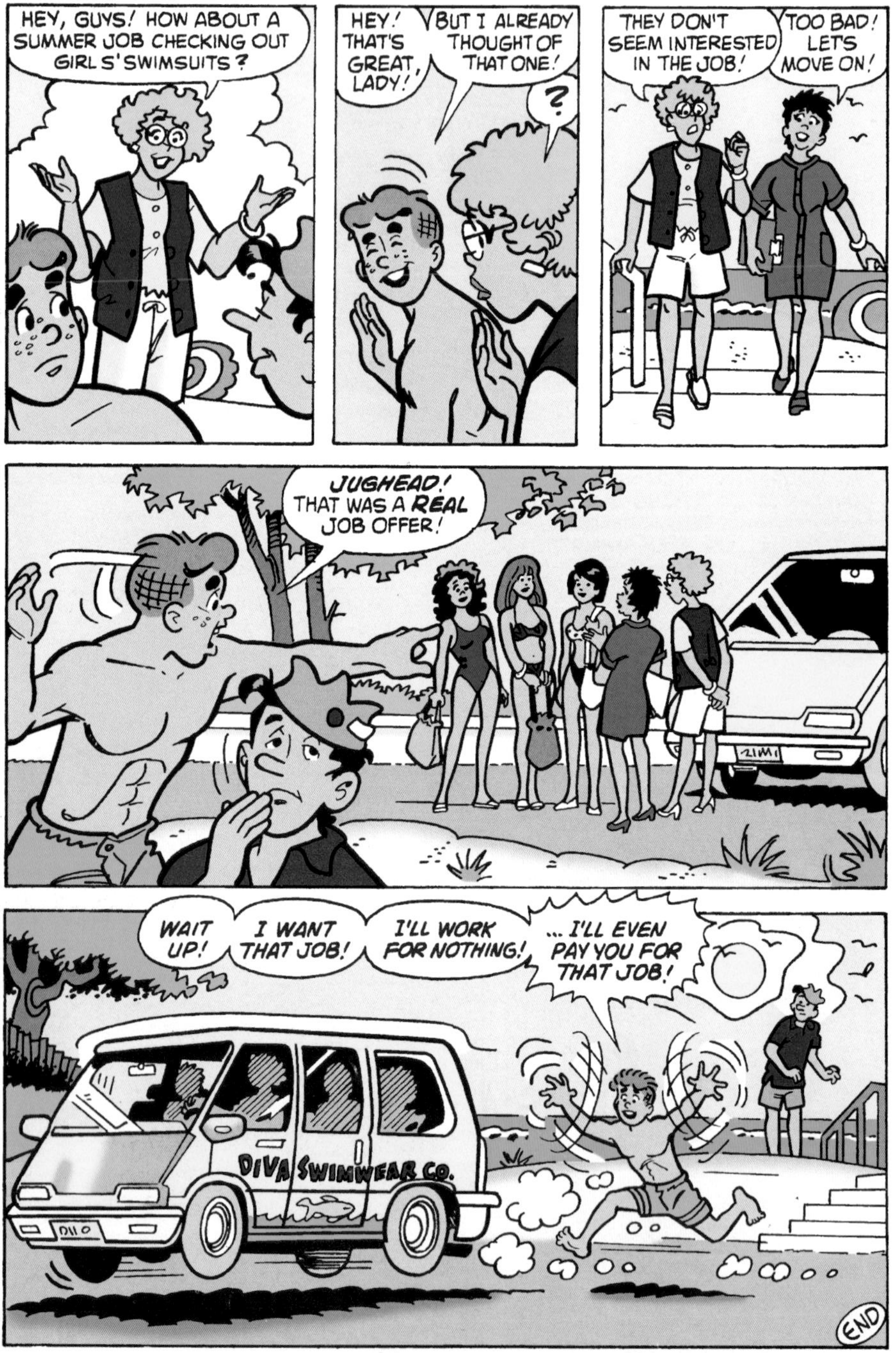
HEY, GUYS! HOW ABOUT A SUMMER JOB CHECKING OUT GIRLS' SWIMSUITS?
HEY! THAT'S GREAT, LADY!
BUT I ALREADY THOUGHT OF THAT ONE!
?
THEY DON'T SEEM INTERESTED IN THE JOB!
TOO BAD! LET'S MOVE ON!
JUGHEAD! THAT WAS A REAL JOB OFFER!
WAIT UP!
I WANT THAT JOB!
I'LL WORK FOR NOTHING!
... I'LL EVEN PAY YOU FOR THAT JOB!
DIVA SWIMWEAR CO.
END

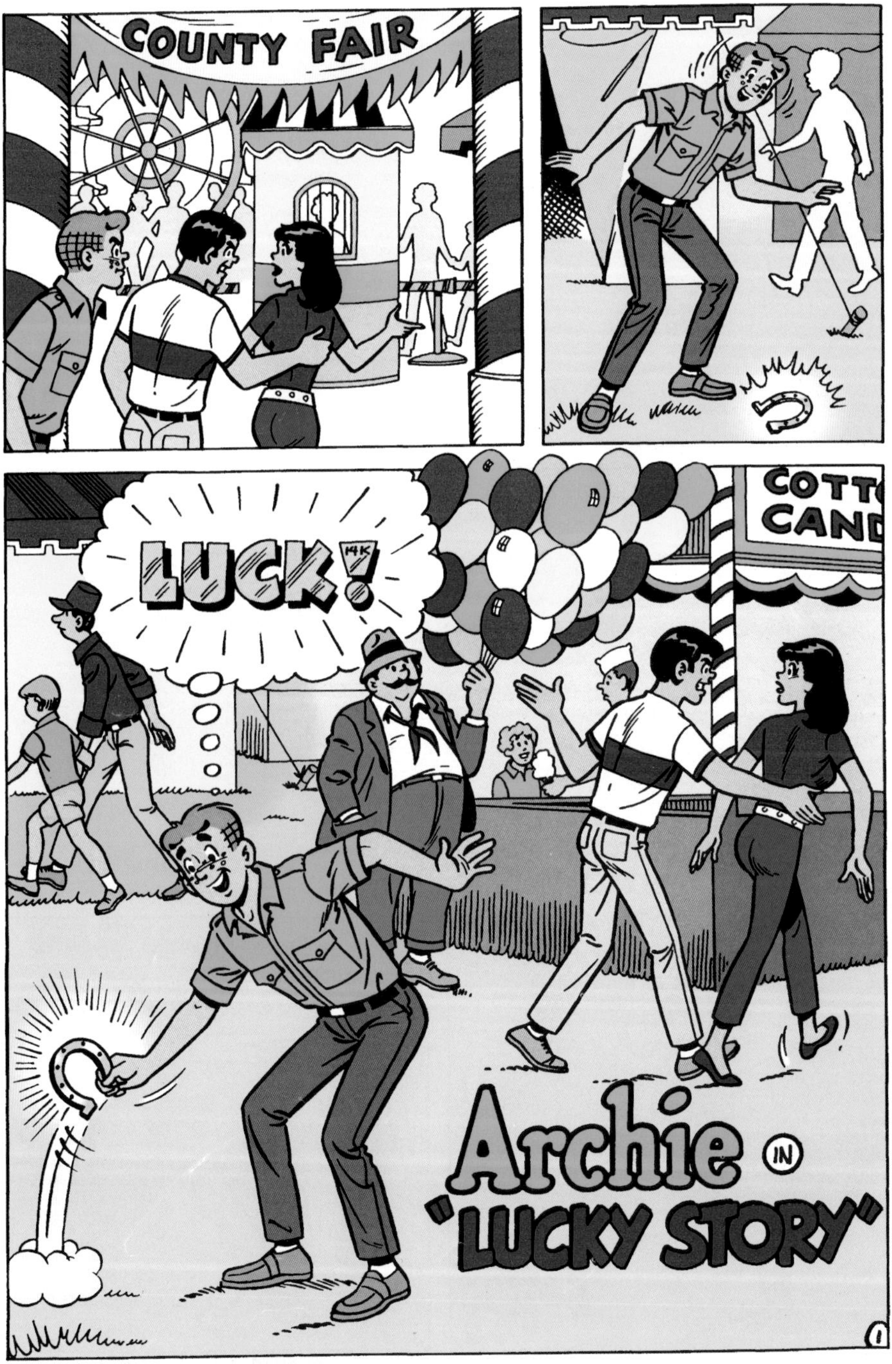
COUNTY FAIR
LUCK!
14K
Archie IN
"LUCKY STORY"
1

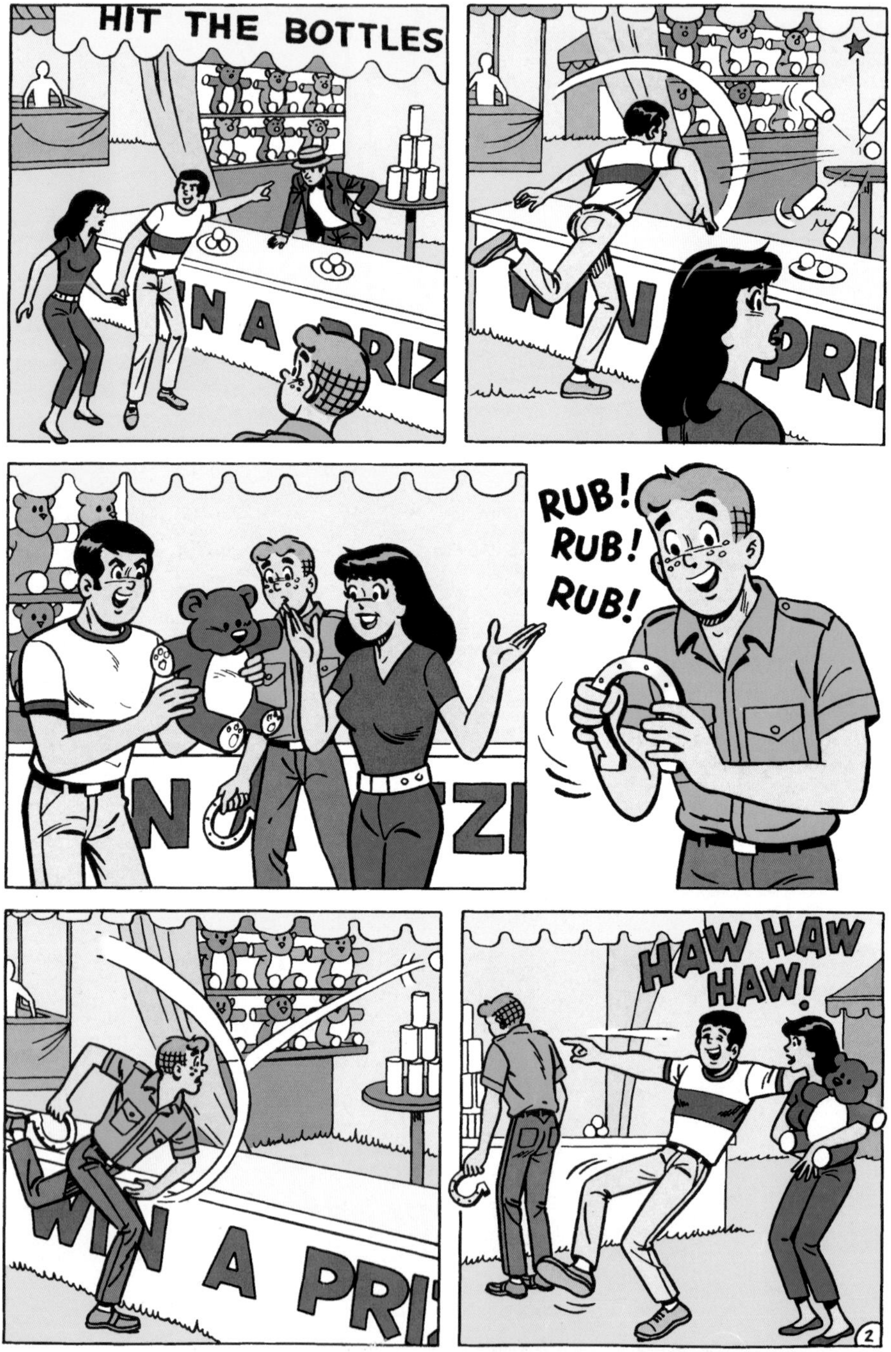
HIT THE BOTTLES
WIN A PRIZE
RUB! RUB! RUB!
HAW HAW HAW!
2

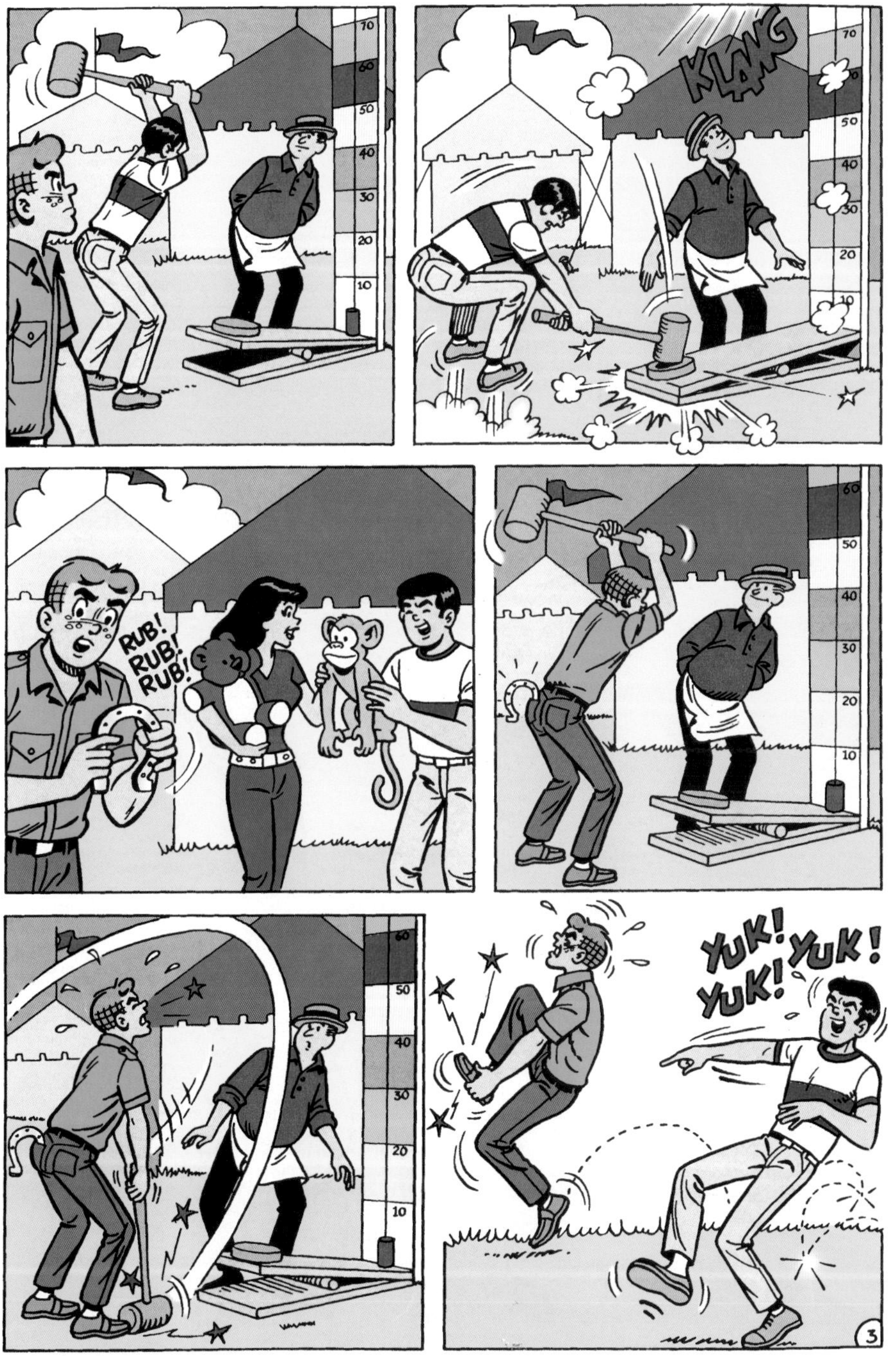
KLANG
RUB! RUB! RUB!
YUK! YUK! YUK!
3

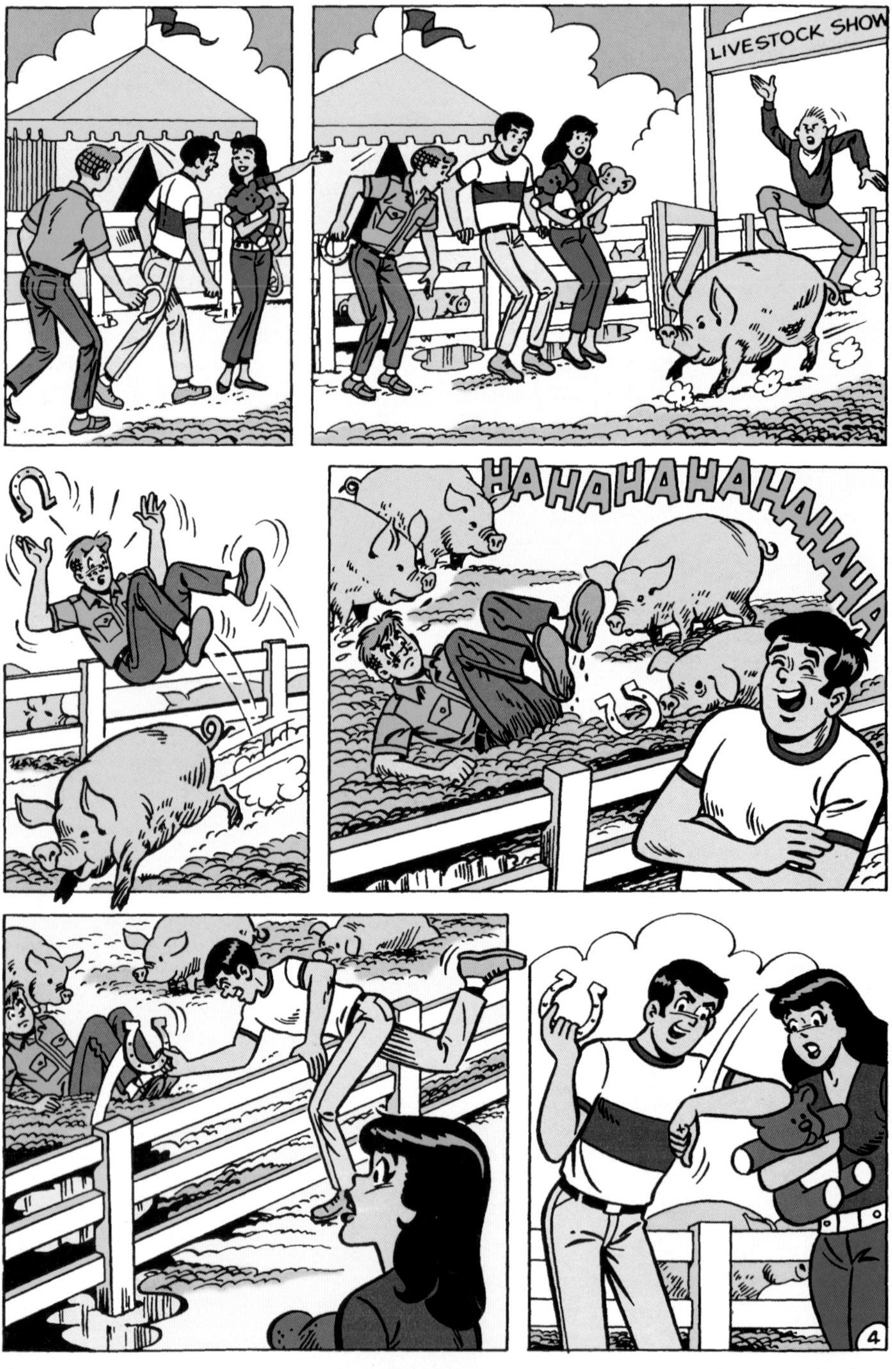
LIVESTOCK SHOW
HAHAHAHAHAHAHAHAHA
4

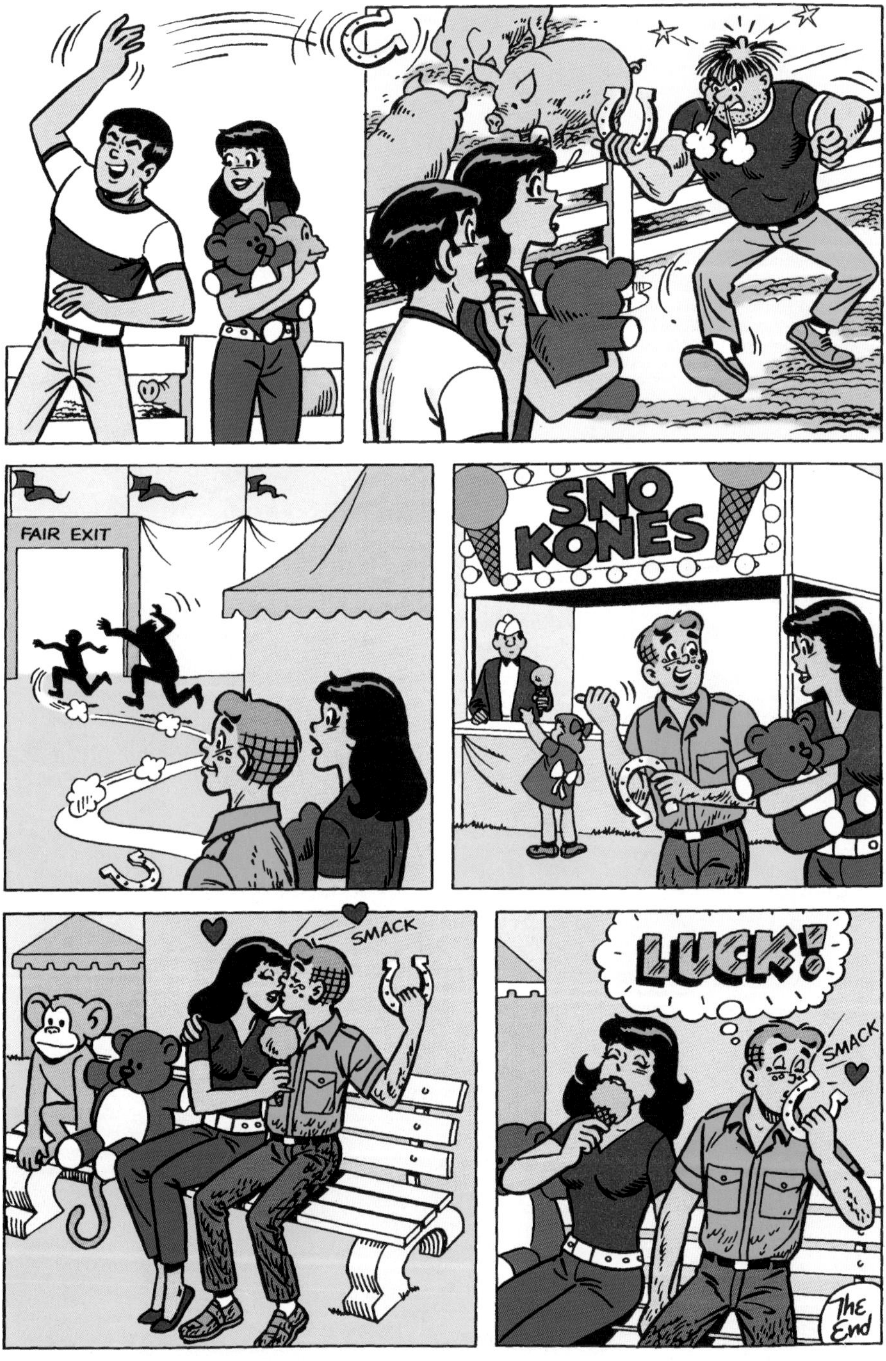
FAIR EXIT
SNO KONES
SMACK
LUCK!
SMACK
THE End

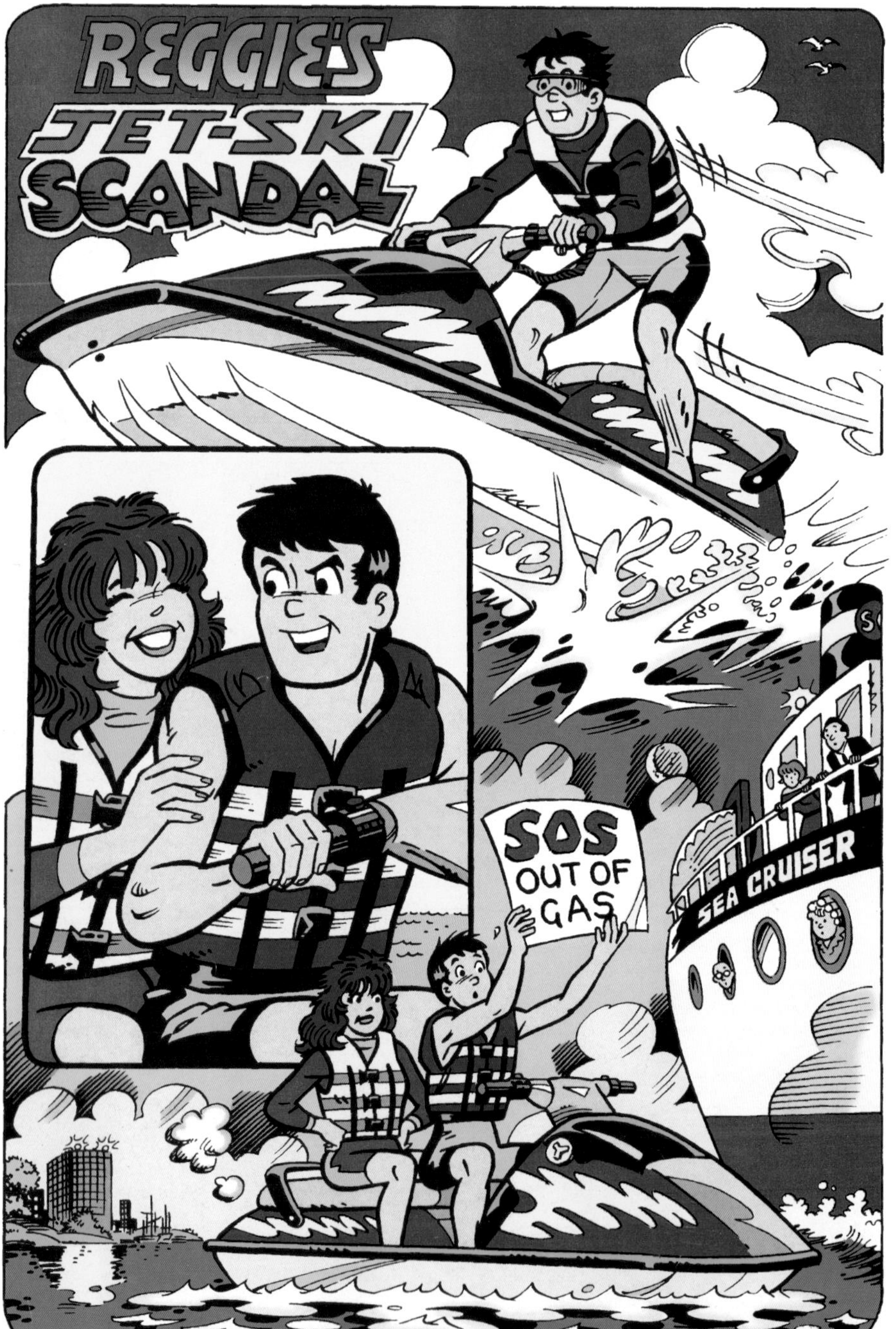
REGGIE'S
JET-SKI
SCANDAL
SOS
OUT OF
GAS
SEA CRUISER

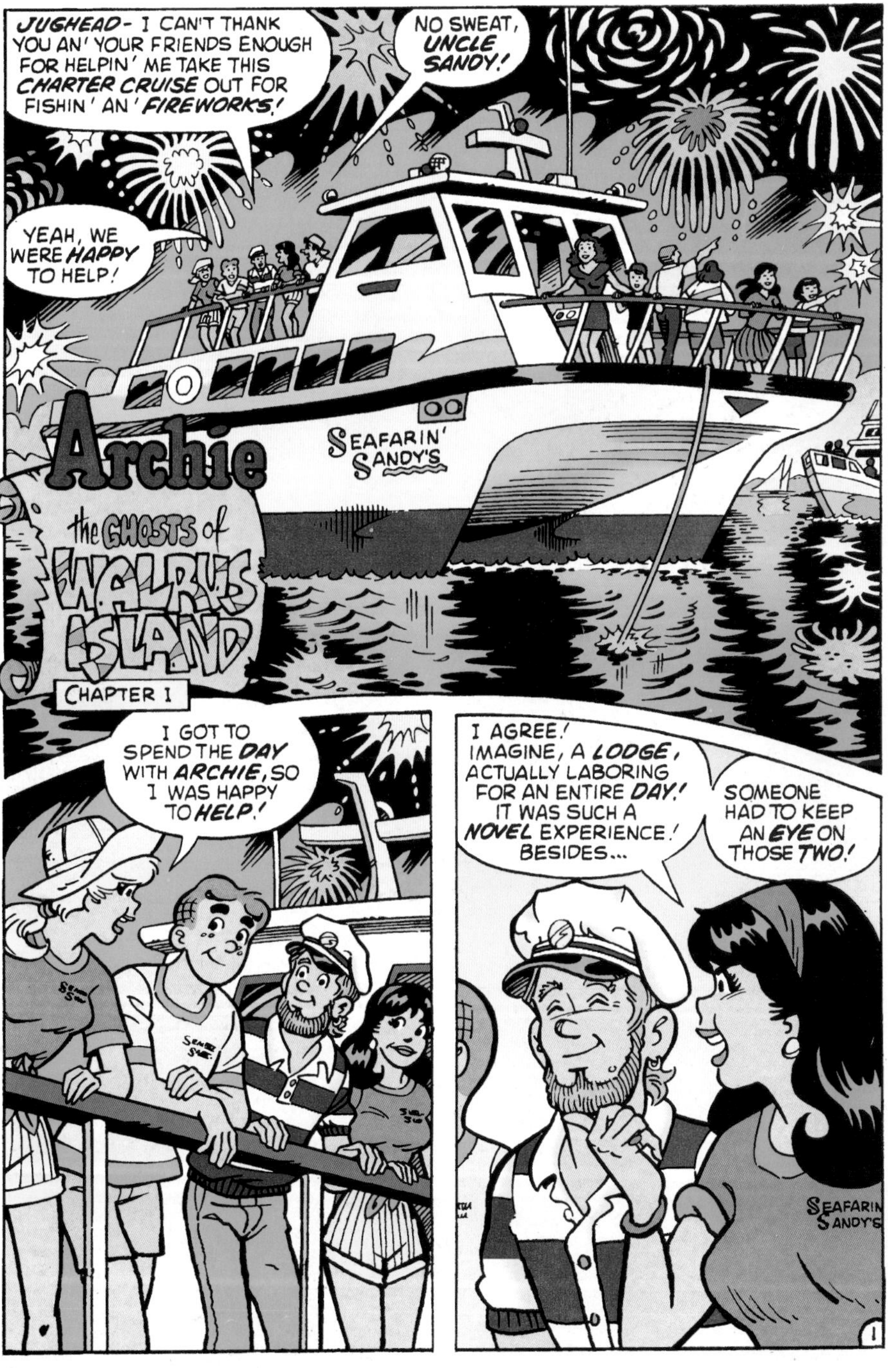
JUGHEAD- I CAN'T THANK YOU AN' YOUR FRIENDS ENOUGH FOR HELPIN' ME TAKE THIS CHARTER CRUISE OUT FOR FISHIN' AN' FIREWORKS!
NO SWEAT, UNCLE SANDY!
YEAH, WE WERE HAPPY TO HELP!
SEAFARIN' SANDY'S
Archie
the GHOSTS of WALRUS ISLAND
CHAPTER 1
I GOT TO SPEND THE DAY WITH ARCHIE, SO I WAS HAPPY TO HELP!
I AGREE! IMAGINE, A LODGE, ACTUALLY LABORING FOR AN ENTIRE DAY! IT WAS SUCH A NOVEL EXPERIENCE! BESIDES...
SOMEONE HAD TO KEEP AN EYE ON THOSE TWO!
SEAFARIN SANDY'S
1

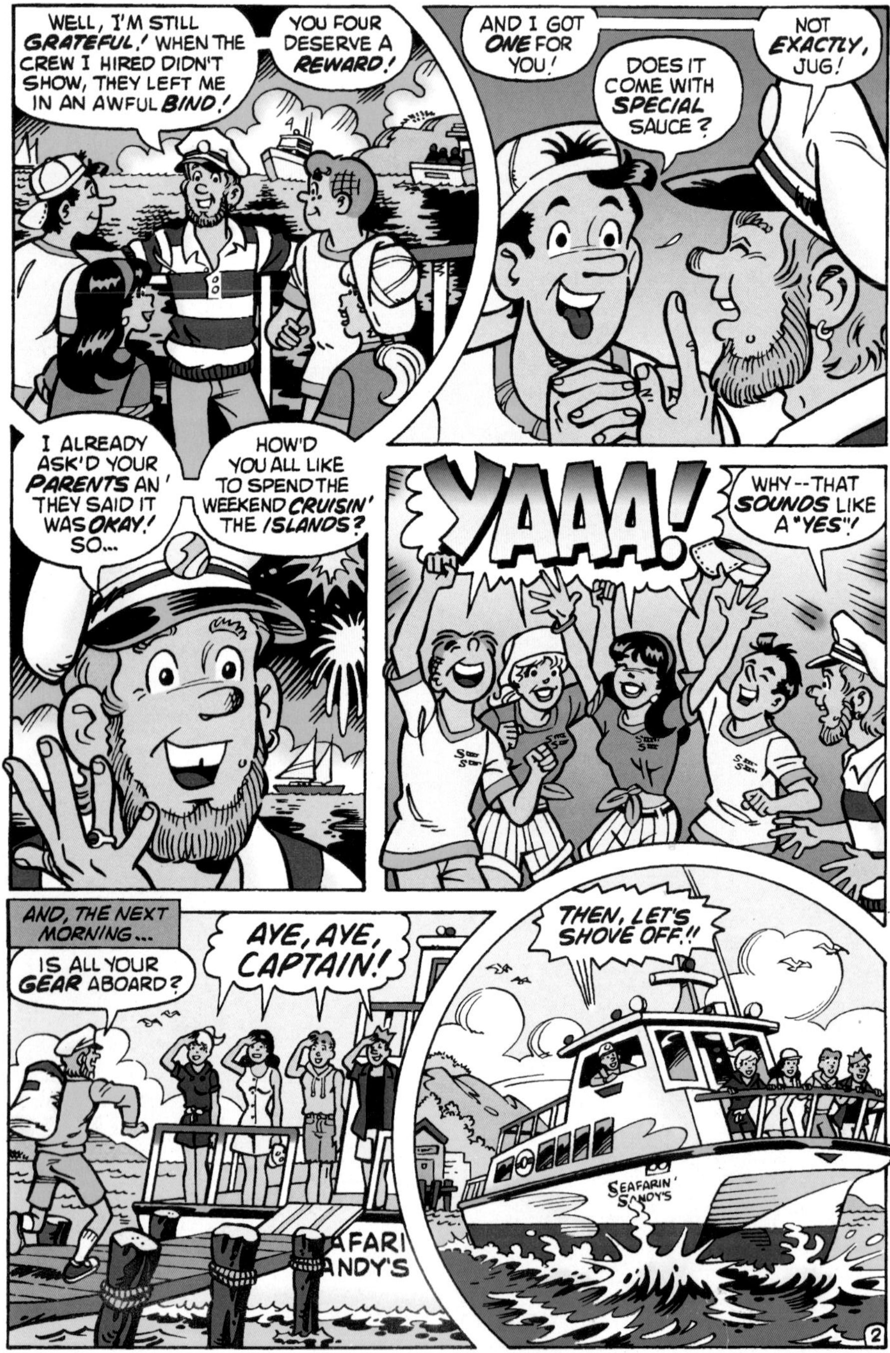
WELL, I'M STILL GRATEFUL! WHEN THE CREW I HIRED DIDN'T SHOW, THEY LEFT ME IN AN AWFUL BIND!
YOU FOUR DESERVE A REWARD!
AND I GOT ONE FOR YOU!
DOES IT COME WITH SPECIAL SAUCE?
NOT EXACTLY, JUG!
I ALREADY ASK'D YOUR PARENTS AN' THEY SAID IT WAS OKAY! SO...
HOW'D YOU ALL LIKE TO SPEND THE WEEKEND CRUISIN' THE ISLANDS?
YAAA!
WHY--THAT SOUNDS LIKE A "YES"!
AND, THE NEXT MORNING...
IS ALL YOUR GEAR ABOARD?
AYE, AYE, CAPTAIN!
SAFARI SANDY'S
THEN, LET'S SHOVE OFF!!
SEAFARIN' SANDY'S
2

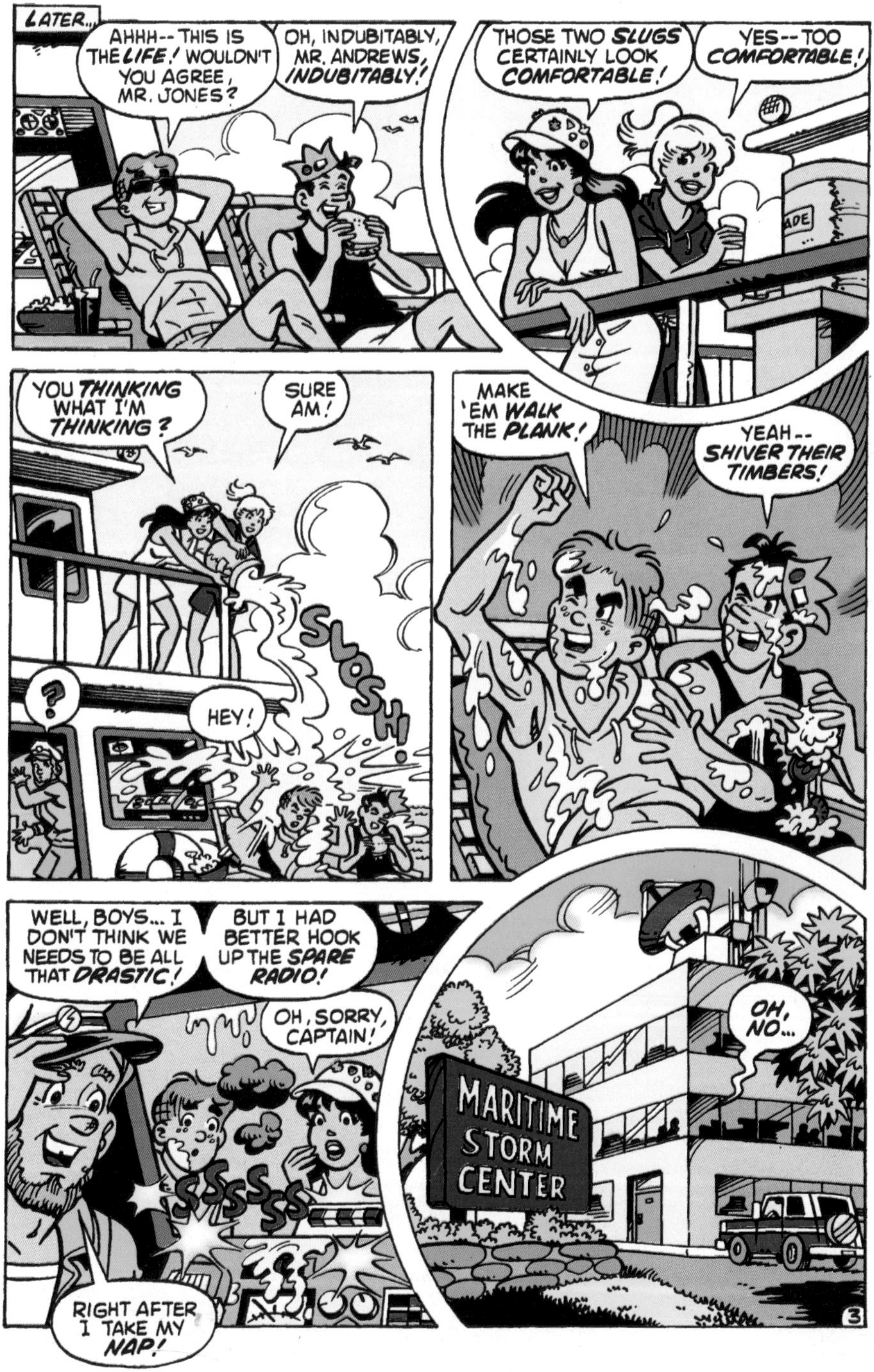
LATER...
AHHH-- THIS IS THE LIFE! WOULDN'T YOU AGREE, MR. JONES?
OH, INDUBITABLY, MR. ANDREWS, INDUBITABLY!
THOSE TWO SLUGS CERTAINLY LOOK COMFORTABLE!
YES-- TOO COMFORTABLE!
YOU THINKING WHAT I'M THINKING?
SURE AM!
SLOSH!
?
HEY!
MAKE 'EM WALK THE PLANK!
YEAH -- SHIVER THEIR TIMBERS!
WELL, BOYS... I DON'T THINK WE NEEDS TO BE ALL THAT DRASTIC!
BUT I HAD BETTER HOOK UP THE SPARE RADIO!
OH, SORRY, CAPTAIN!
SSSSSS
RIGHT AFTER I TAKE MY NAP!
MARITIME STORM CENTER
OH, NO...
3

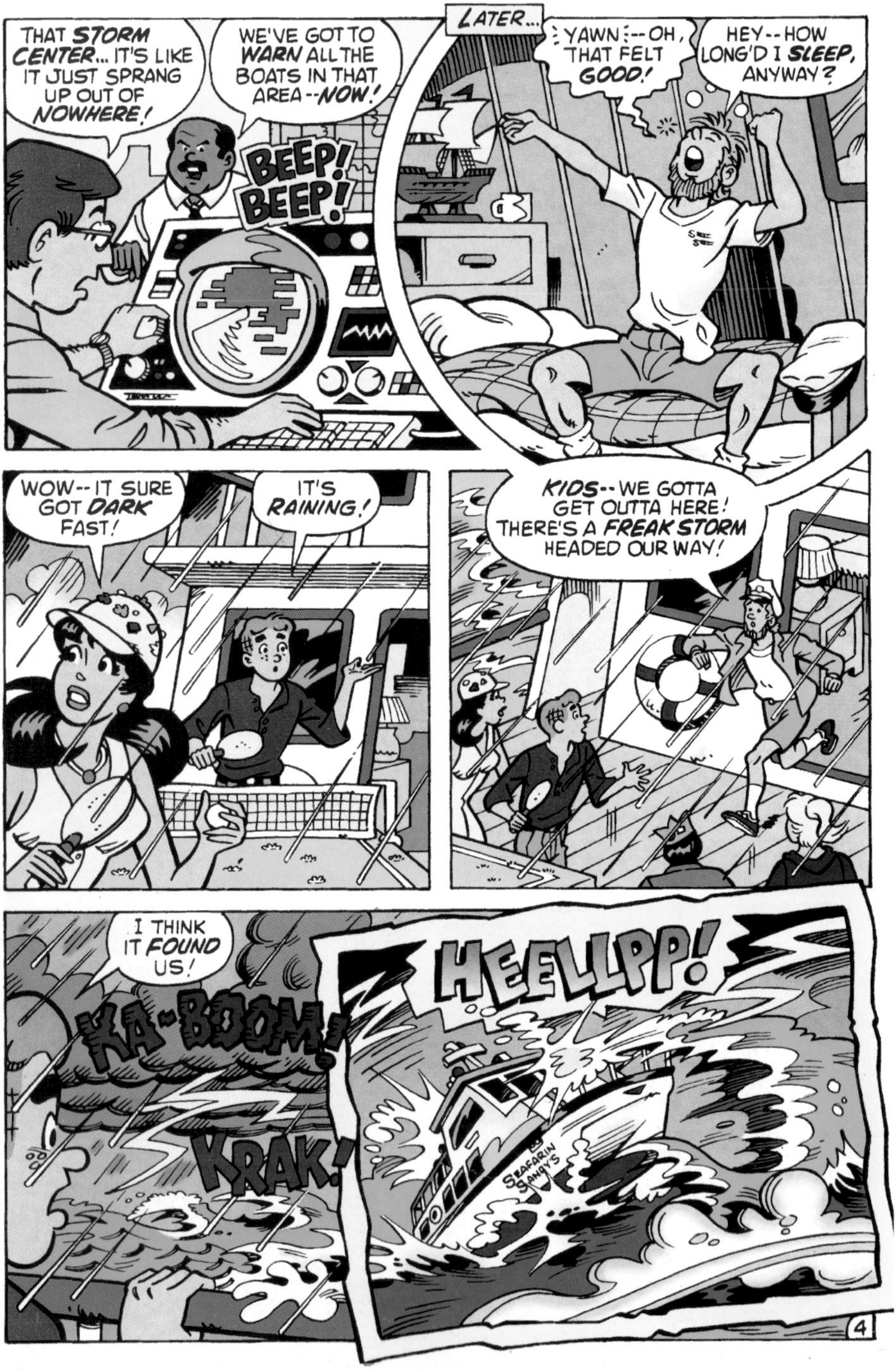
THAT STORM CENTER... IT'S LIKE IT JUST SPRANG UP OUT OF NOWHERE!
WE'VE GOT TO WARN ALL THE BOATS IN THAT AREA--NOW!
BEEP! BEEP!
LATER...
YAWN!--OH, THAT FELT GOOD!
HEY--HOW LONG'D I SLEEP, ANYWAY?
WOW--IT SURE GOT DARK FAST!
IT'S RAINING!
KIDS--WE GOTTA GET OUTTA HERE! THERE'S A FREAK STORM HEADED OUR WAY!
I THINK IT FOUND US!
KA-BOOM!
KRAK!
HEELLPP!
SEAFARIN SAMMY'S
4

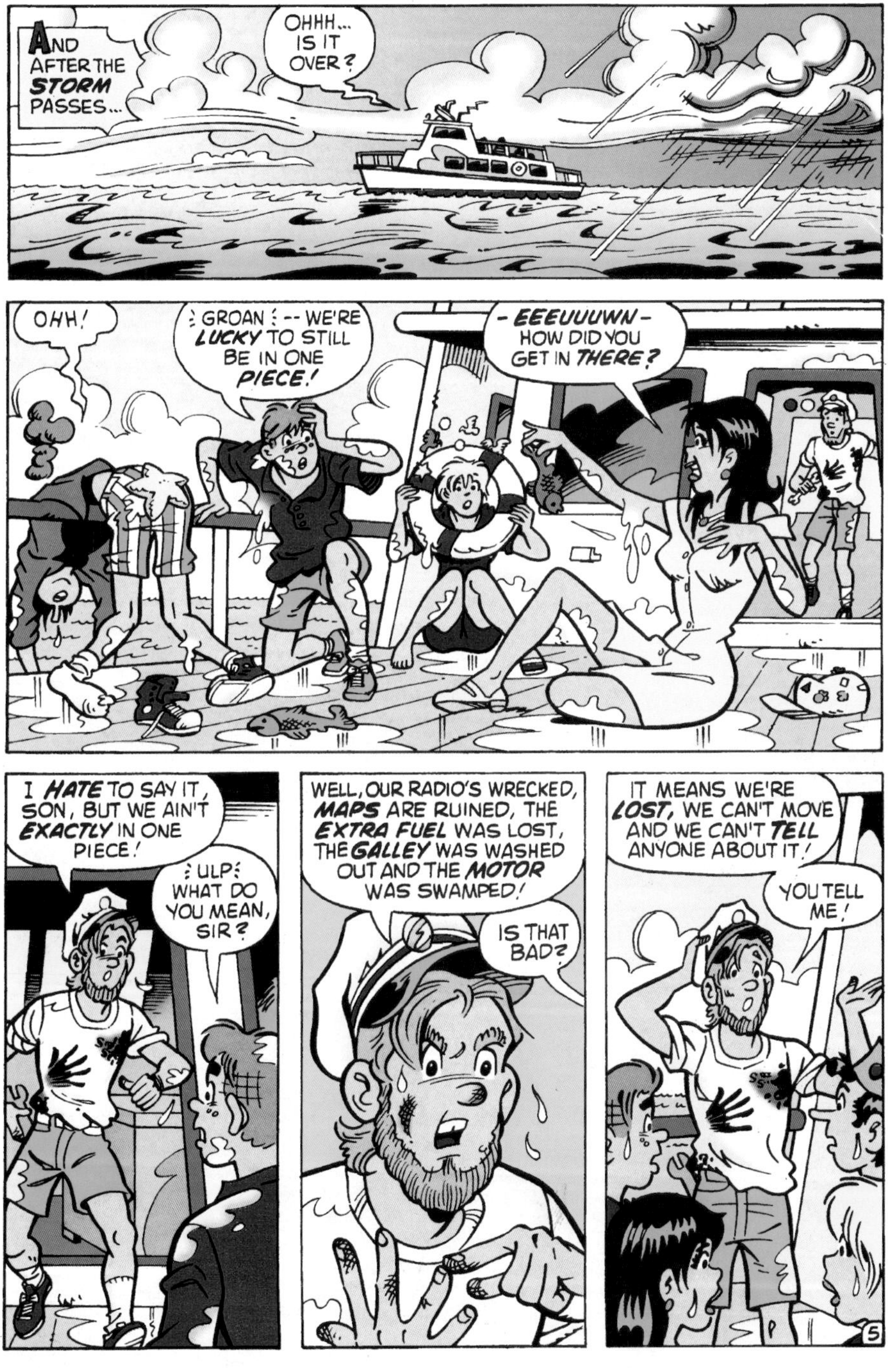
AND AFTER THE STORM PASSES...
OHHH... IS IT OVER?
OHH!
GROAN -- WE'RE LUCKY TO STILL BE IN ONE PIECE!
-EEEUUUWN- HOW DID YOU GET IN THERE?
I HATE TO SAY IT, SON, BUT WE AIN'T EXACTLY IN ONE PIECE!
ULP! WHAT DO YOU MEAN, SIR?
WELL, OUR RADIO'S WRECKED, MAPS ARE RUINED, THE EXTRA FUEL WAS LOST, THE GALLEY WAS WASHED OUT AND THE MOTOR WAS SWAMPED!
IS THAT BAD?
IT MEANS WE'RE LOST, WE CAN'T MOVE AND WE CAN'T TELL ANYONE ABOUT IT!
YOU TELL ME!
5

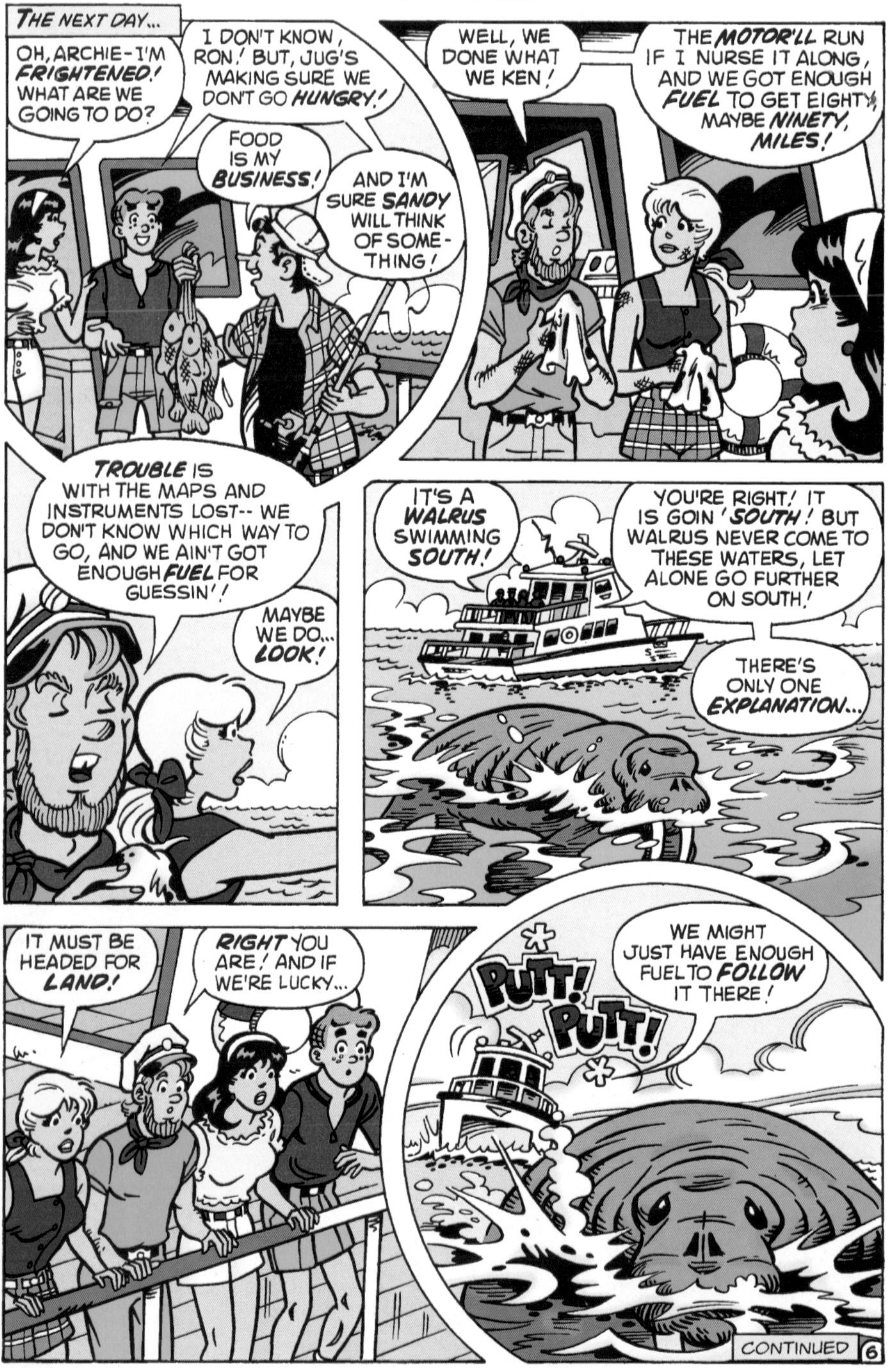
THE NEXT DAY...
OH, ARCHIE-I'M FRIGHTENED! WHAT ARE WE GOING TO DO?
I DON'T KNOW, RON! BUT, JUG'S MAKING SURE WE DON'T GO HUNGRY!
FOOD IS MY BUSINESS!
AND I'M SURE SANDY WILL THINK OF SOME-THING!
WELL, WE DONE WHAT WE KEN!
THE MOTOR'LL RUN IF I NURSE IT ALONG, AND WE GOT ENOUGH FUEL TO GET EIGHTY, MAYBE NINETY, MILES!
TROUBLE IS WITH THE MAPS AND INSTRUMENTS LOST-- WE DON'T KNOW WHICH WAY TO GO, AND WE AIN'T GOT ENOUGH FUEL FOR GUESSIN'!
MAYBE WE DO... LOOK!
IT'S A WALRUS SWIMMING SOUTH!
YOU'RE RIGHT! IT IS GOIN' SOUTH! BUT WALRUS NEVER COME TO THESE WATERS, LET ALONE GO FURTHER ON SOUTH!
THERE'S ONLY ONE EXPLANATION...
IT MUST BE HEADED FOR LAND!
RIGHT YOU ARE! AND IF WE'RE LUCKY...
WE MIGHT JUST HAVE ENOUGH FUEL TO FOLLOW IT THERE!
PUTT! PUTT!
CONTINUED
6

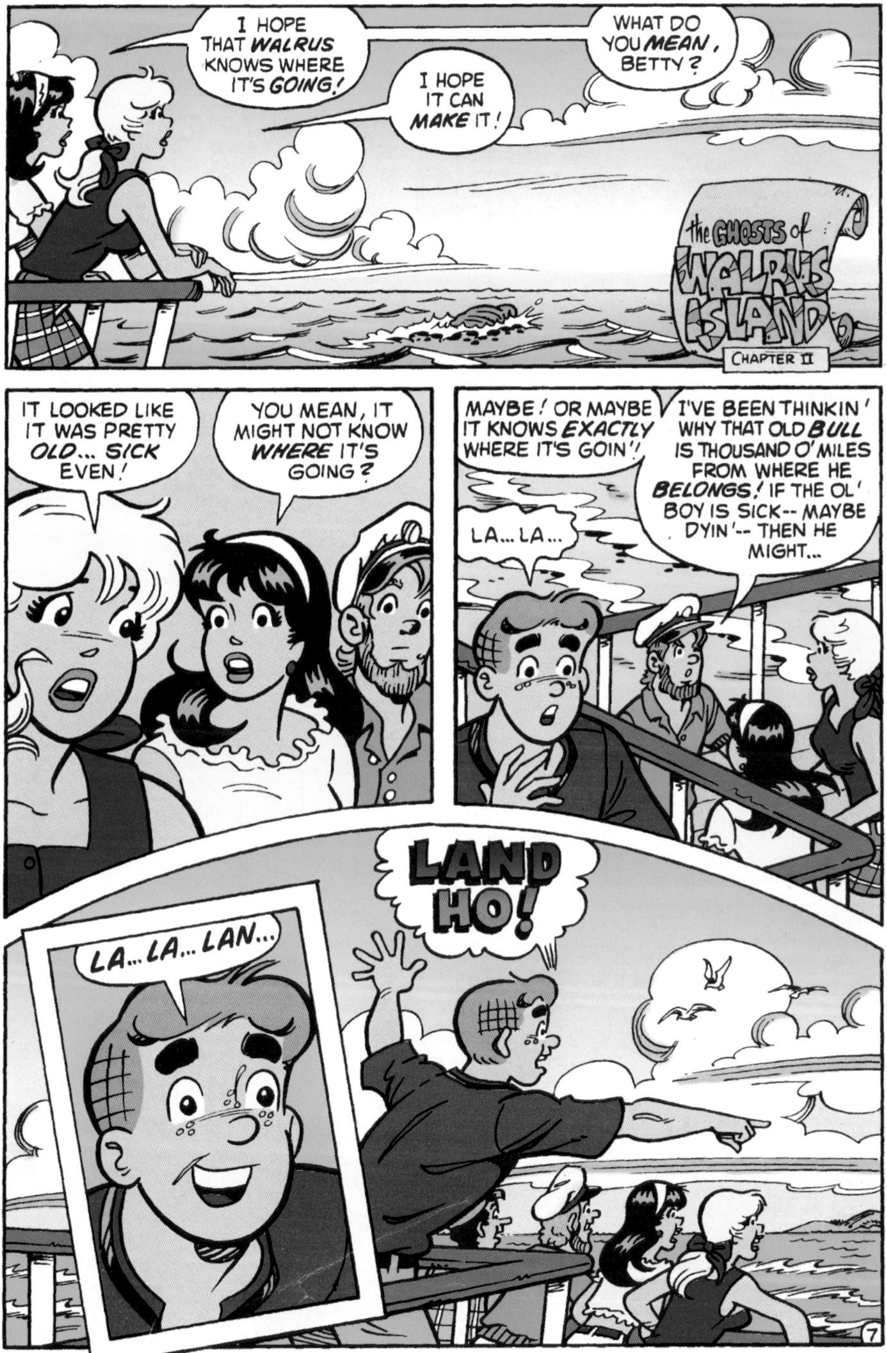

I HOPE THAT WALRUS KNOWS WHERE IT'S GOING!
I HOPE IT CAN MAKE IT!
WHAT DO YOU MEAN, BETTY?
the GHOSTS of WALRUS ISLAND
CHAPTER II
IT LOOKED LIKE IT WAS PRETTY OLD... SICK EVEN!
YOU MEAN, IT MIGHT NOT KNOW WHERE IT'S GOING?
MAYBE! OR MAYBE IT KNOWS EXACTLY WHERE IT'S GOIN'!
I'VE BEEN THINKIN' WHY THAT OLD BULL IS THOUSAND O' MILES FROM WHERE HE BELONGS! IF THE OL' BOY IS SICK-- MAYBE DYIN'-- THEN HE MIGHT...
LA... LA...
LA... LA... LAN...
LAND HO!
7

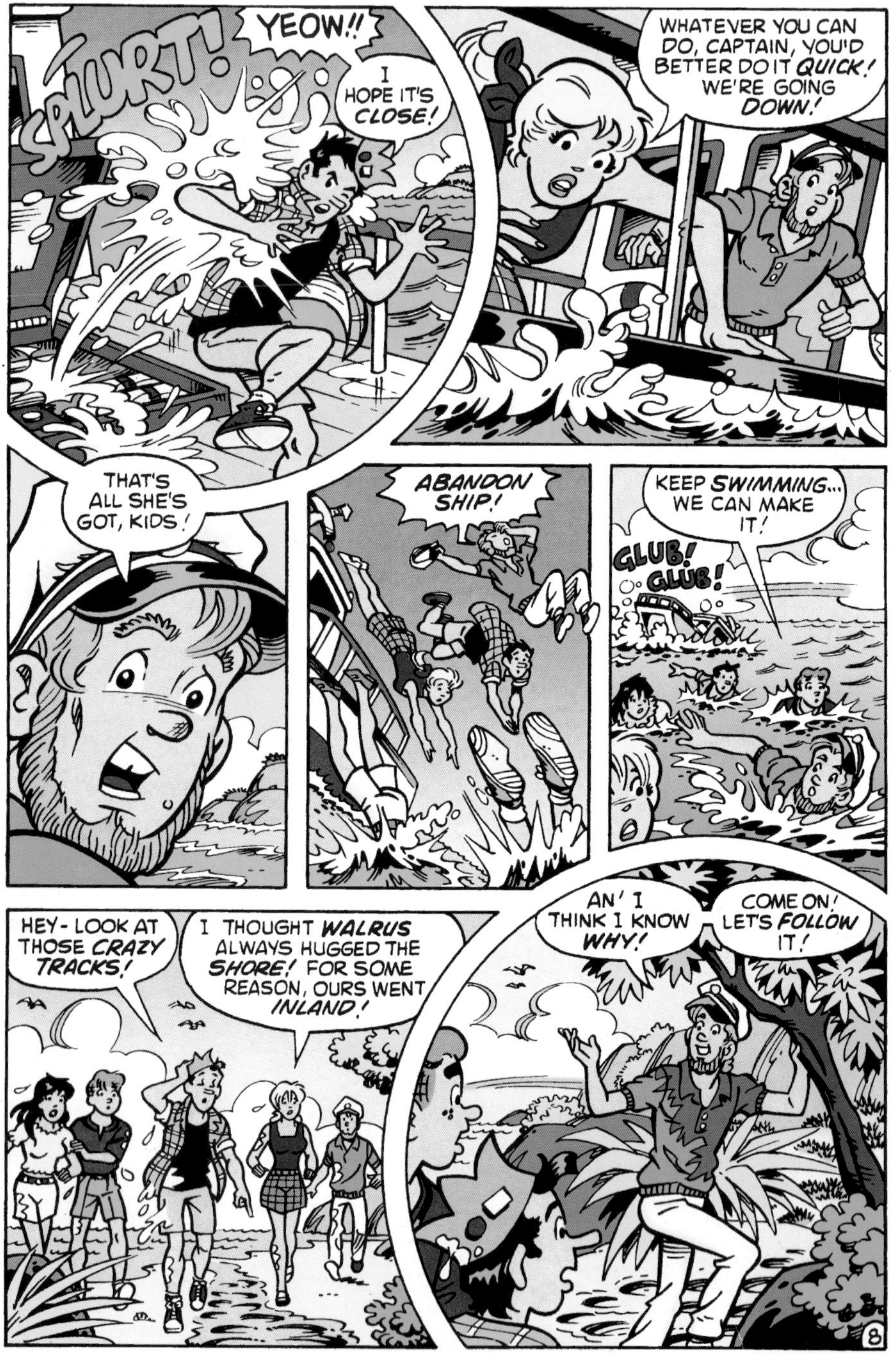
SPLURT!
YEOW!!
I HOPE IT'S CLOSE!
WHATEVER YOU CAN DO, CAPTAIN, YOU'D BETTER DO IT QUICK! WE'RE GOING DOWN!
THAT'S ALL SHE'S GOT, KIDS!
ABANDON SHIP!
KEEP SWIMMING... WE CAN MAKE IT!
GLUB! GLUB!
HEY- LOOK AT THOSE CRAZY TRACKS!
I THOUGHT WALRUS ALWAYS HUGGED THE SHORE! FOR SOME REASON, OURS WENT INLAND!
AN' I THINK I KNOW WHY!
COME ON! LET'S FOLLOW IT!
8

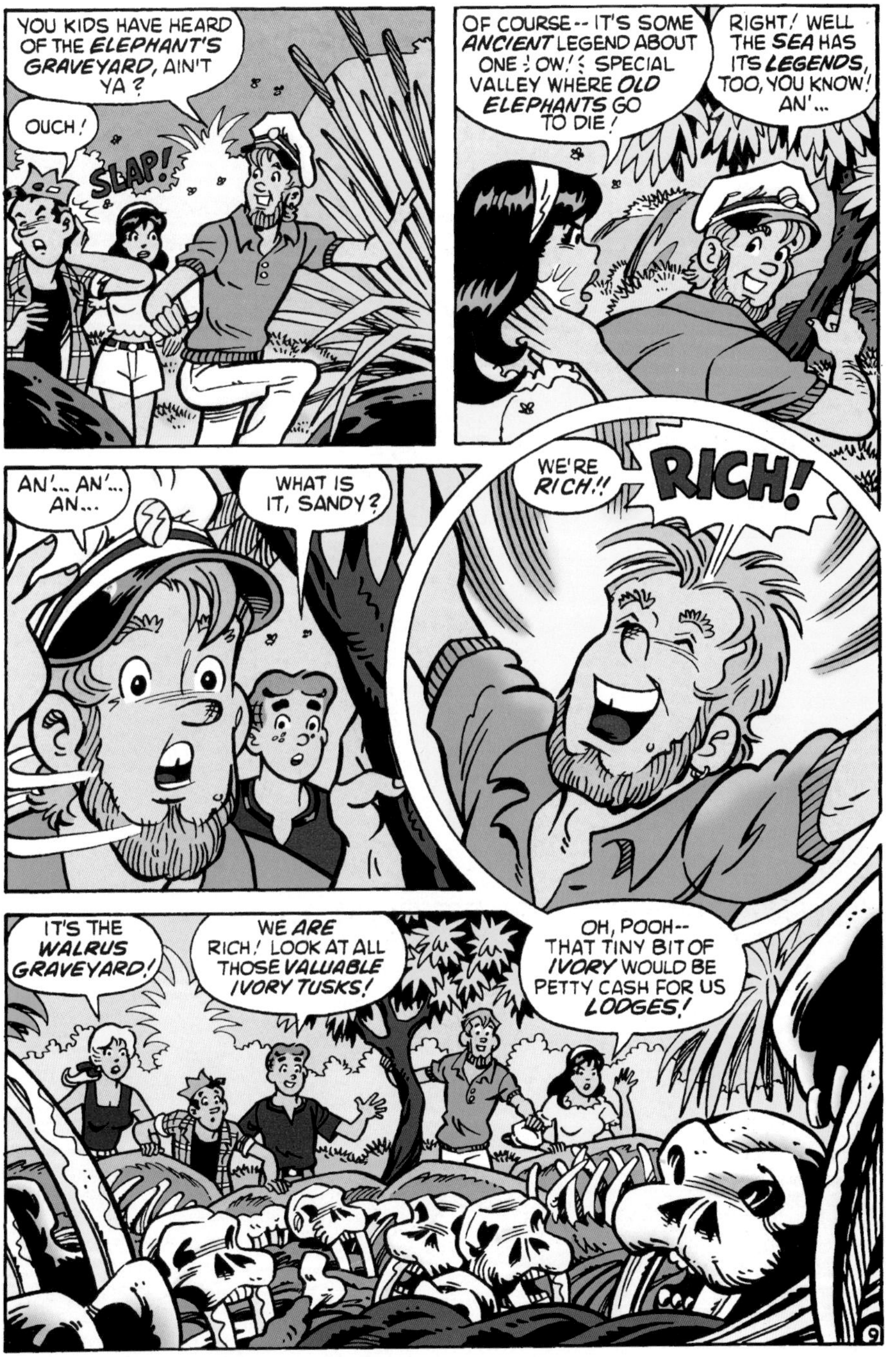
YOU KIDS HAVE HEARD OF THE ELEPHANT'S GRAVEYARD, AIN'T YA?
OUCH!
SLAP!
OF COURSE -- IT'S SOME ANCIENT LEGEND ABOUT ONE -OW!- SPECIAL VALLEY WHERE OLD ELEPHANTS GO TO DIE!
RIGHT! WELL THE SEA HAS ITS LEGENDS, TOO, YOU KNOW! AN'...
AN'... AN'... AN...
WHAT IS IT, SANDY?
WE'RE RICH!!
RICH!
IT'S THE WALRUS GRAVEYARD!
WE ARE RICH! LOOK AT ALL THOSE VALUABLE IVORY TUSKS!
OH, POOH-- THAT TINY BIT OF IVORY WOULD BE PETTY CASH FOR US LODGES!
9

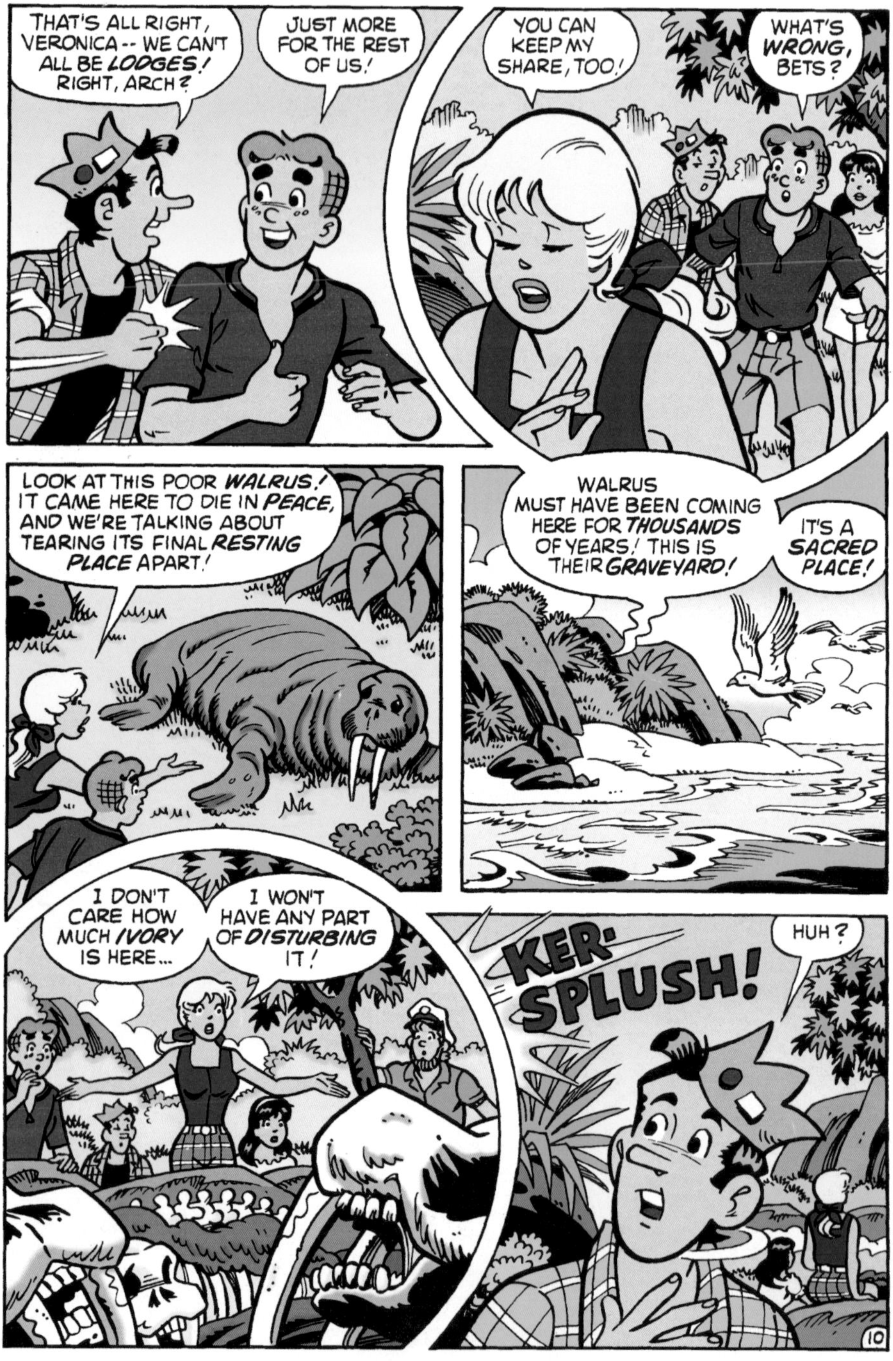
THAT'S ALL RIGHT, VERONICA -- WE CAN'T ALL BE LODGES! RIGHT, ARCH?
JUST MORE FOR THE REST OF US!
YOU CAN KEEP MY SHARE, TOO!
WHAT'S WRONG, BETS?
LOOK AT THIS POOR WALRUS! IT CAME HERE TO DIE IN PEACE, AND WE'RE TALKING ABOUT TEARING ITS FINAL RESTING PLACE APART!
WALRUS MUST HAVE BEEN COMING HERE FOR THOUSANDS OF YEARS! THIS IS THEIR GRAVEYARD!
IT'S A SACRED PLACE!
I DON'T CARE HOW MUCH IVORY IS HERE...
I WON'T HAVE ANY PART OF DISTURBING IT!
KER-SPLUSH!
HUH?
10

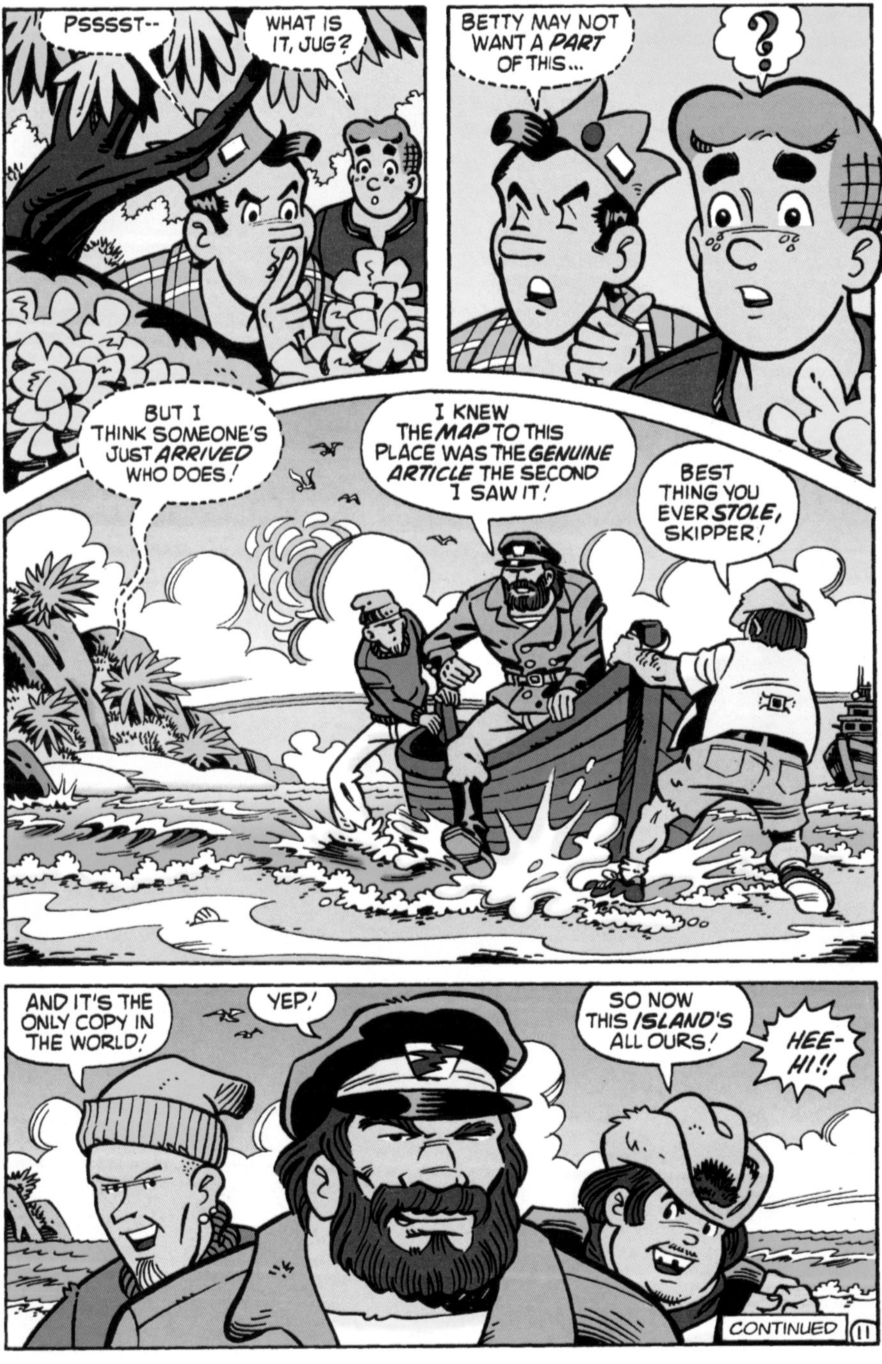
PSSSST--
WHAT IS IT, JUG?
BETTY MAY NOT WANT A PART OF THIS...
?
BUT I THINK SOMEONE'S JUST ARRIVED WHO DOES!
I KNEW THE MAP TO THIS PLACE WAS THE GENUINE ARTICLE THE SECOND I SAW IT!
BEST THING YOU EVER STOLE, SKIPPER!
AND IT'S THE ONLY COPY IN THE WORLD!
YEP!
SO NOW THIS ISLAND'S ALL OURS!
HEE-HI!!
CONTINUED
11

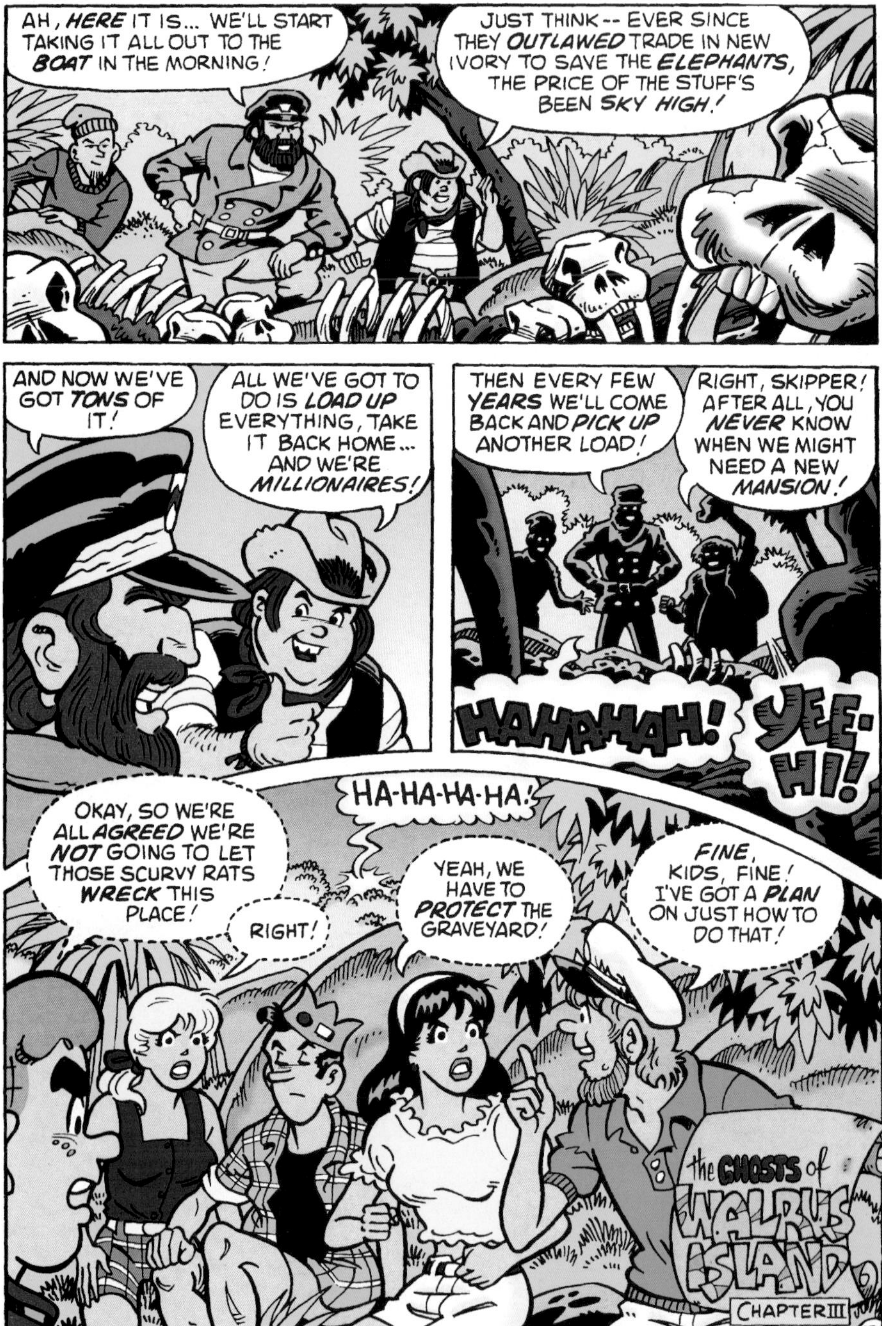
AH, HERE IT IS... WE'LL START TAKING IT ALL OUT TO THE BOAT IN THE MORNING!
JUST THINK -- EVER SINCE THEY OUTLAWED TRADE IN NEW IVORY TO SAVE THE ELEPHANTS, THE PRICE OF THE STUFF'S BEEN SKY HIGH!
AND NOW WE'VE GOT TONS OF IT!
ALL WE'VE GOT TO DO IS LOAD UP EVERYTHING, TAKE IT BACK HOME... AND WE'RE MILLIONAIRES!
THEN EVERY FEW YEARS WE'LL COME BACK AND PICK UP ANOTHER LOAD!
RIGHT, SKIPPER! AFTER ALL, YOU NEVER KNOW WHEN WE MIGHT NEED A NEW MANSION!
HAHAHAH!
YEE-HI!
HA-HA-HA-HA!
OKAY, SO WE'RE ALL AGREED WE'RE NOT GOING TO LET THOSE SCURVY RATS WRECK THIS PLACE!
RIGHT!
YEAH, WE HAVE TO PROTECT THE GRAVEYARD!
FINE, KIDS, FINE! I'VE GOT A PLAN ON JUST HOW TO DO THAT!
the GHOSTS of WALRUS ISLAND
CHAPTER III
12

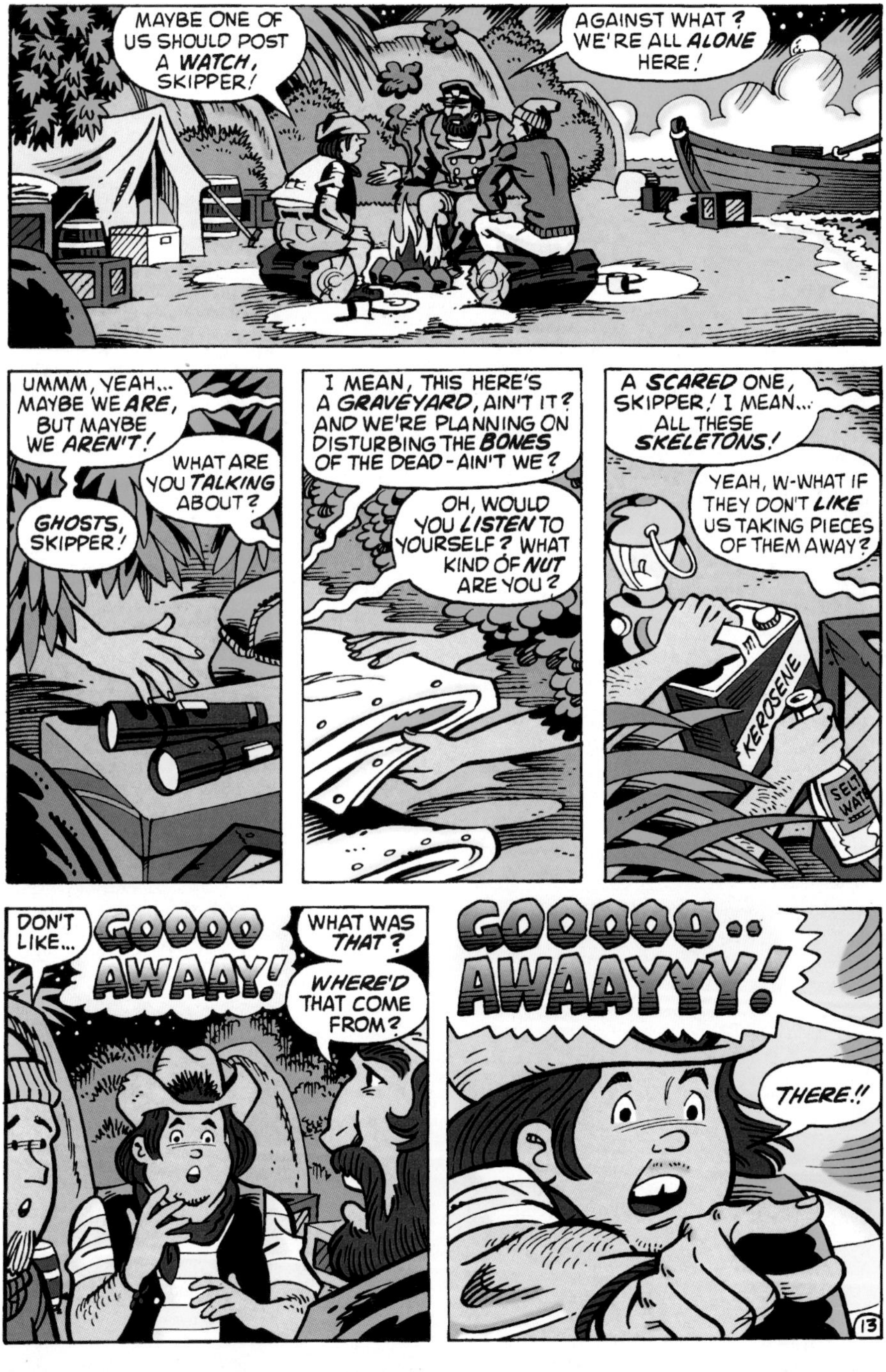
MAYBE ONE OF US SHOULD POST A WATCH, SKIPPER!
AGAINST WHAT? WE'RE ALL ALONE HERE!
UMMM, YEAH... MAYBE WE ARE, BUT MAYBE WE AREN'T!
WHAT ARE YOU TALKING ABOUT?
GHOSTS, SKIPPER!
I MEAN, THIS HERE'S A GRAVEYARD, AIN'T IT? AND WE'RE PLANNING ON DISTURBING THE BONES OF THE DEAD - AIN'T WE?
OH, WOULD YOU LISTEN TO YOURSELF? WHAT KIND OF NUT ARE YOU?
A SCARED ONE, SKIPPER! I MEAN... ALL THESE SKELETONS!
YEAH, W-WHAT IF THEY DON'T LIKE US TAKING PIECES OF THEM AWAY?
KEROSENE
DON'T LIKE...
GOOOO AWAAAY!
WHAT WAS THAT?
WHERE'D THAT COME FROM?
GOOOOO.. AWAAAYYY!
THERE!!
13

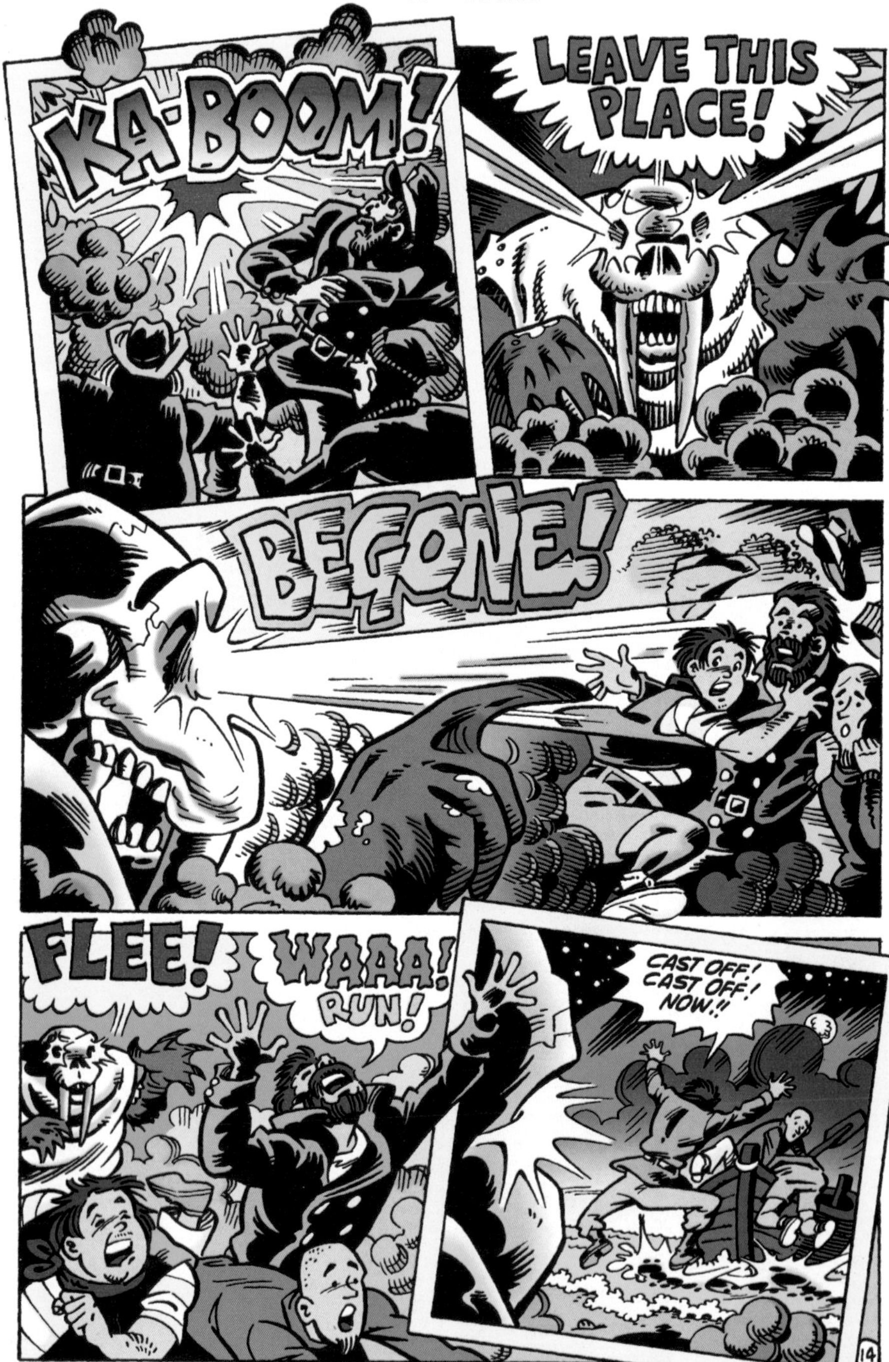
KA-BOOM!
LEAVE THIS PLACE!
BEGONE!
FLEE!
WAAA! RUN!
CAST OFF! CAST OFF! NOW.!!
14

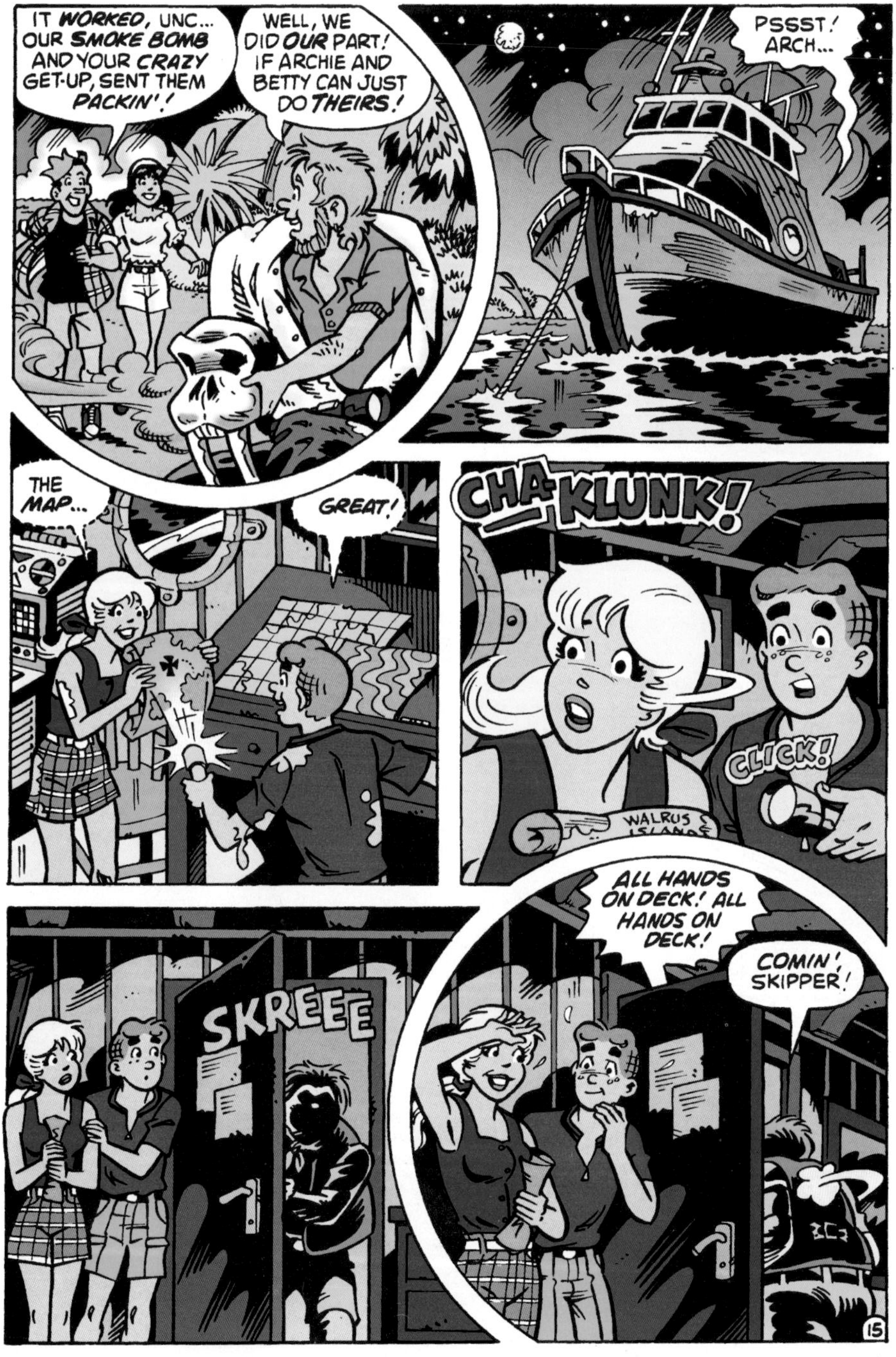
IT WORKED, UNC... OUR SMOKE BOMB AND YOUR CRAZY GET-UP, SENT THEM PACKIN'!
WELL, WE DID OUR PART! IF ARCHIE AND BETTY CAN JUST DO THEIRS!
PSSST! ARCH...
THE MAP...
GREAT!
CHA-KLUNK!
CLICK!
WALRUS ISLAND
SKREEEE
ALL HANDS ON DECK! ALL HANDS ON DECK!
COMIN', SKIPPER!
15

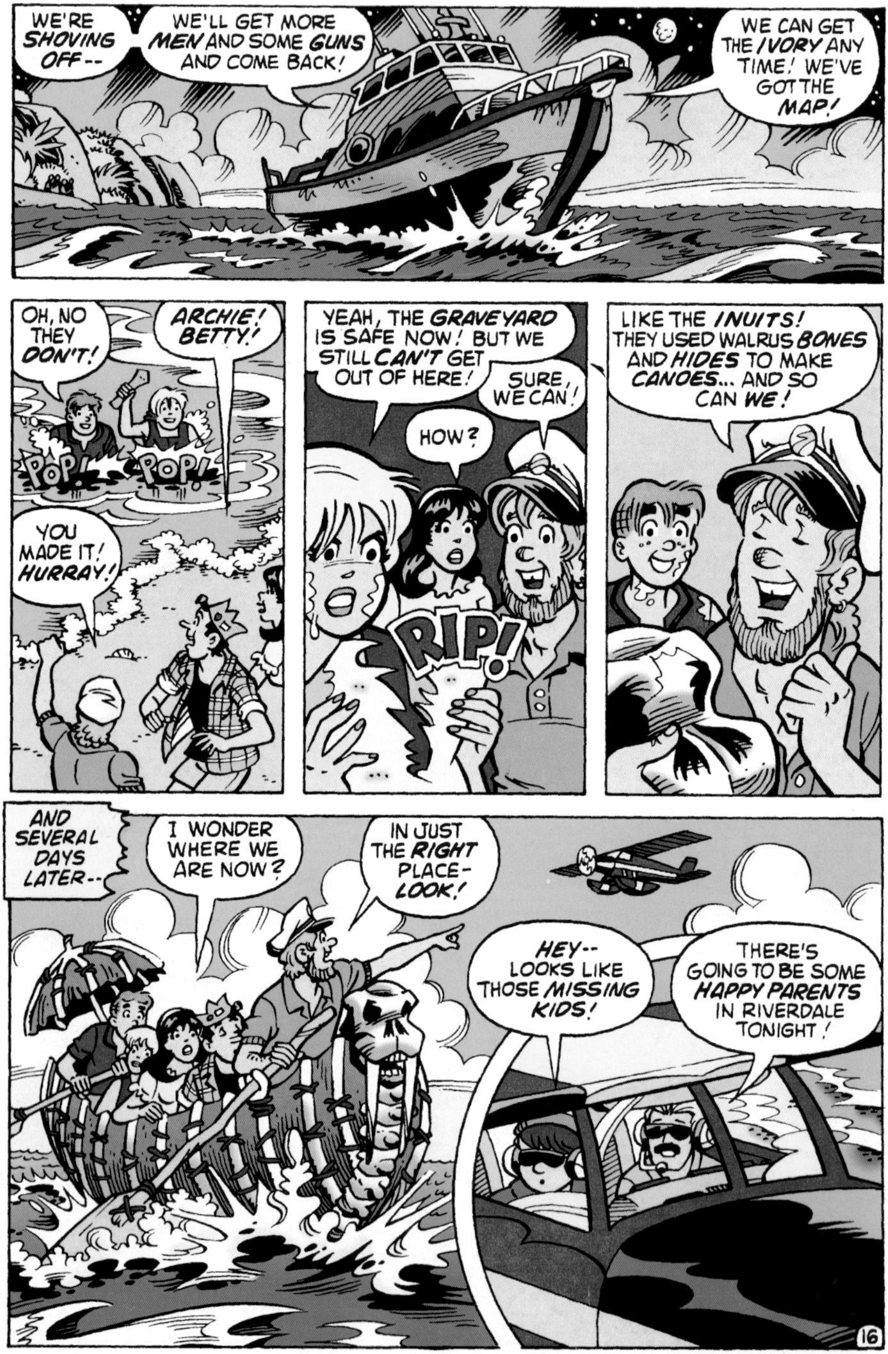
WE'RE SHOVING OFF--
WE'LL GET MORE MEN AND SOME GUNS AND COME BACK!
WE CAN GET THE IVORY ANY TIME! WE'VE GOT THE MAP!
OH, NO THEY DON'T!
ARCHIE! BETTY!
POP! POP!
YOU MADE IT! HURRAY!
YEAH, THE GRAVEYARD IS SAFE NOW! BUT WE STILL CAN'T GET OUT OF HERE!
HOW?
SURE, WE CAN!
RIP!
LIKE THE INUITS! THEY USED WALRUS BONES AND HIDES TO MAKE CANOES... AND SO CAN WE!
AND SEVERAL DAYS LATER--
I WONDER WHERE WE ARE NOW?
IN JUST THE RIGHT PLACE- LOOK!
HEY-- LOOKS LIKE THOSE MISSING KIDS!
THERE'S GOING TO BE SOME HAPPY PARENTS IN RIVERDALE TONIGHT!
16

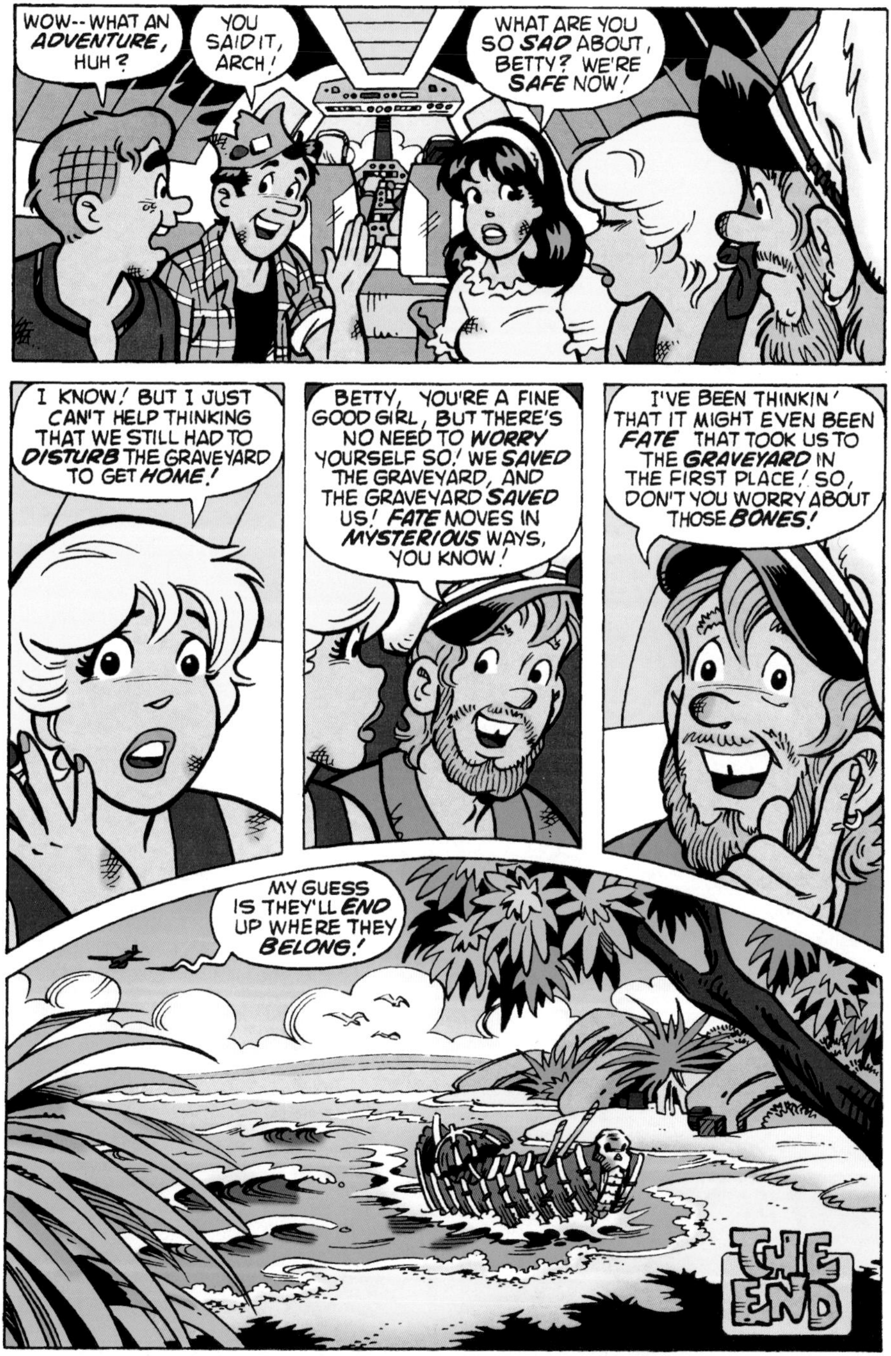
WOW--WHAT AN ADVENTURE, HUH?
YOU SAID IT, ARCH!
WHAT ARE YOU SO SAD ABOUT, BETTY? WE'RE SAFE NOW!
I KNOW! BUT I JUST CAN'T HELP THINKING THAT WE STILL HAD TO DISTURB THE GRAVEYARD TO GET HOME!
BETTY, YOU'RE A FINE GOOD GIRL, BUT THERE'S NO NEED TO WORRY YOURSELF SO! WE SAVED THE GRAVEYARD, AND THE GRAVEYARD SAVED US! FATE MOVES IN MYSTERIOUS WAYS, YOU KNOW!
I'VE BEEN THINKIN' THAT IT MIGHT EVEN BEEN FATE THAT TOOK US TO THE GRAVEYARD IN THE FIRST PLACE! SO, DON'T YOU WORRY ABOUT THOSE BONES!
MY GUESS IS THEY'LL END UP WHERE THEY BELONG!
THE END

Archie in "SHORT SUBJECTS"

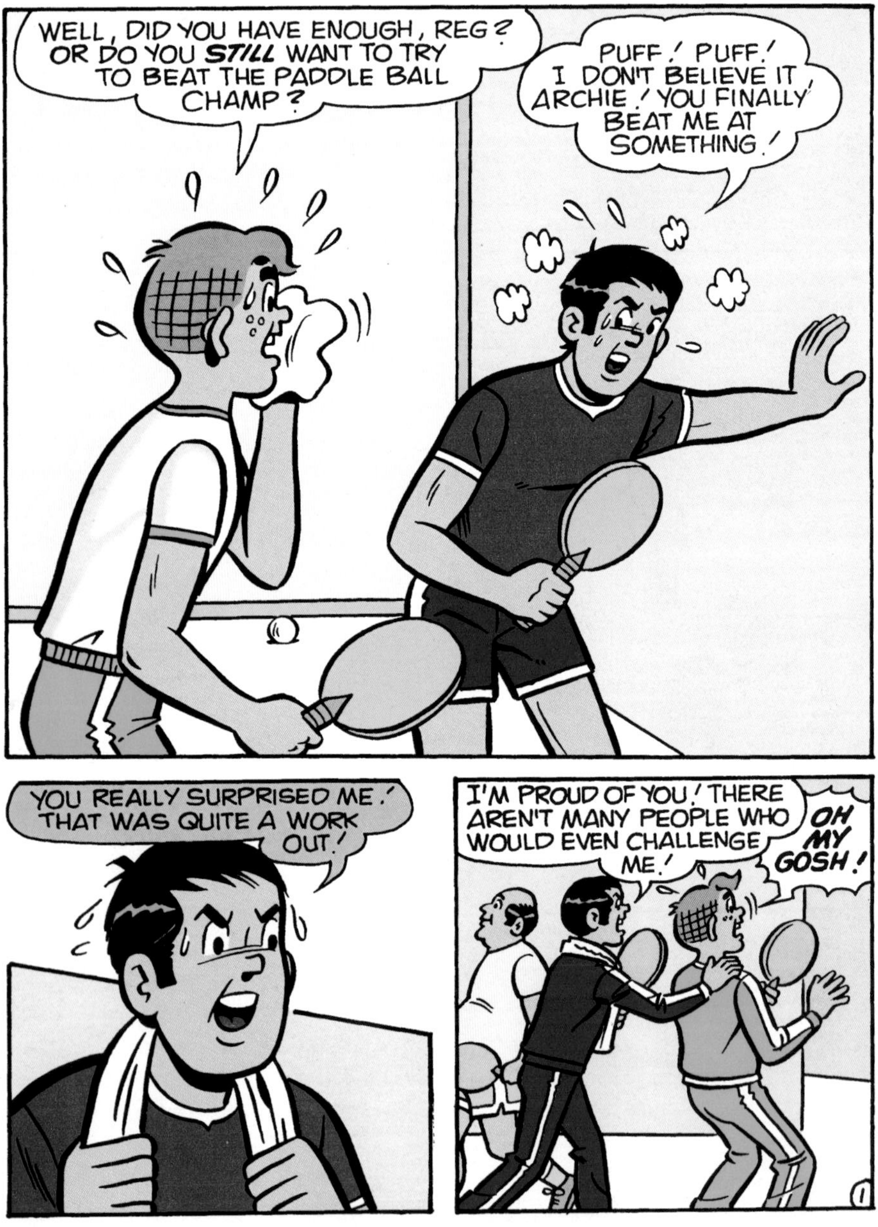
WELL, DID YOU HAVE ENOUGH, REG? OR DO YOU STILL WANT TO TRY TO BEAT THE PADDLE BALL CHAMP?
PUFF! PUFF! I DON'T BELIEVE IT, ARCHIE! YOU FINALLY BEAT ME AT SOMETHING!
YOU REALLY SURPRISED ME! THAT WAS QUITE A WORK OUT!
I'M PROUD OF YOU! THERE AREN'T MANY PEOPLE WHO WOULD EVEN CHALLENGE ME!
OH MY GOSH!
1

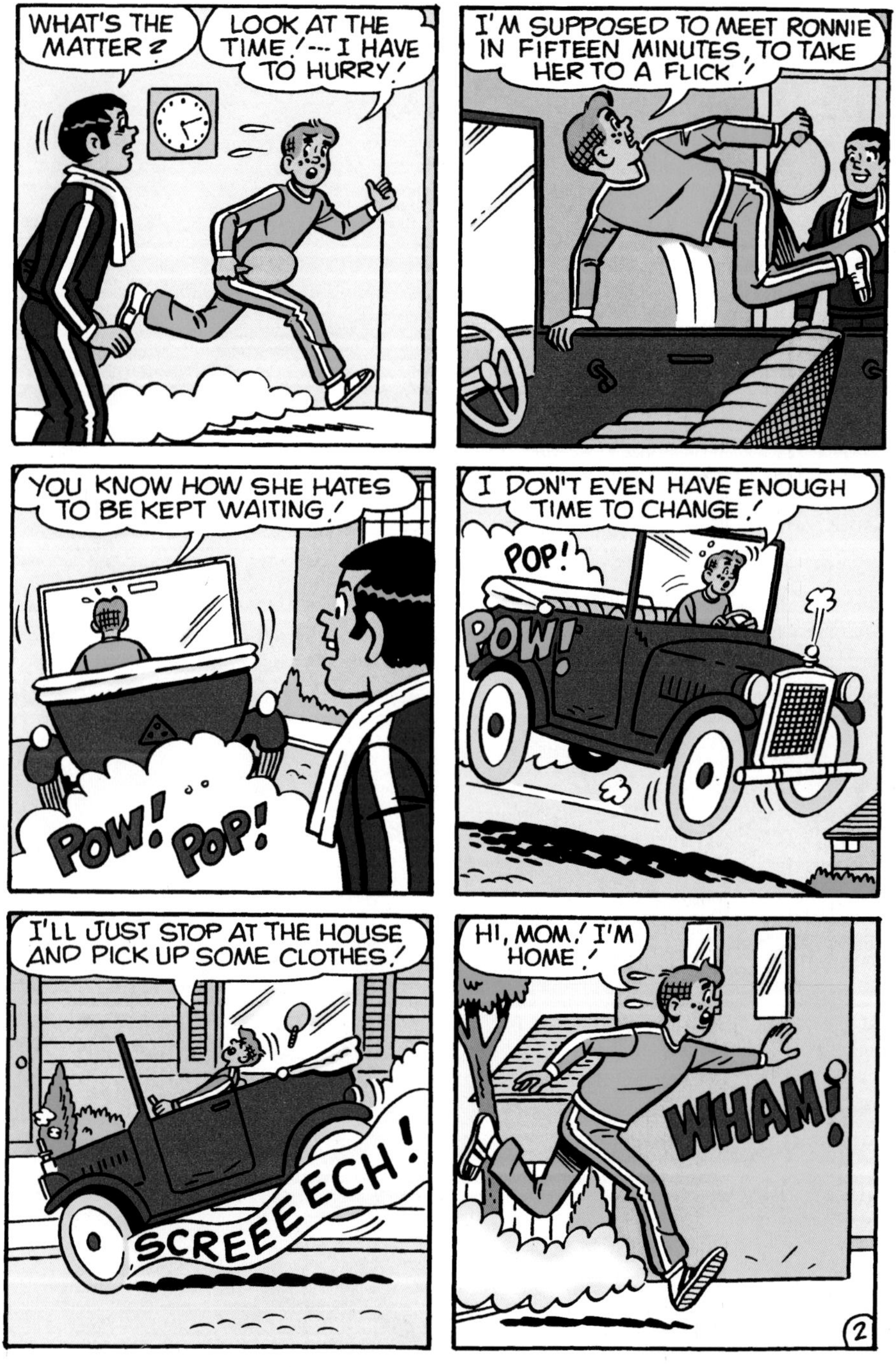
WHAT'S THE MATTER?
LOOK AT THE TIME! -- I HAVE TO HURRY!
I'M SUPPOSED TO MEET RONNIE IN FIFTEEN MINUTES, TO TAKE HER TO A FLICK!
YOU KNOW HOW SHE HATES TO BE KEPT WAITING!
POW! POP!
I DON'T EVEN HAVE ENOUGH TIME TO CHANGE!
POP!
POW!
I'LL JUST STOP AT THE HOUSE AND PICK UP SOME CLOTHES!
SCREEEECH!
HI, MOM! I'M HOME!
WHAM!
2

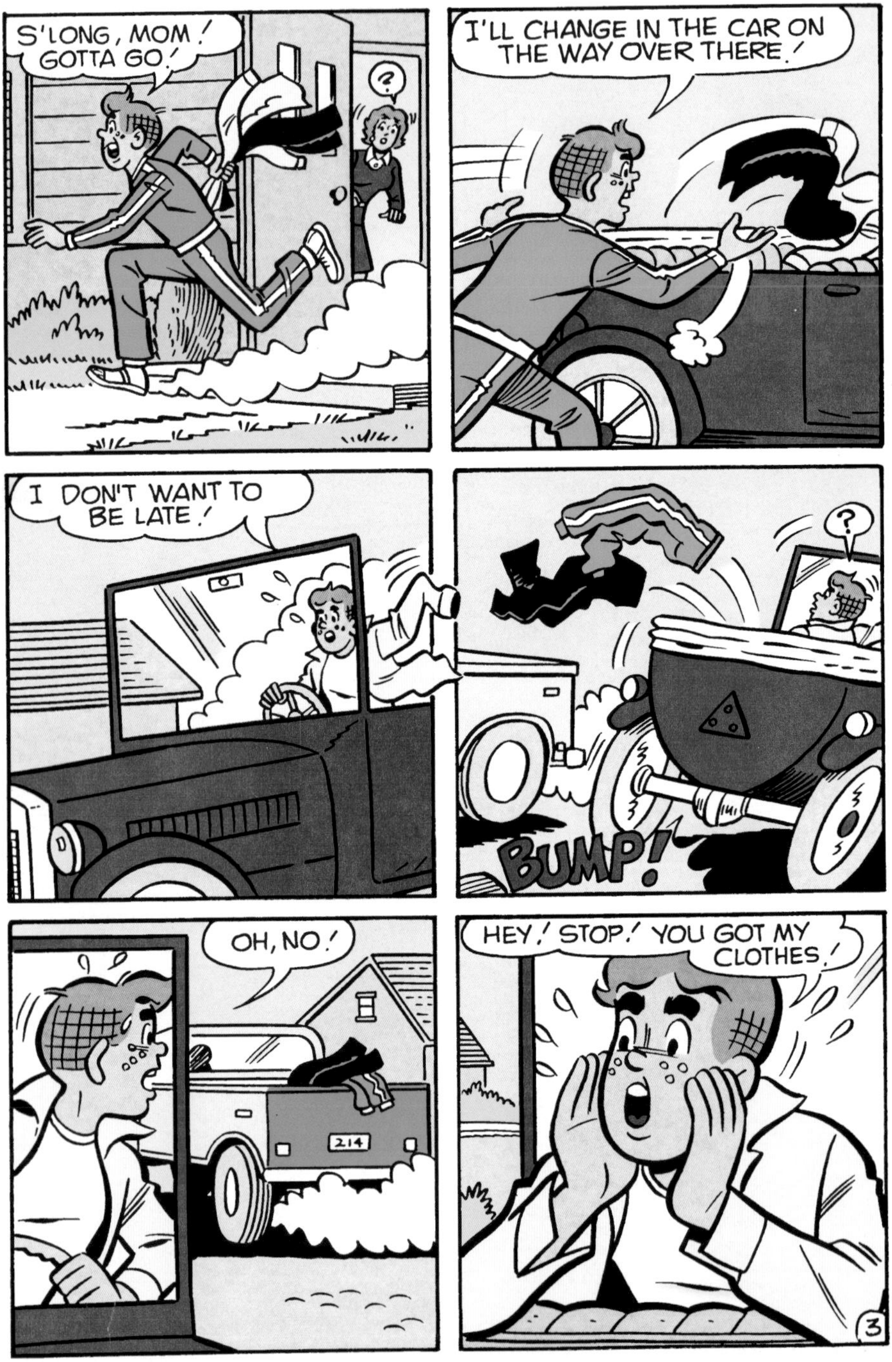
S'LONG, MOM! GOTTA GO!
I'LL CHANGE IN THE CAR ON THE WAY OVER THERE!
I DON'T WANT TO BE LATE!
BUMP!
OH, NO!
HEY! STOP! YOU GOT MY CLOTHES!
3

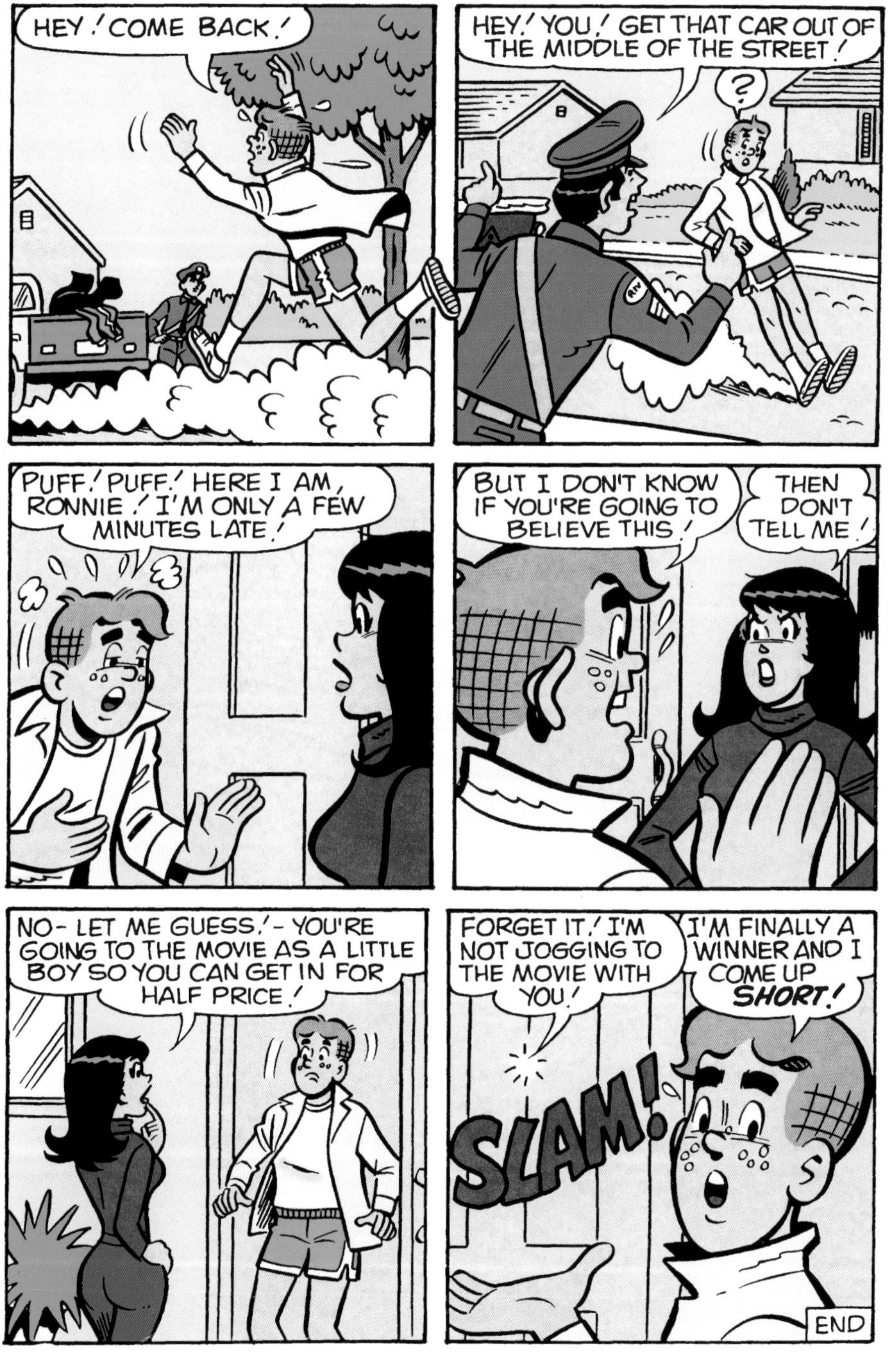
HEY! COME BACK!
HEY! YOU! GET THAT CAR OUT OF THE MIDDLE OF THE STREET!
?
PUFF! PUFF! HERE I AM, RONNIE! I'M ONLY A FEW MINUTES LATE!
BUT I DON'T KNOW IF YOU'RE GOING TO BELIEVE THIS!
THEN DON'T TELL ME!
NO- LET ME GUESS! - YOU'RE GOING TO THE MOVIE AS A LITTLE BOY SO YOU CAN GET IN FOR HALF PRICE!
FORGET IT! I'M NOT JOGGING TO THE MOVIE WITH YOU!
SLAM!
I'M FINALLY A WINNER AND I COME UP SHORT!
END

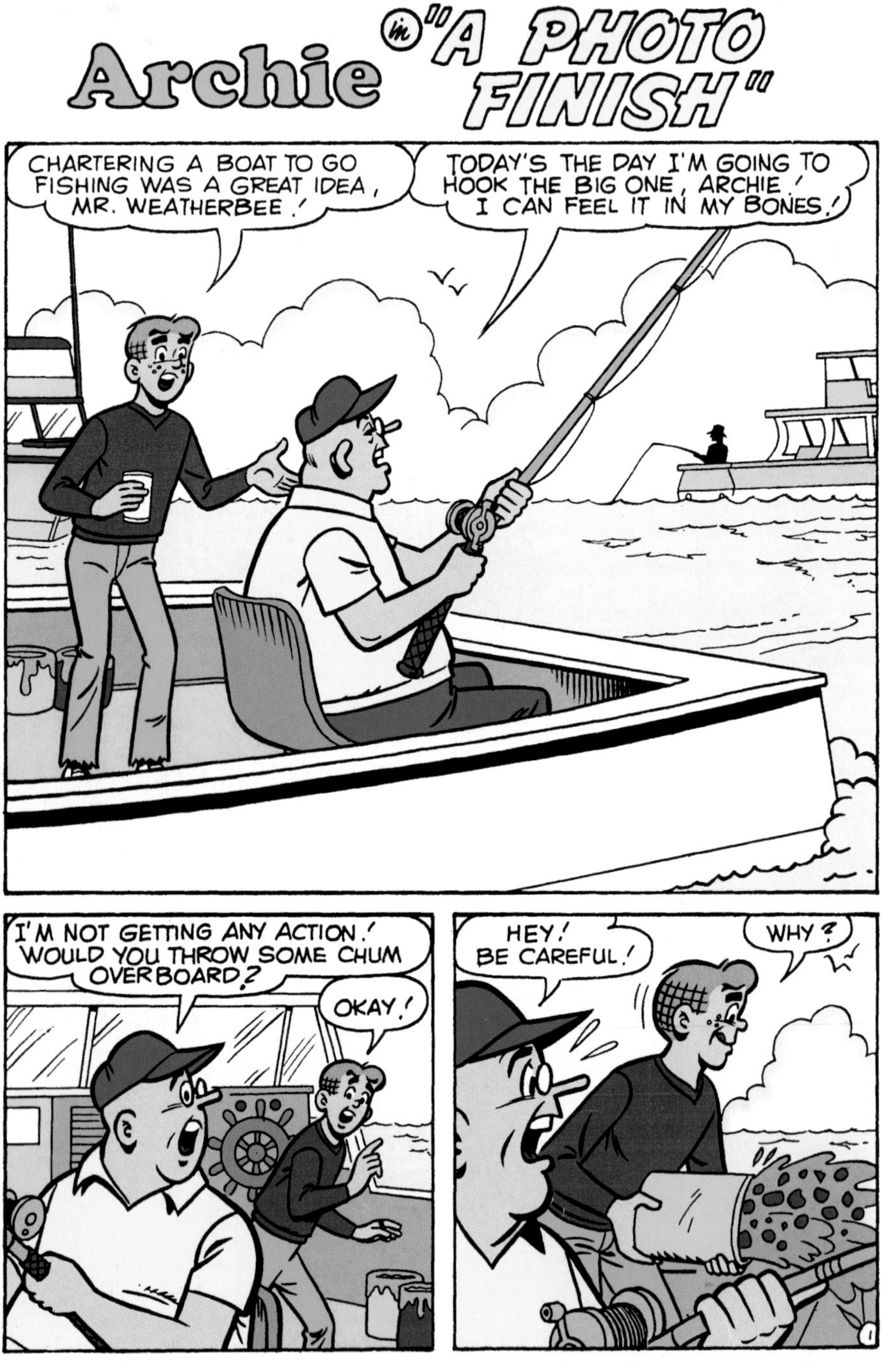
Archie in "A PHOTO FINISH"
CHARTERING A BOAT TO GO FISHING WAS A GREAT IDEA, MR. WEATHERBEE!
TODAY'S THE DAY I'M GOING TO HOOK THE BIG ONE, ARCHIE! I CAN FEEL IT IN MY BONES!
I'M NOT GETTING ANY ACTION! WOULD YOU THROW SOME CHUM OVERBOARD?
OKAY!
HEY! BE CAREFUL!
WHY?
1

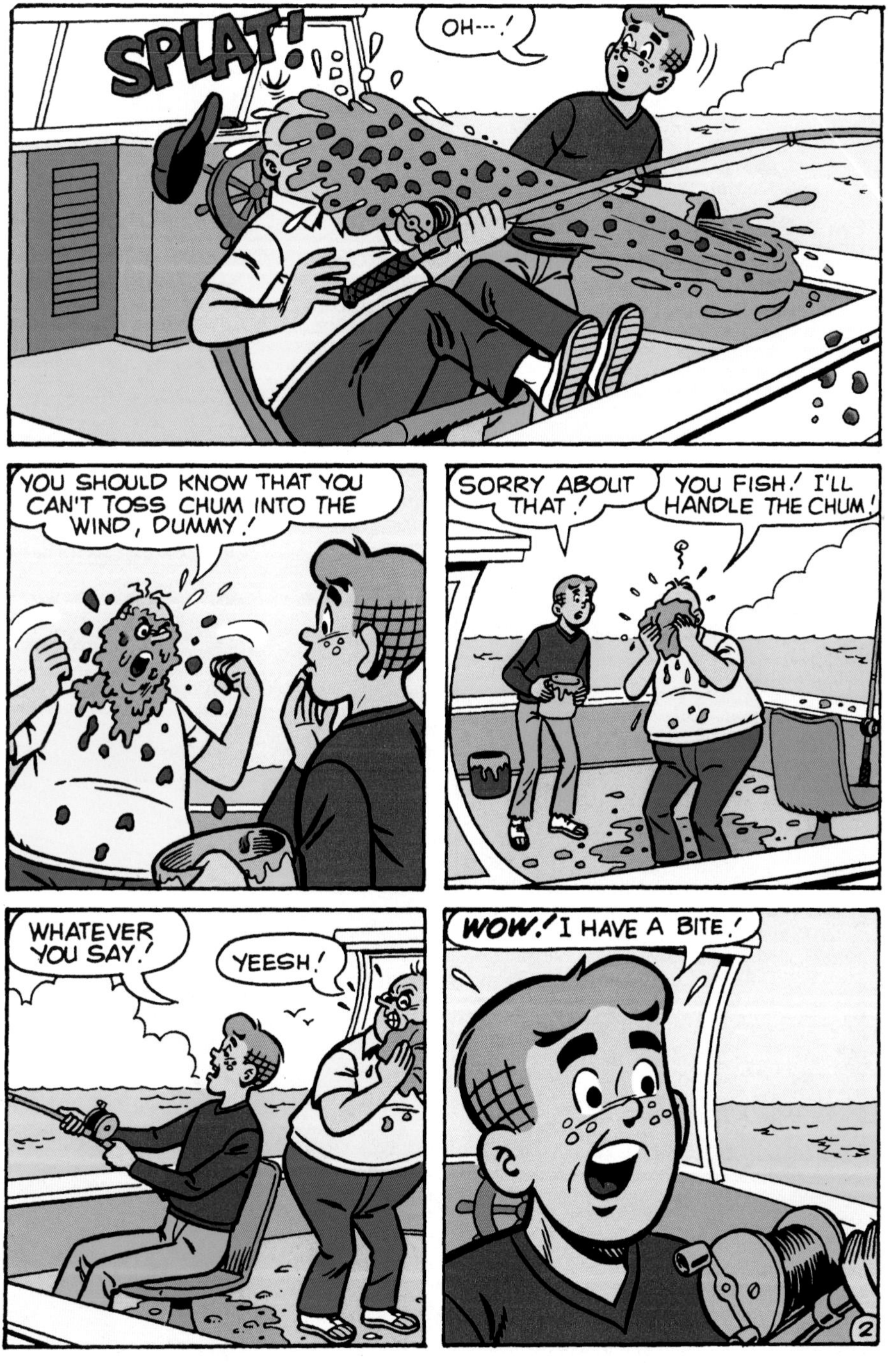
SPLAT!
OH---!
YOU SHOULD KNOW THAT YOU CAN'T TOSS CHUM INTO THE WIND, DUMMY!
SORRY ABOUT THAT!
YOU FISH! I'LL HANDLE THE CHUM!
WHATEVER YOU SAY!
YEESH!
WOW! I HAVE A BITE!
2

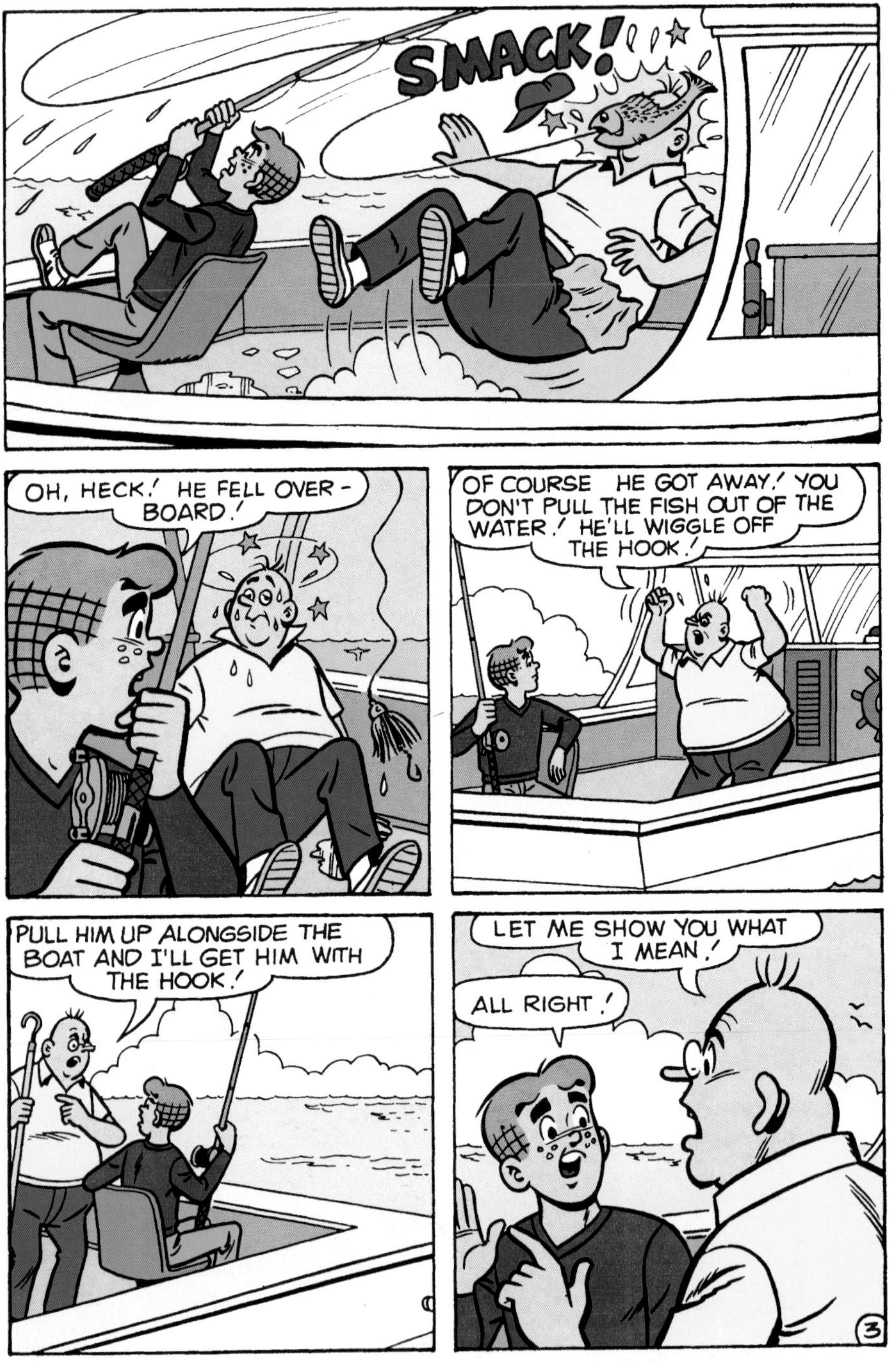
SMACK!
OH, HECK! HE FELL OVER-BOARD!
OF COURSE HE GOT AWAY! YOU DON'T PULL THE FISH OUT OF THE WATER! HE'LL WIGGLE OFF THE HOOK!
PULL HIM UP ALONGSIDE THE BOAT AND I'LL GET HIM WITH THE HOOK!
LET ME SHOW YOU WHAT I MEAN!
ALL RIGHT!
3

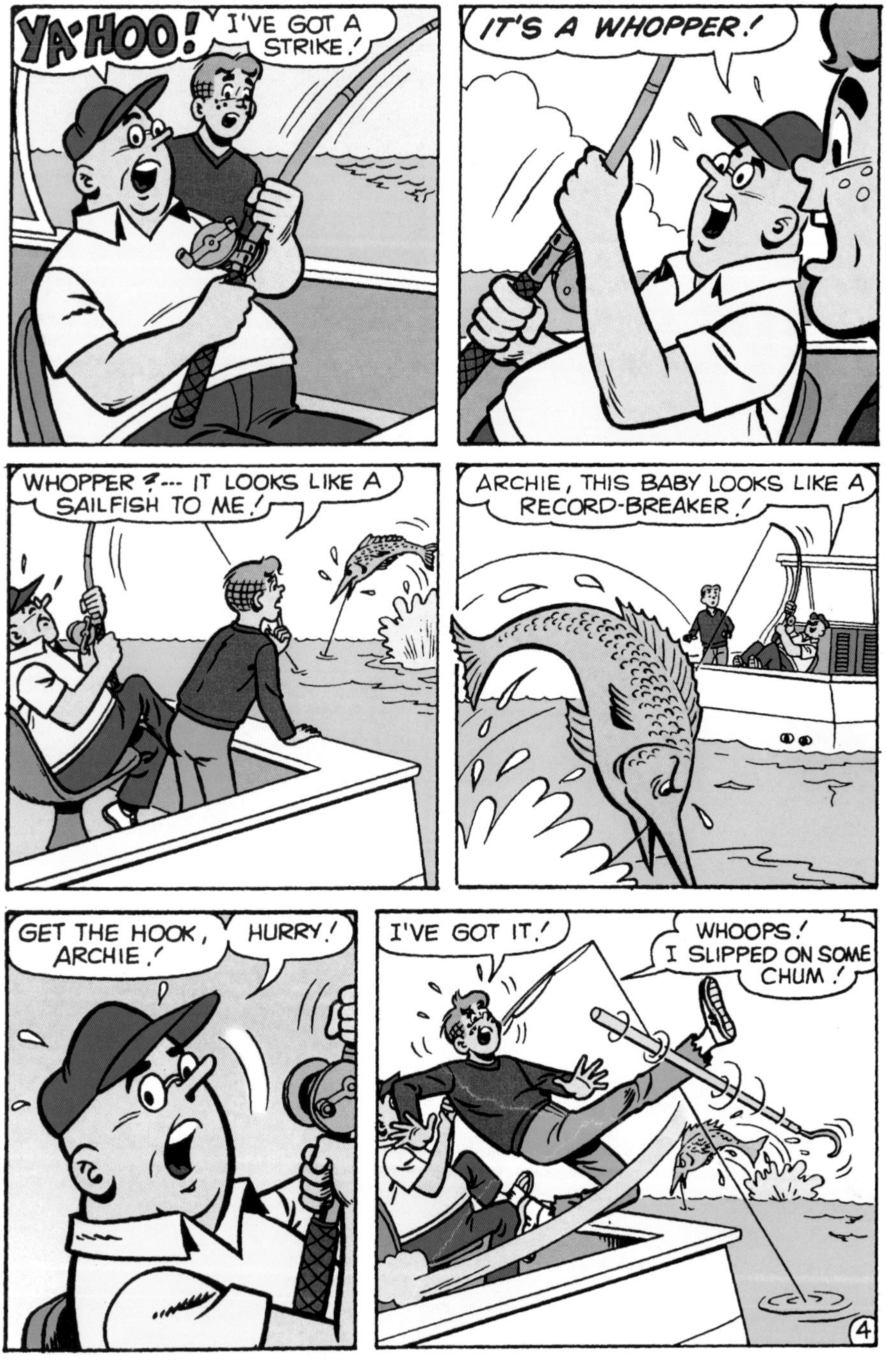
YA-HOO!
I'VE GOT A STRIKE!
IT'S A WHOPPER!
WHOPPER ?--- IT LOOKS LIKE A SAILFISH TO ME!
ARCHIE, THIS BABY LOOKS LIKE A RECORD-BREAKER!
GET THE HOOK, ARCHIE!
HURRY!
I'VE GOT IT!
WHOOPS! I SLIPPED ON SOME CHUM!
4

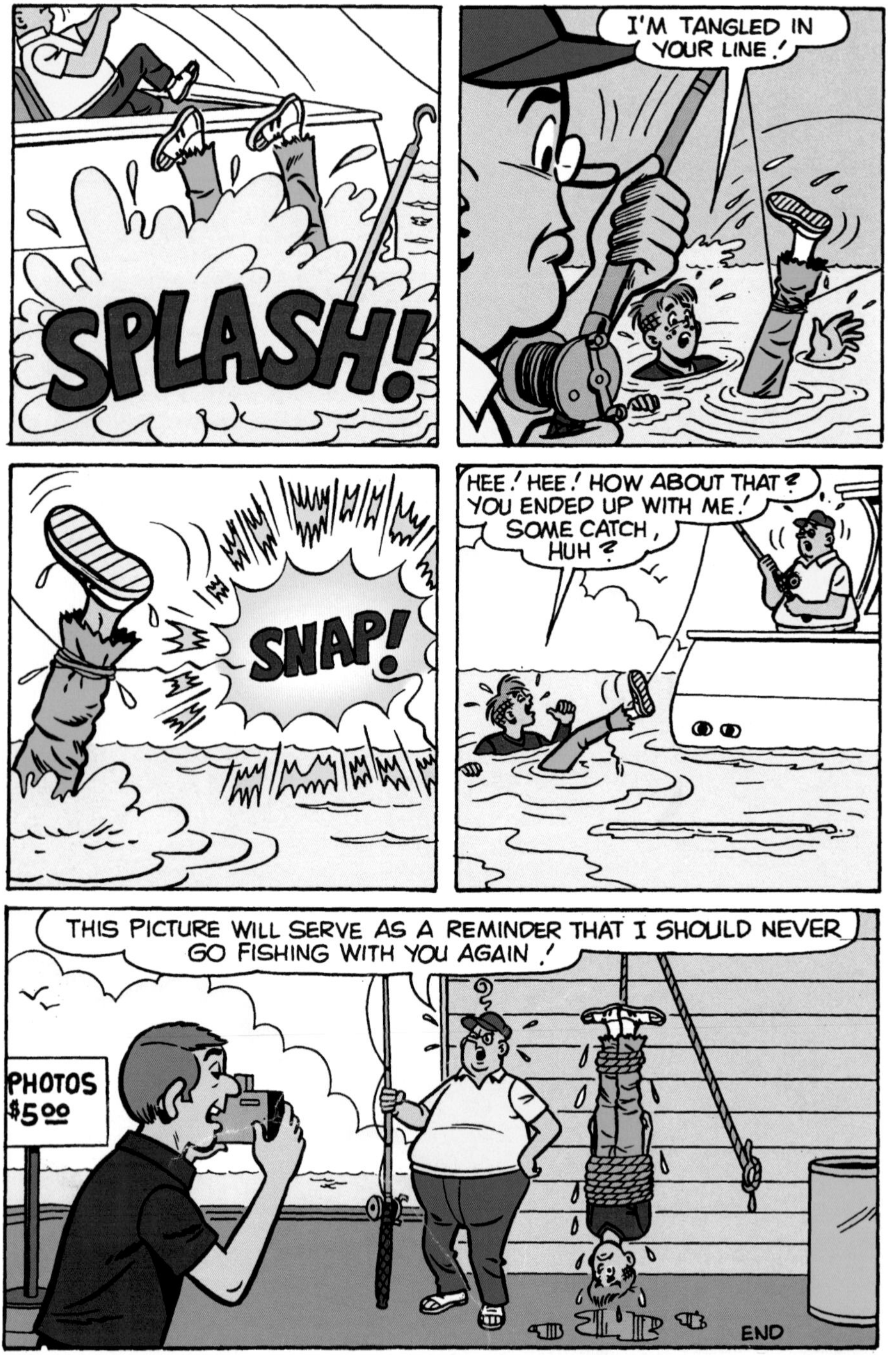
SPLASH!
I'M TANGLED IN YOUR LINE!
SNAP!
HEE! HEE! HOW ABOUT THAT? YOU ENDED UP WITH ME! SOME CATCH, HUH?
THIS PICTURE WILL SERVE AS A REMINDER THAT I SHOULD NEVER GO FISHING WITH YOU AGAIN!
PHOTOS $5.00
END

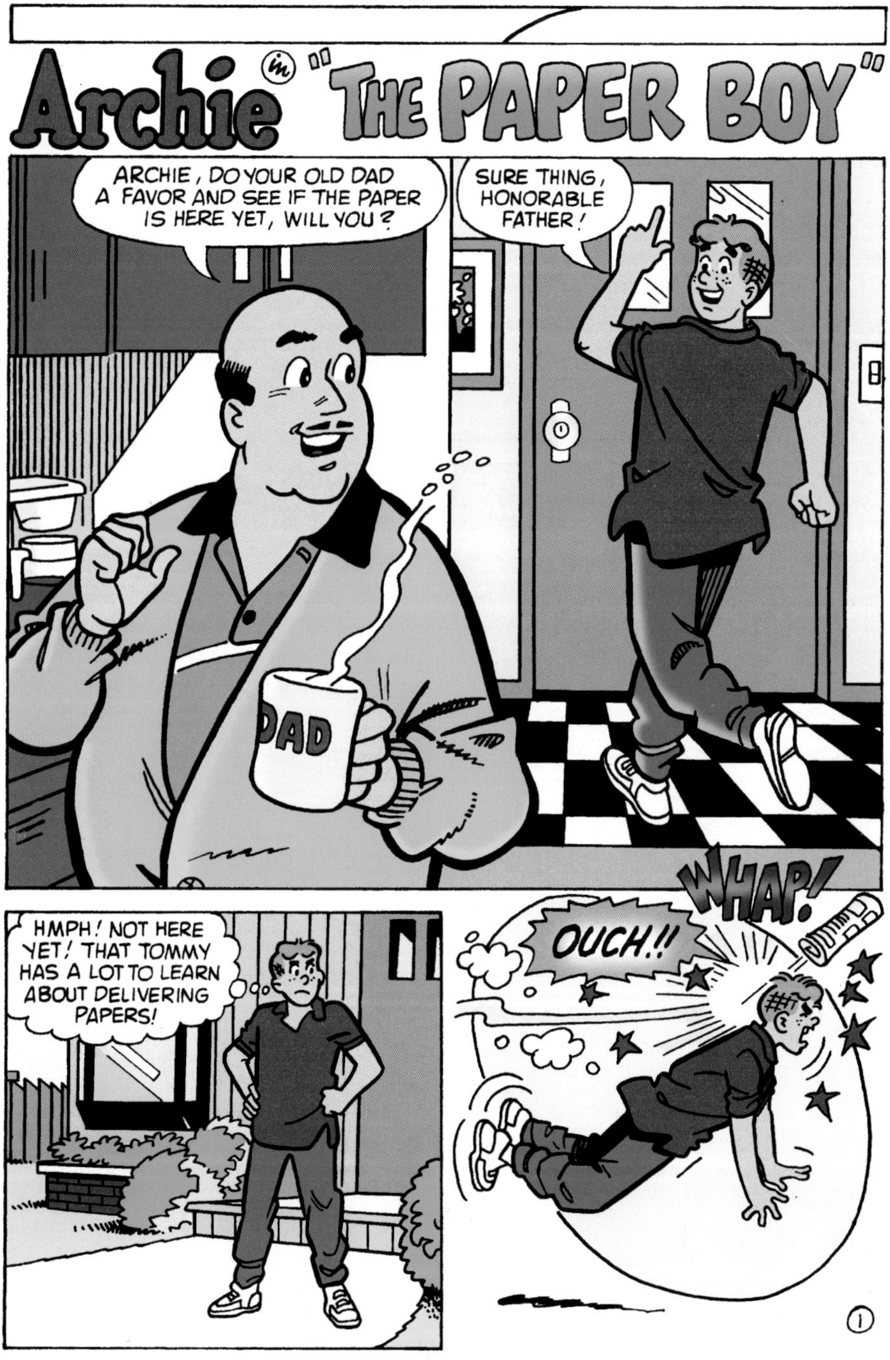
Archie in "THE PAPER BOY"
ARCHIE, DO YOUR OLD DAD A FAVOR AND SEE IF THE PAPER IS HERE YET, WILL YOU?
SURE THING, HONORABLE FATHER!
DAD
HMPH! NOT HERE YET! THAT TOMMY HAS A LOT TO LEARN ABOUT DELIVERING PAPERS!
WHAP!
OUCH!!
1

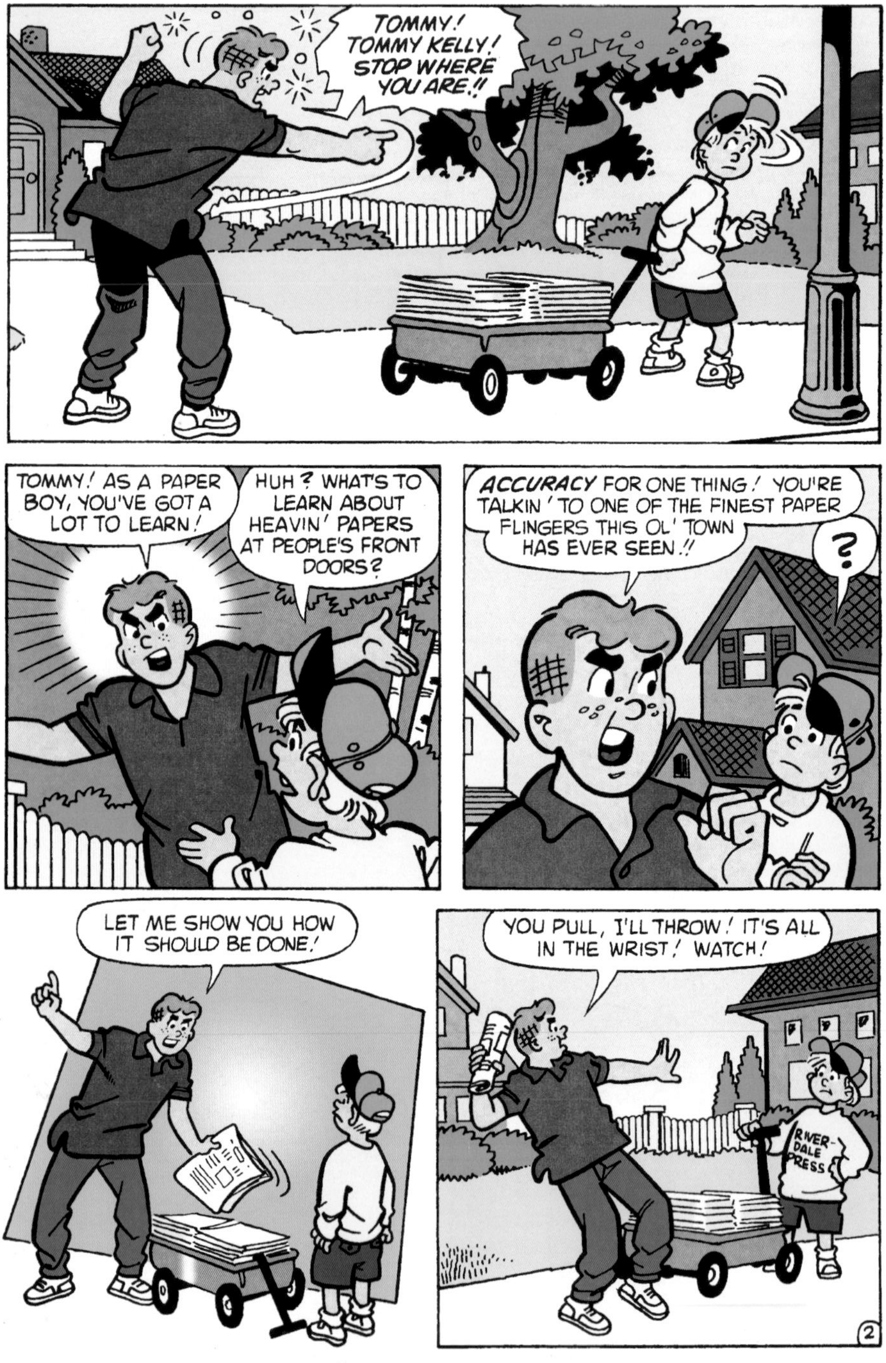
TOMMY! TOMMY KELLY! STOP WHERE YOU ARE!!
TOMMY! AS A PAPER BOY, YOU'VE GOT A LOT TO LEARN!
HUH? WHAT'S TO LEARN ABOUT HEAVIN' PAPERS AT PEOPLE'S FRONT DOORS?
ACCURACY FOR ONE THING! YOU'RE TALKIN' TO ONE OF THE FINEST PAPER FLINGERS THIS OL' TOWN HAS EVER SEEN!!
?
LET ME SHOW YOU HOW IT SHOULD BE DONE!
YOU PULL, I'LL THROW! IT'S ALL IN THE WRIST! WATCH!
RIVER-DALE PRESS
2

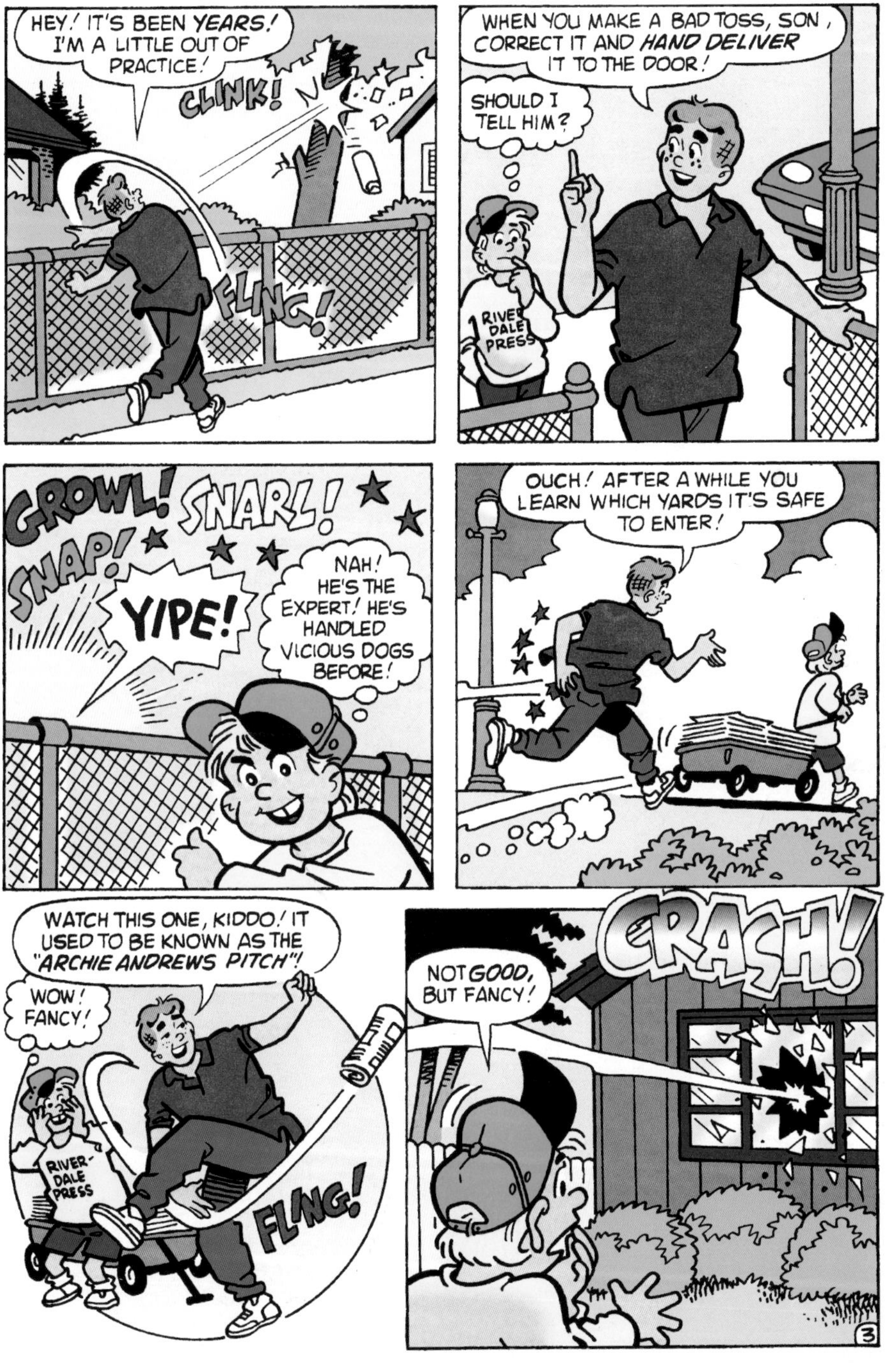
HEY! IT'S BEEN YEARS! I'M A LITTLE OUT OF PRACTICE!
CLINK!
FLING!
WHEN YOU MAKE A BAD TOSS, SON, CORRECT IT AND HAND DELIVER IT TO THE DOOR!
SHOULD I TELL HIM?
RIVER DALE PRESS
GROWL!
SNARL!
SNAP!
YIPE!
NAH! HE'S THE EXPERT! HE'S HANDLED VICIOUS DOGS BEFORE!
OUCH! AFTER A WHILE YOU LEARN WHICH YARDS IT'S SAFE TO ENTER!
WATCH THIS ONE, KIDDO! IT USED TO BE KNOWN AS THE "ARCHIE ANDREWS PITCH"!
WOW! FANCY!
RIVER-DALE PRESS
FLING!
CRASH!
NOT GOOD, BUT FANCY!
3

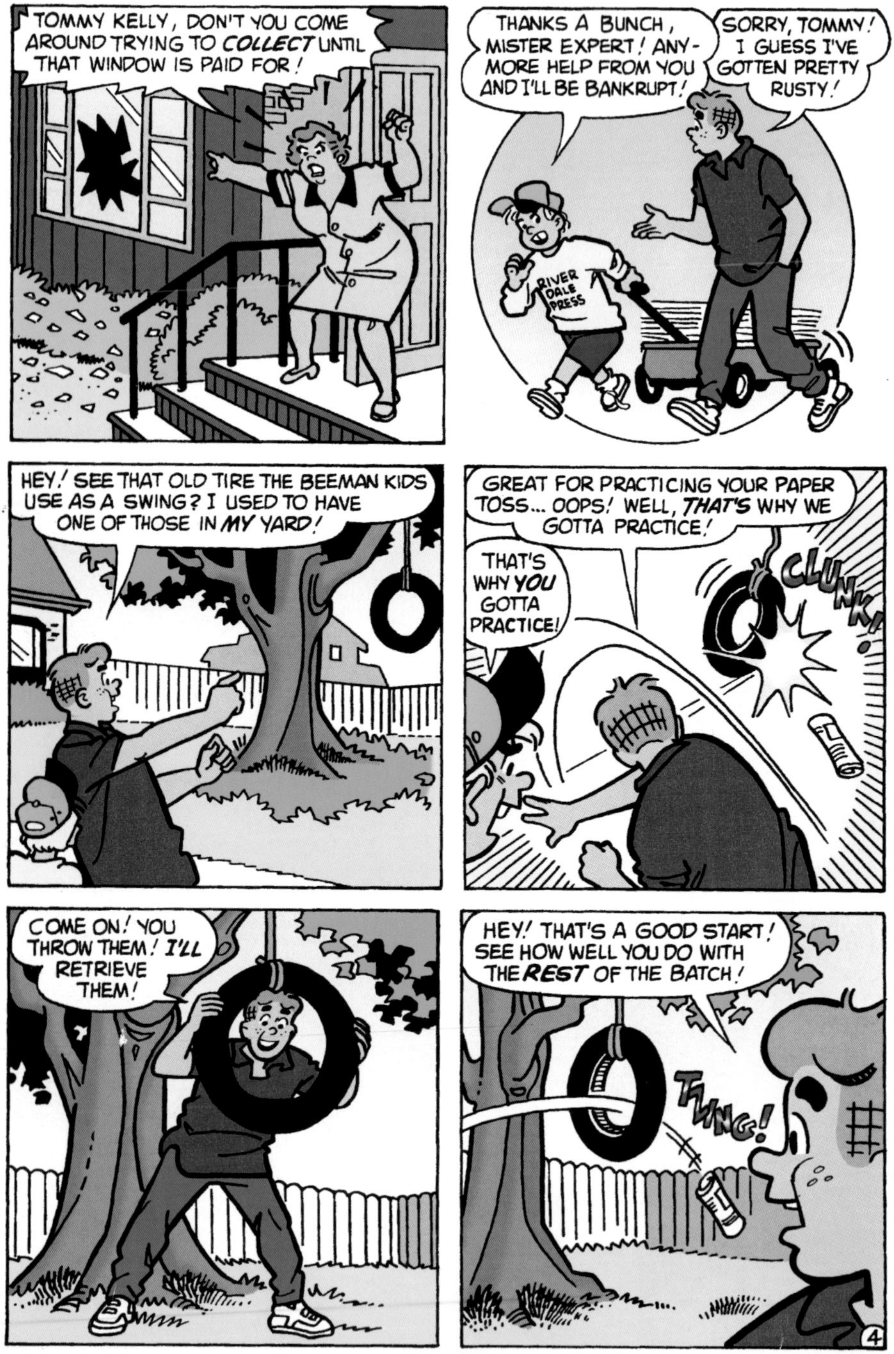
TOMMY KELLY, DON'T YOU COME AROUND TRYING TO COLLECT UNTIL THAT WINDOW IS PAID FOR!
THANKS A BUNCH, MISTER EXPERT! ANY-MORE HELP FROM YOU AND I'LL BE BANKRUPT!
SORRY, TOMMY! I GUESS I'VE GOTTEN PRETTY RUSTY!
RIVER DALE PRESS
HEY! SEE THAT OLD TIRE THE BEEMAN KIDS USE AS A SWING? I USED TO HAVE ONE OF THOSE IN MY YARD!
GREAT FOR PRACTICING YOUR PAPER TOSS... OOPS! WELL, THAT'S WHY WE GOTTA PRACTICE!
THAT'S WHY YOU GOTTA PRACTICE!
CLUNK!
COME ON! YOU THROW THEM! I'LL RETRIEVE THEM!
HEY! THAT'S A GOOD START! SEE HOW WELL YOU DO WITH THE REST OF THE BATCH!
TWUNG!
4

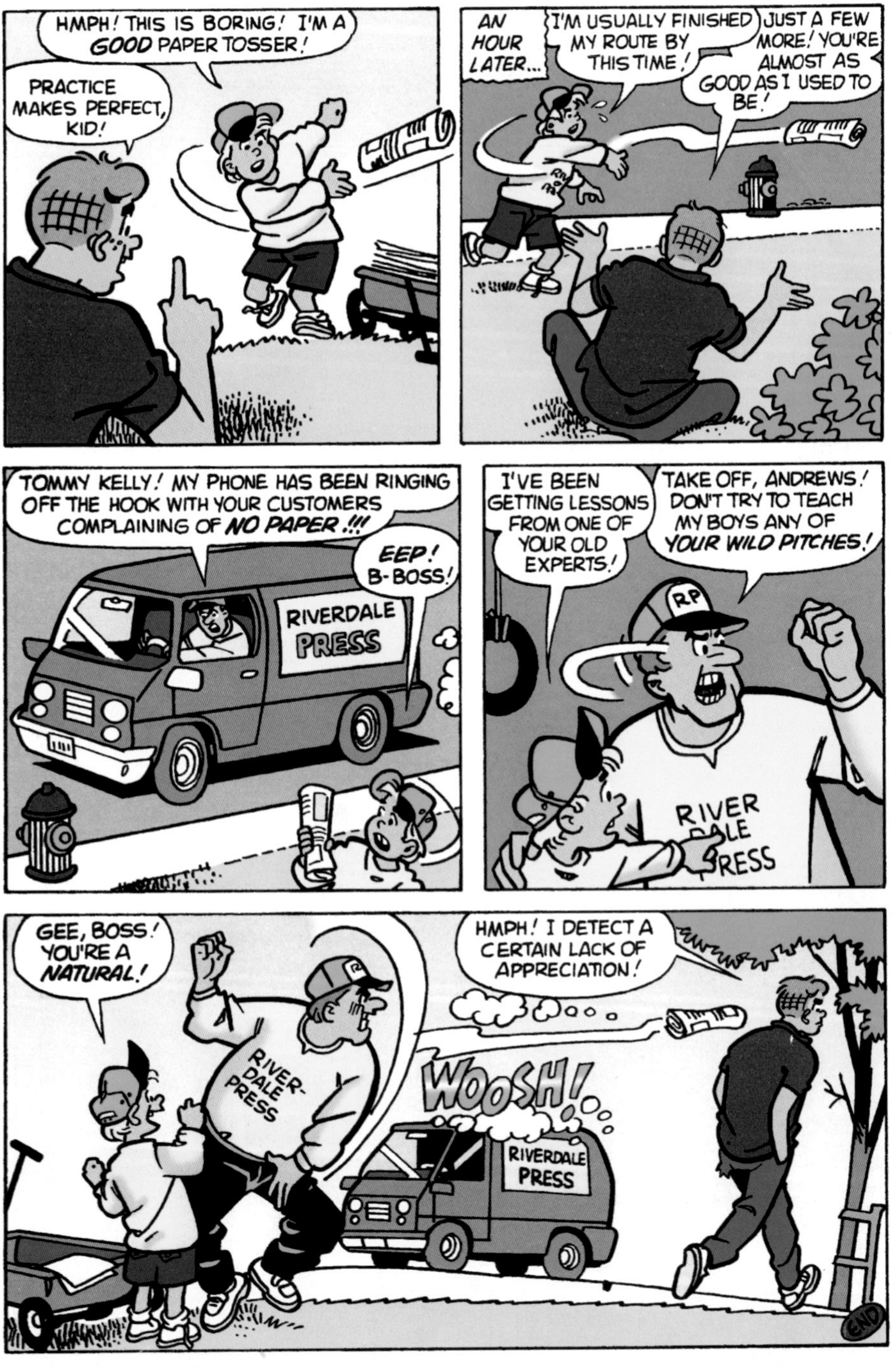
HMPH! THIS IS BORING! I'M A GOOD PAPER TOSSER!
PRACTICE MAKES PERFECT, KID!
AN HOUR LATER...
I'M USUALLY FINISHED MY ROUTE BY THIS TIME!
JUST A FEW MORE! YOU'RE ALMOST AS GOOD AS I USED TO BE!
TOMMY KELLY! MY PHONE HAS BEEN RINGING OFF THE HOOK WITH YOUR CUSTOMERS COMPLAINING OF NO PAPER!!!
RIVERDALE PRESS
EEP! B-BOSS!
I'VE BEEN GETTING LESSONS FROM ONE OF YOUR OLD EXPERTS!
TAKE OFF, ANDREWS! DON'T TRY TO TEACH MY BOYS ANY OF YOUR WILD PITCHES!
RP
RIVER DALE PRESS
GEE, BOSS! YOU'RE A NATURAL!
HMPH! I DETECT A CERTAIN LACK OF APPRECIATION!
RIVER-DALE PRESS
WOOSH!
RIVERDALE PRESS
END

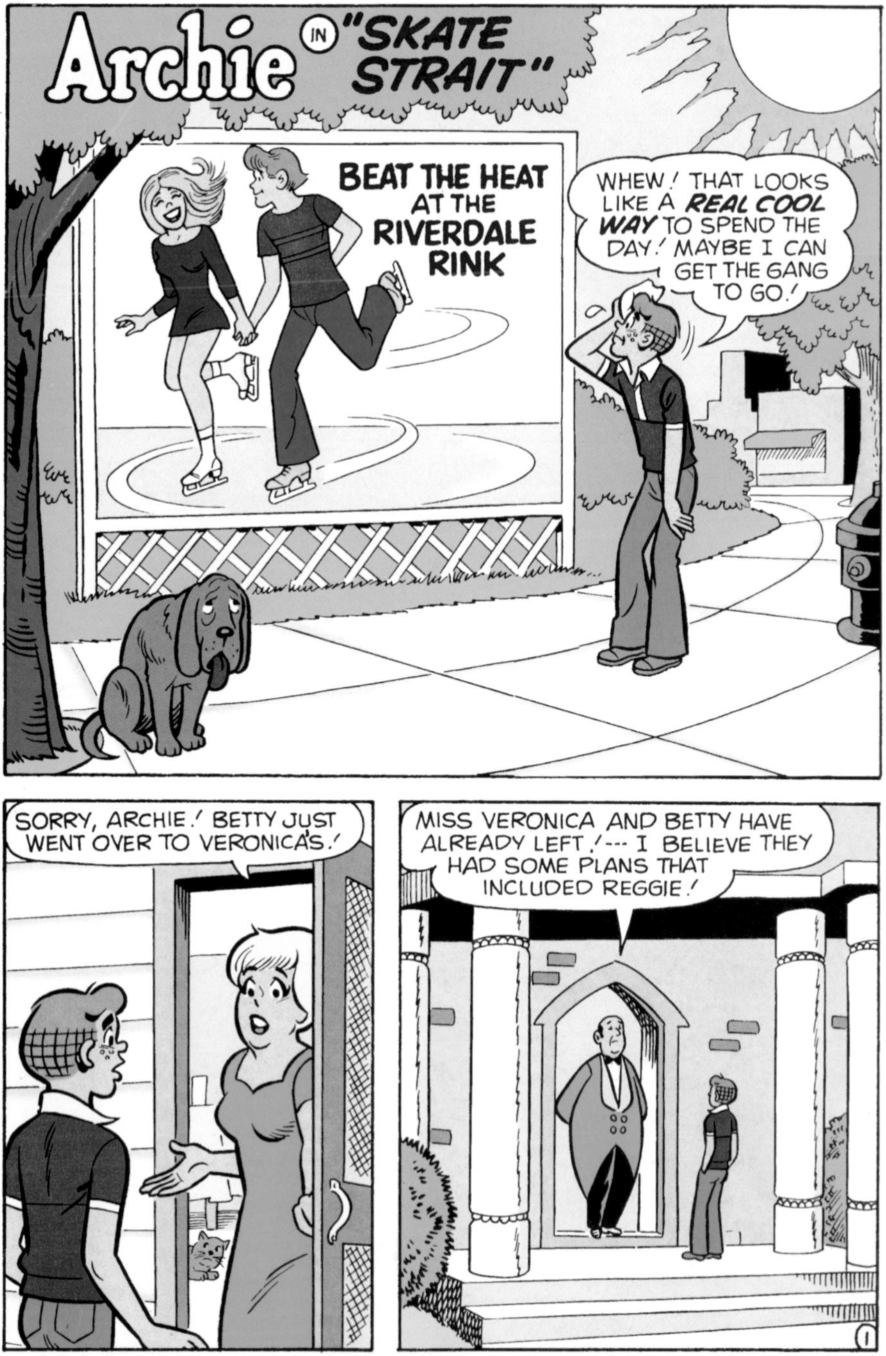
Archie IN "SKATE STRAIT"
BEAT THE HEAT AT THE RIVERDALE RINK
WHEW! THAT LOOKS LIKE A REAL COOL WAY TO SPEND THE DAY! MAYBE I CAN GET THE GANG TO GO!
SORRY, ARCHIE! BETTY JUST WENT OVER TO VERONICA'S!
MISS VERONICA AND BETTY HAVE ALREADY LEFT! --- I BELIEVE THEY HAD SOME PLANS THAT INCLUDED REGGIE!
1

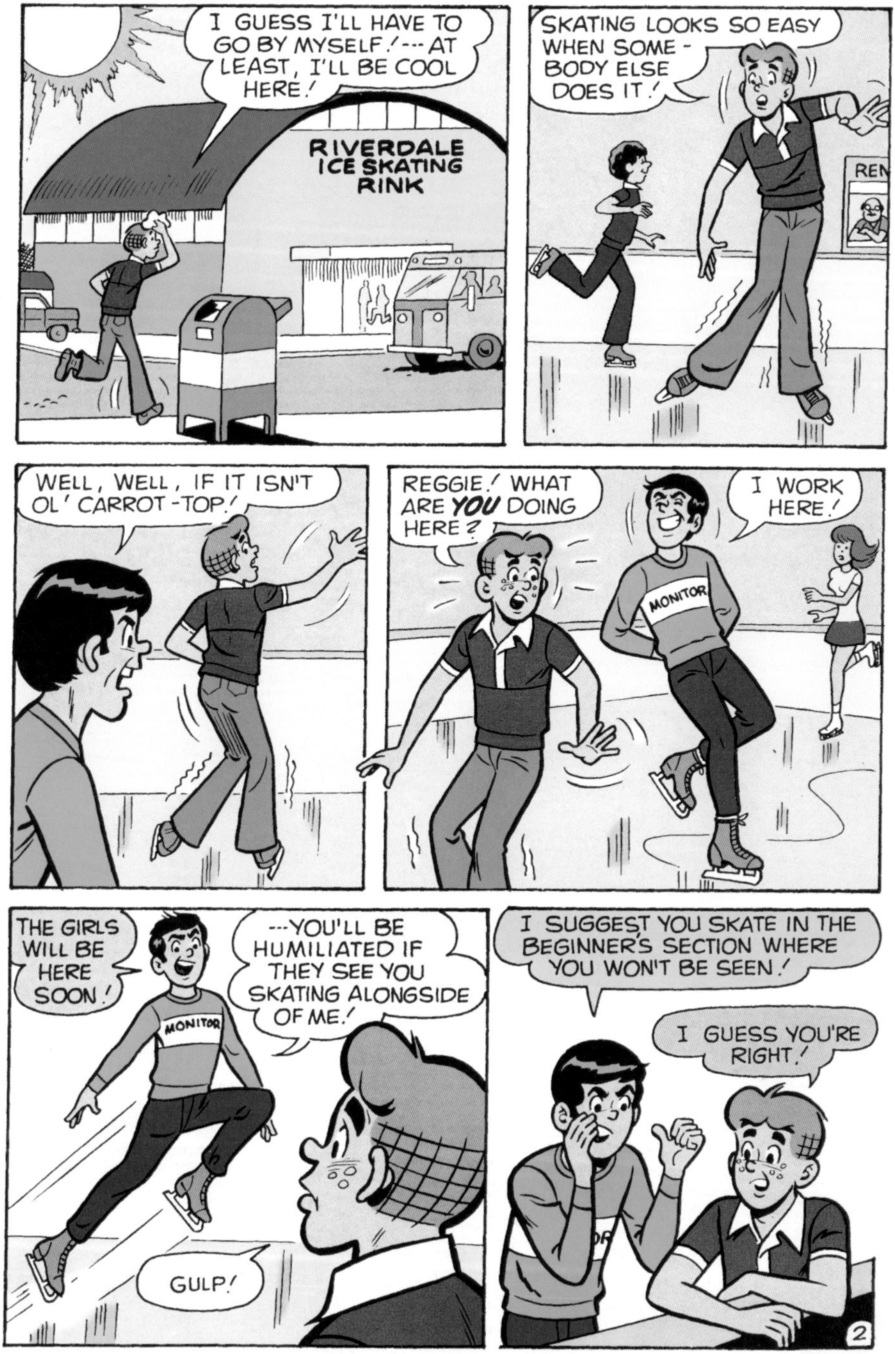
I GUESS I'LL HAVE TO GO BY MYSELF! --- AT LEAST, I'LL BE COOL HERE!
RIVERDALE ICE SKATING RINK
SKATING LOOKS SO EASY WHEN SOMEBODY ELSE DOES IT!
REN
WELL, WELL, IF IT ISN'T OL' CARROT-TOP!
REGGIE! WHAT ARE YOU DOING HERE?
I WORK HERE!
MONITOR
THE GIRLS WILL BE HERE SOON!
---YOU'LL BE HUMILIATED IF THEY SEE YOU SKATING ALONGSIDE OF ME!
MONITOR
GULP!
I SUGGEST YOU SKATE IN THE BEGINNER'S SECTION WHERE YOU WON'T BE SEEN!
I GUESS YOU'RE RIGHT!
2

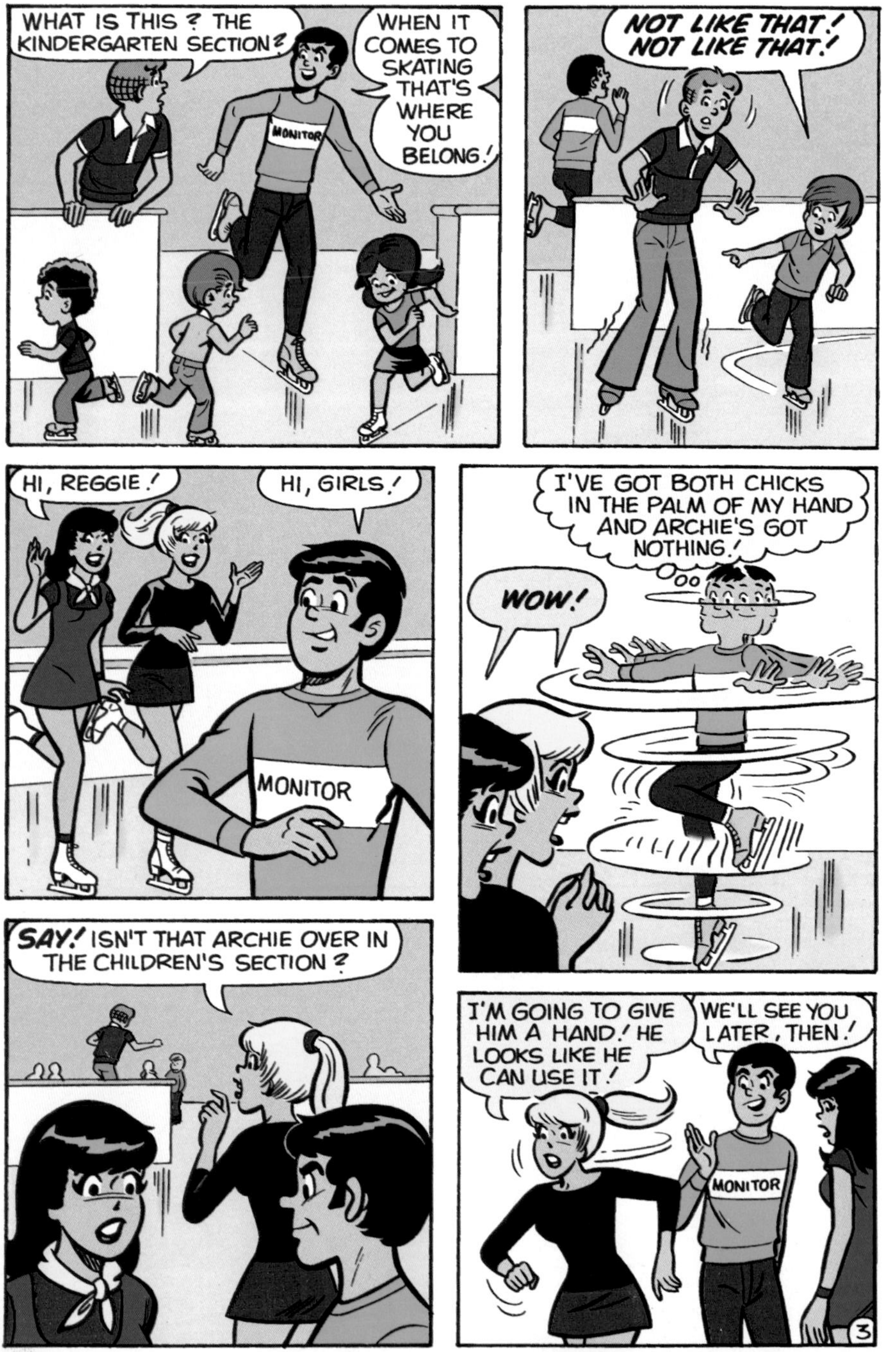
WHAT IS THIS? THE KINDERGARTEN SECTION?
WHEN IT COMES TO SKATING THAT'S WHERE YOU BELONG!
MONITOR
NOT LIKE THAT! NOT LIKE THAT!
HI, REGGIE!
HI, GIRLS!
MONITOR
I'VE GOT BOTH CHICKS IN THE PALM OF MY HAND AND ARCHIE'S GOT NOTHING!
WOW!
SAY! ISN'T THAT ARCHIE OVER IN THE CHILDREN'S SECTION?
I'M GOING TO GIVE HIM A HAND! HE LOOKS LIKE HE CAN USE IT!
WE'LL SEE YOU LATER, THEN!
MONITOR
3

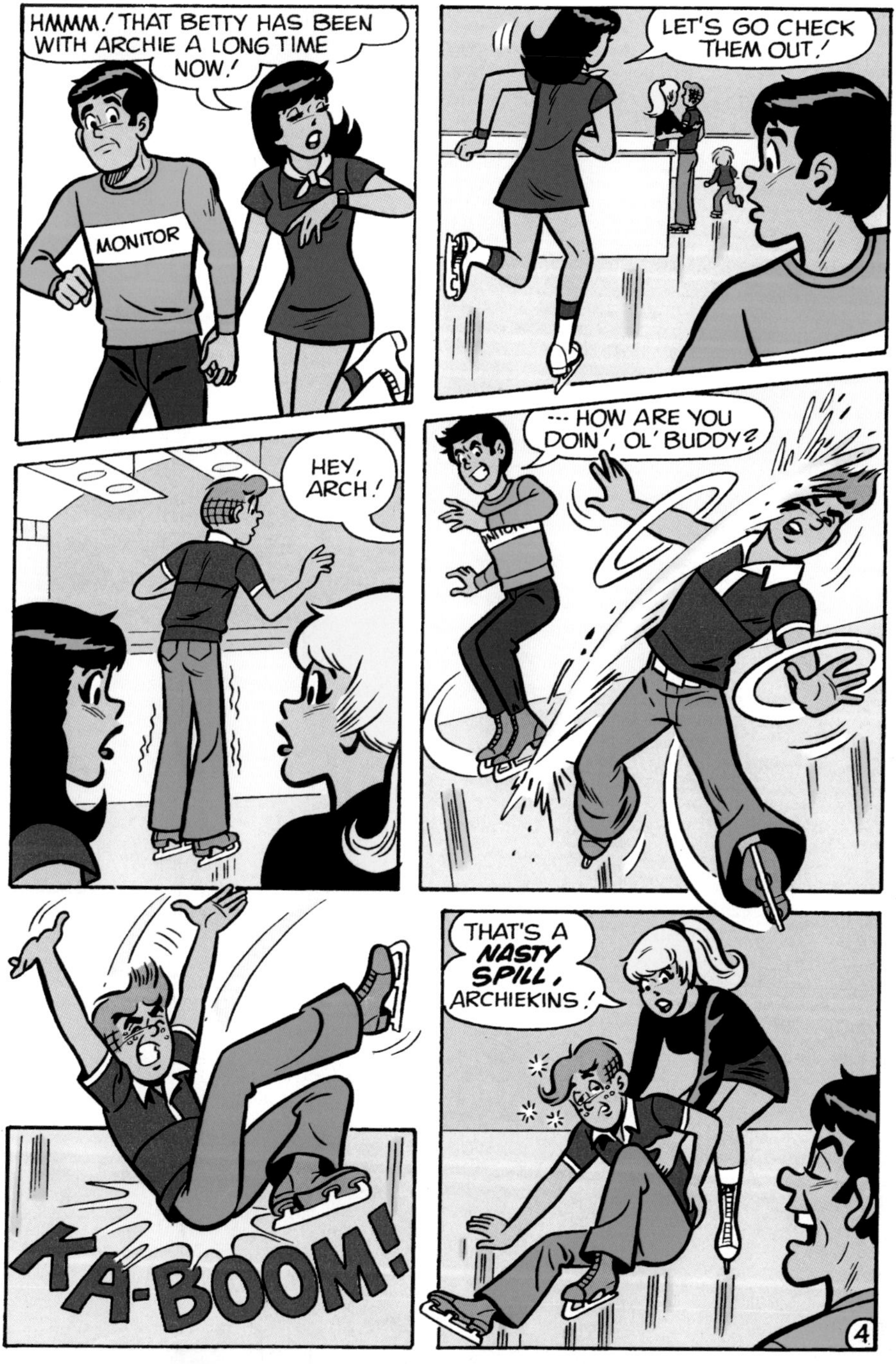
HMMM! THAT BETTY HAS BEEN WITH ARCHIE A LONG TIME NOW!
MONITOR
LET'S GO CHECK THEM OUT!
HEY, ARCH!
--- HOW ARE YOU DOIN', OL' BUDDY?
KA-BOOM!
THAT'S A NASTY SPILL, ARCHIEKINS!
4

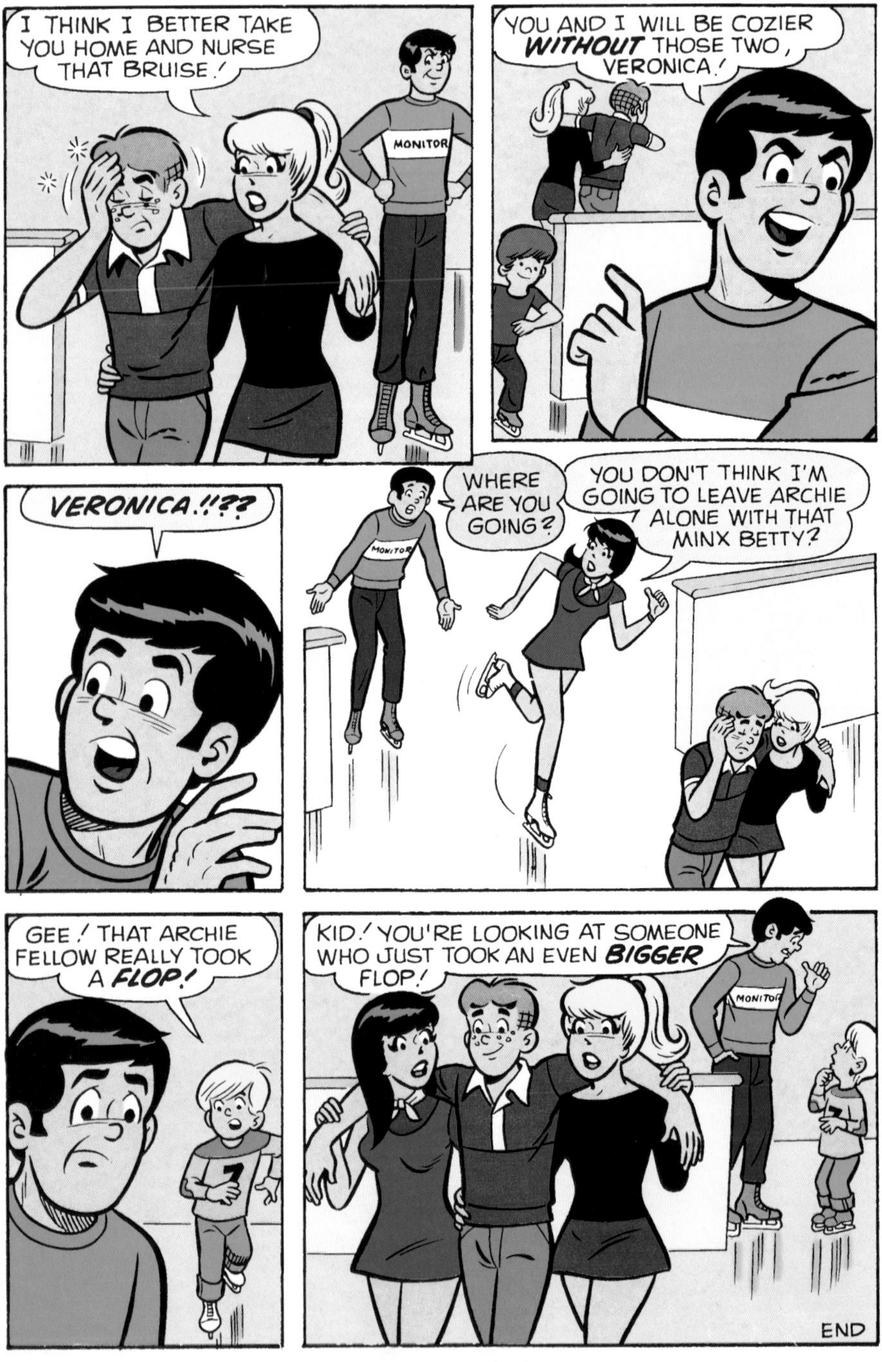
I THINK I BETTER TAKE YOU HOME AND NURSE THAT BRUISE!
MONITOR
YOU AND I WILL BE COZIER WITHOUT THOSE TWO, VERONICA!
VERONICA!!??
WHERE ARE YOU GOING?
MONITOR
YOU DON'T THINK I'M GOING TO LEAVE ARCHIE ALONE WITH THAT MINX BETTY?
GEE! THAT ARCHIE FELLOW REALLY TOOK A FLOP!
KID! YOU'RE LOOKING AT SOMEONE WHO JUST TOOK AN EVEN BIGGER FLOP!
MONITOR
END

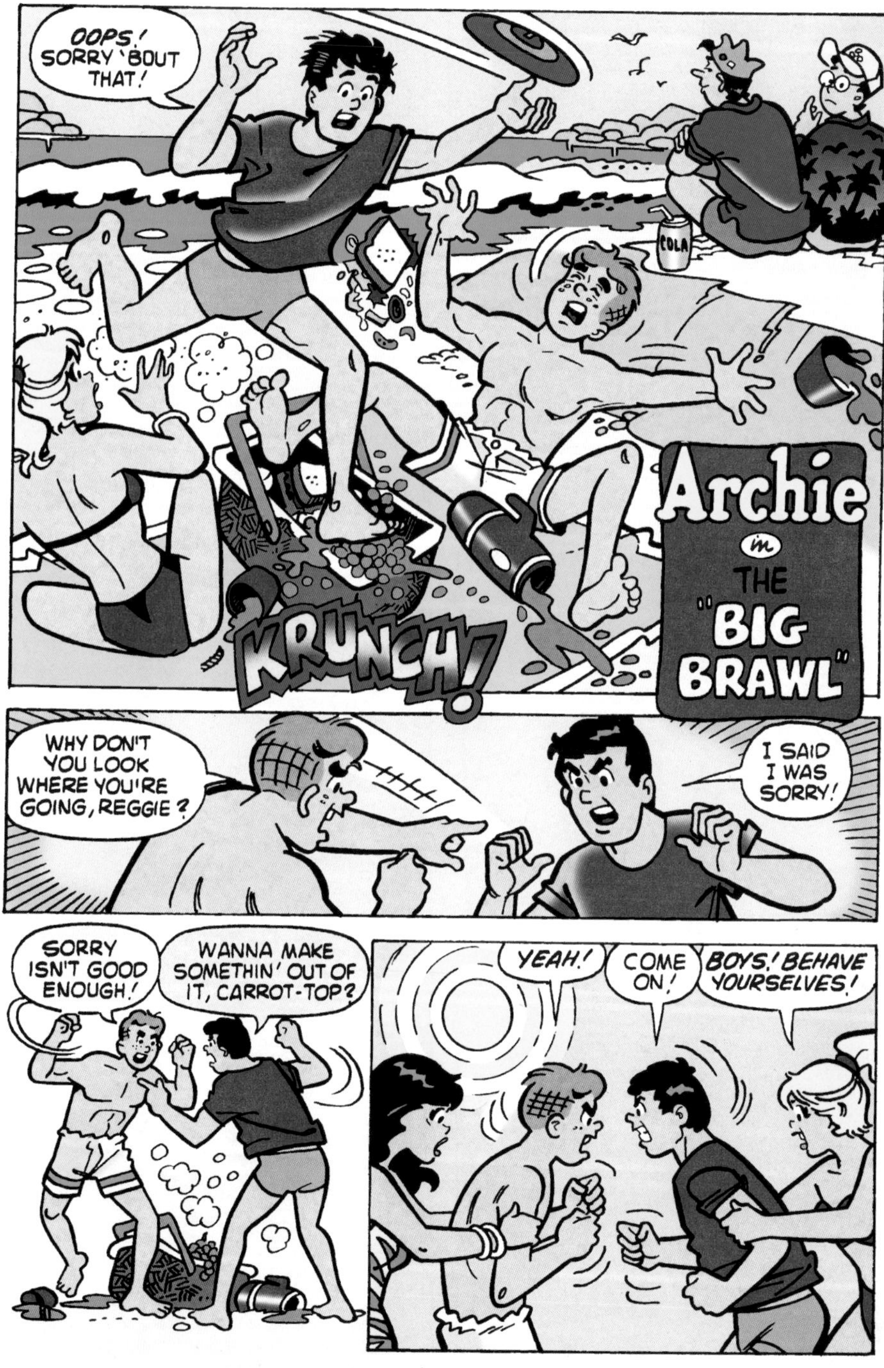
OOPS! SORRY 'BOUT THAT!
COLA
KRUNCH!
Archie in THE "BIG BRAWL"
WHY DON'T YOU LOOK WHERE YOU'RE GOING, REGGIE?
I SAID I WAS SORRY!
SORRY ISN'T GOOD ENOUGH!
WANNA MAKE SOMETHIN' OUT OF IT, CARROT-TOP?
YEAH!
COME ON!
BOYS! BEHAVE YOURSELVES!

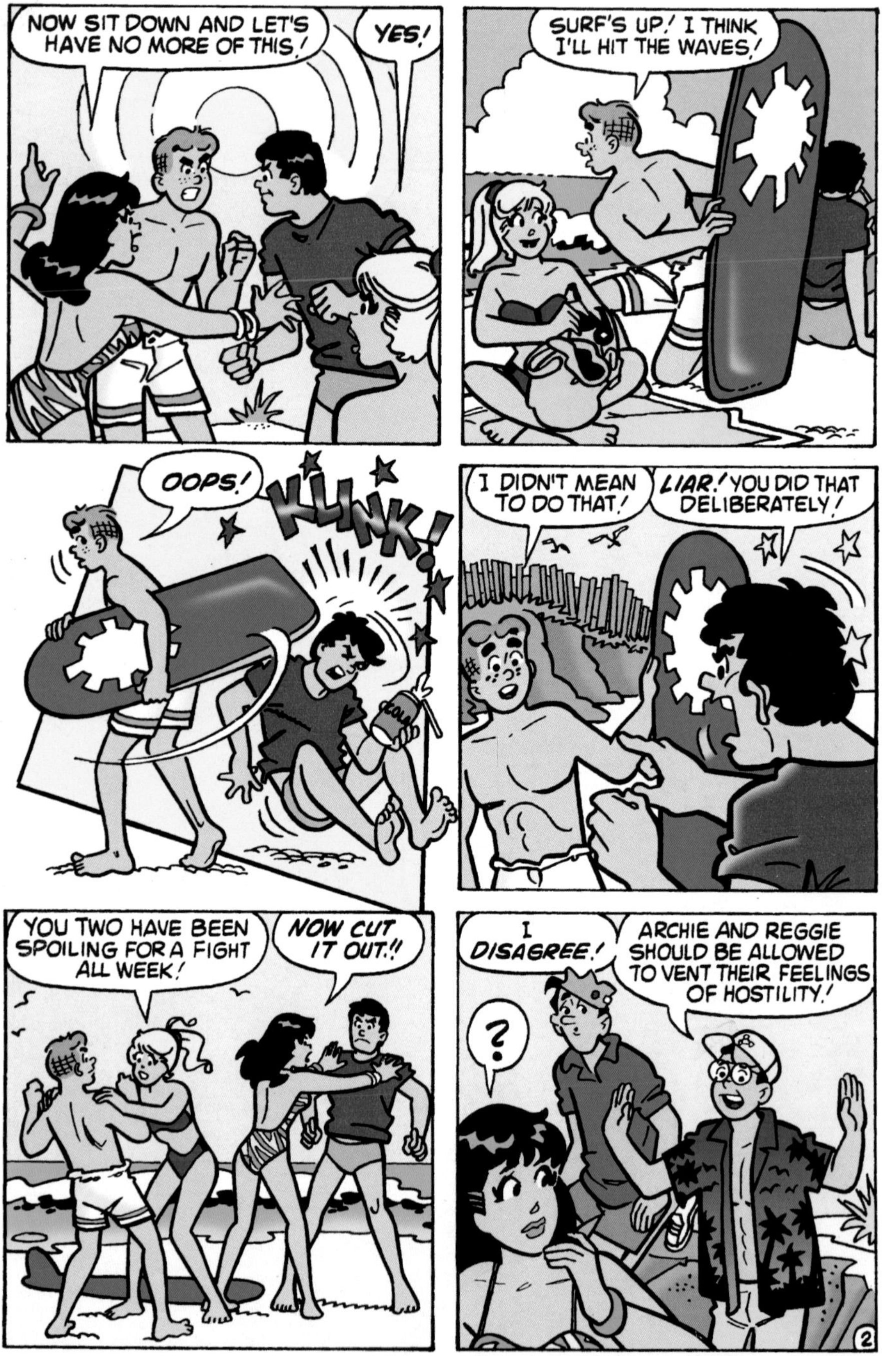
NOW SIT DOWN AND LET'S HAVE NO MORE OF THIS!
YES!
SURF'S UP! I THINK I'LL HIT THE WAVES!
OOPS!
KLUNK!
COLA
I DIDN'T MEAN TO DO THAT!
LIAR! YOU DID THAT DELIBERATELY!
YOU TWO HAVE BEEN SPOILING FOR A FIGHT ALL WEEK!
NOW CUT IT OUT!!
?
I DISAGREE!
ARCHIE AND REGGIE SHOULD BE ALLOWED TO VENT THEIR FEELINGS OF HOSTILITY!
2

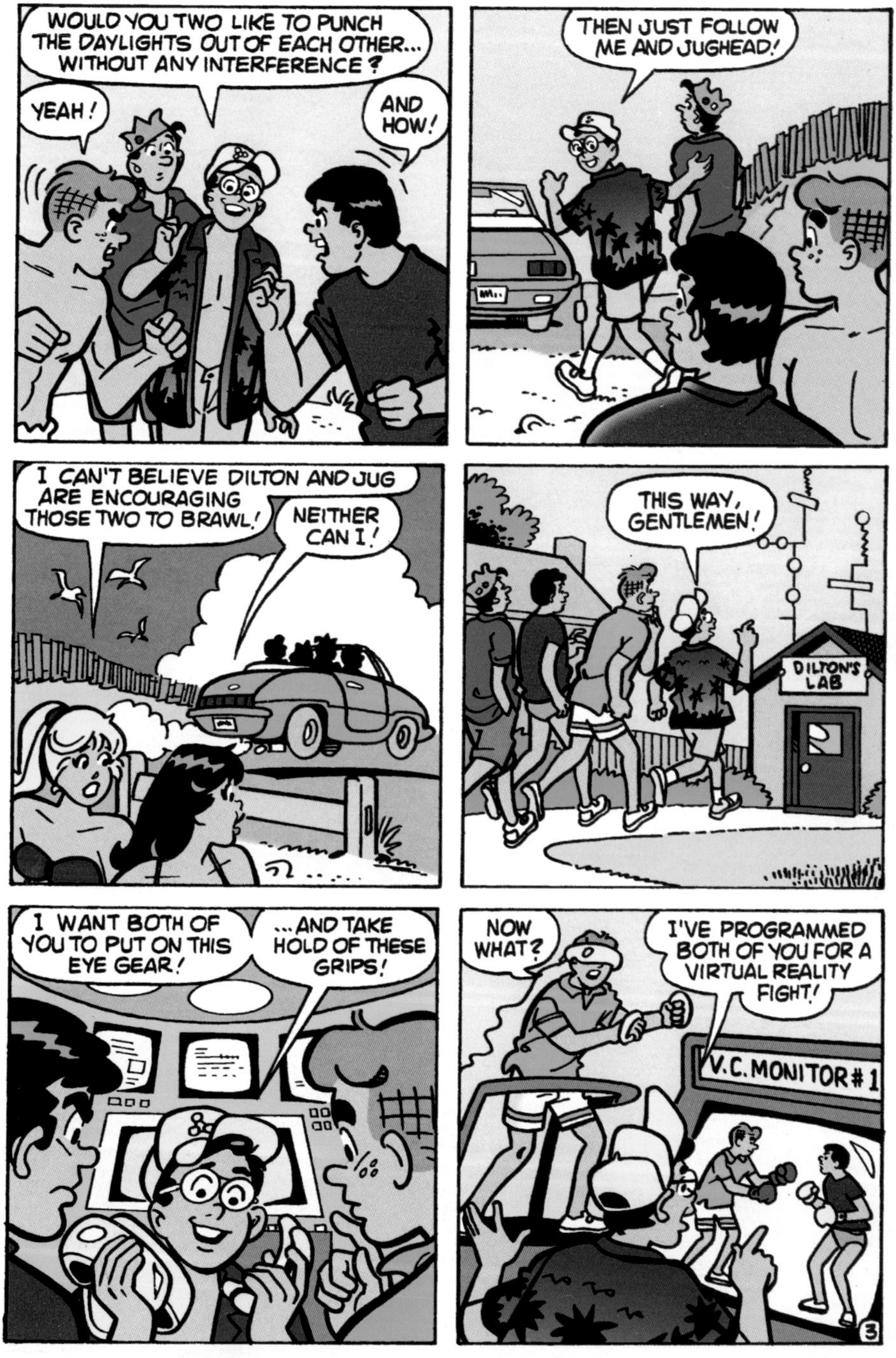
WOULD YOU TWO LIKE TO PUNCH THE DAYLIGHTS OUT OF EACH OTHER... WITHOUT ANY INTERFERENCE?
YEAH!
AND HOW!
THEN JUST FOLLOW ME AND JUGHEAD!
I CAN'T BELIEVE DILTON AND JUG ARE ENCOURAGING THOSE TWO TO BRAWL!
NEITHER CAN I!
THIS WAY, GENTLEMEN!
DILTON'S LAB
I WANT BOTH OF YOU TO PUT ON THIS EYE GEAR!
...AND TAKE HOLD OF THESE GRIPS!
NOW WHAT?
I'VE PROGRAMMED BOTH OF YOU FOR A VIRTUAL REALITY FIGHT!
V.C. MONITOR #1
3

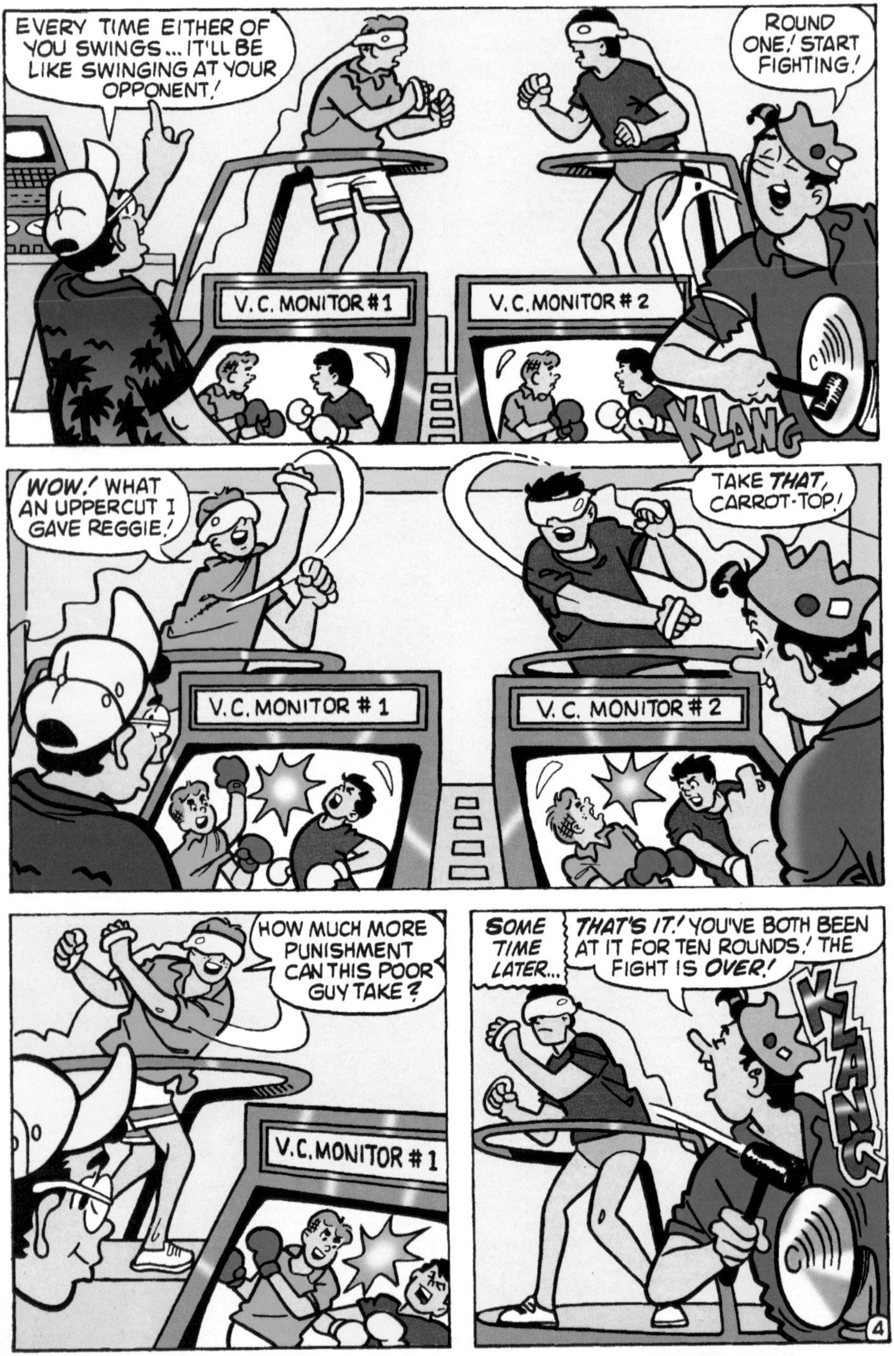
EVERY TIME EITHER OF YOU SWINGS... IT'LL BE LIKE SWINGING AT YOUR OPPONENT!
ROUND ONE! START FIGHTING!
V.C. MONITOR #1
V.C. MONITOR #2
KLANG
WOW! WHAT AN UPPERCUT I GAVE REGGIE!
TAKE THAT, CARROT-TOP!
V.C. MONITOR #1
V.C. MONITOR #2
HOW MUCH MORE PUNISHMENT CAN THIS POOR GUY TAKE?
V.C. MONITOR #1
SOME TIME LATER...
THAT'S IT! YOU'VE BOTH BEEN AT IT FOR TEN ROUNDS! THE FIGHT IS OVER!
KLANG
4

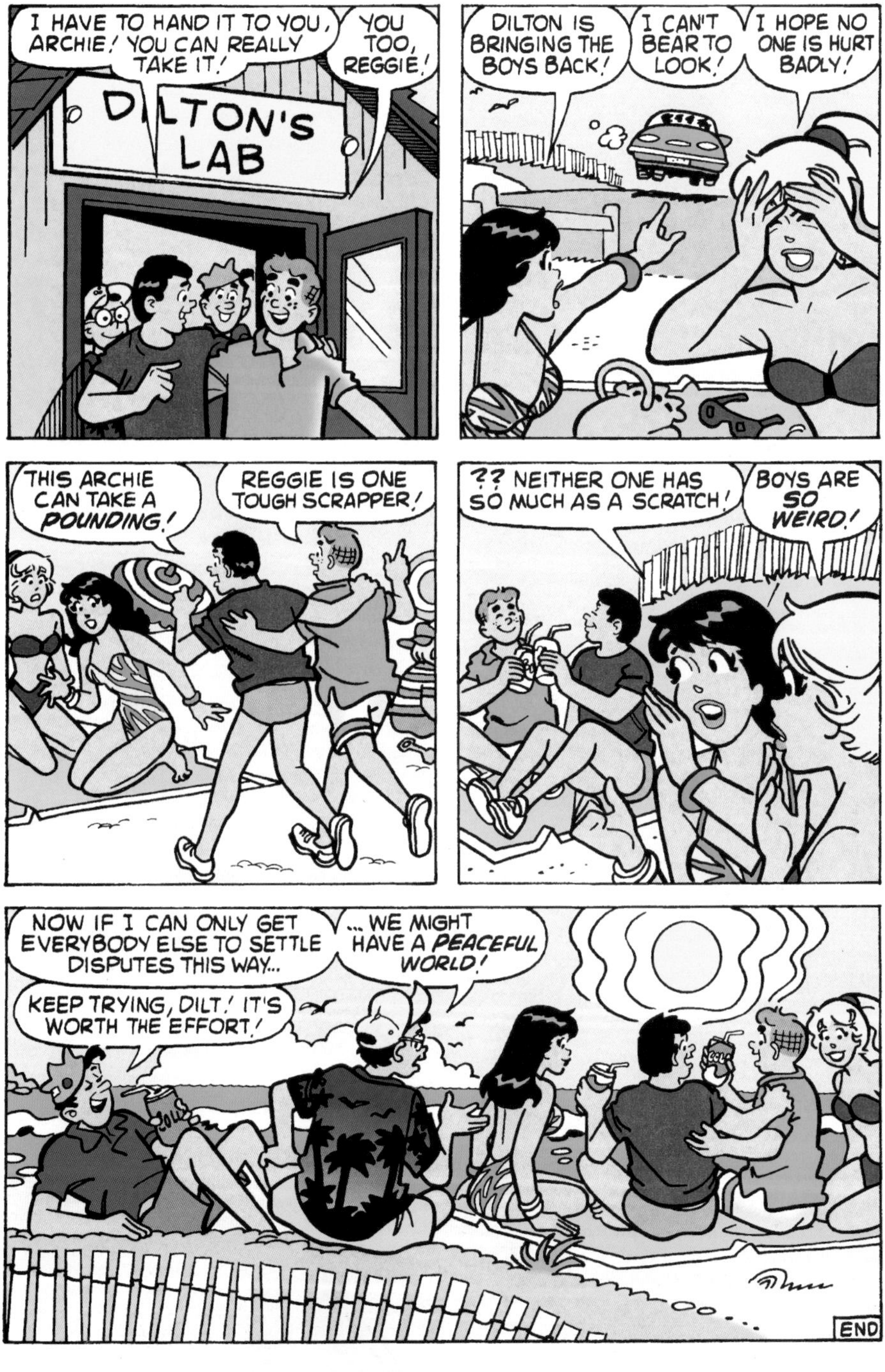
I HAVE TO HAND IT TO YOU, ARCHIE! YOU CAN REALLY TAKE IT!
YOU TOO, REGGIE!
DILTON'S LAB
DILTON IS BRINGING THE BOYS BACK!
I CAN'T BEAR TO LOOK!
I HOPE NO ONE IS HURT BADLY!
THIS ARCHIE CAN TAKE A POUNDING!
REGGIE IS ONE TOUGH SCRAPPER!
?? NEITHER ONE HAS SO MUCH AS A SCRATCH!
BOYS ARE SO WEIRD!
NOW IF I CAN ONLY GET EVERYBODY ELSE TO SETTLE DISPUTES THIS WAY...
... WE MIGHT HAVE A PEACEFUL WORLD!
KEEP TRYING, DILT! IT'S WORTH THE EFFORT!
END

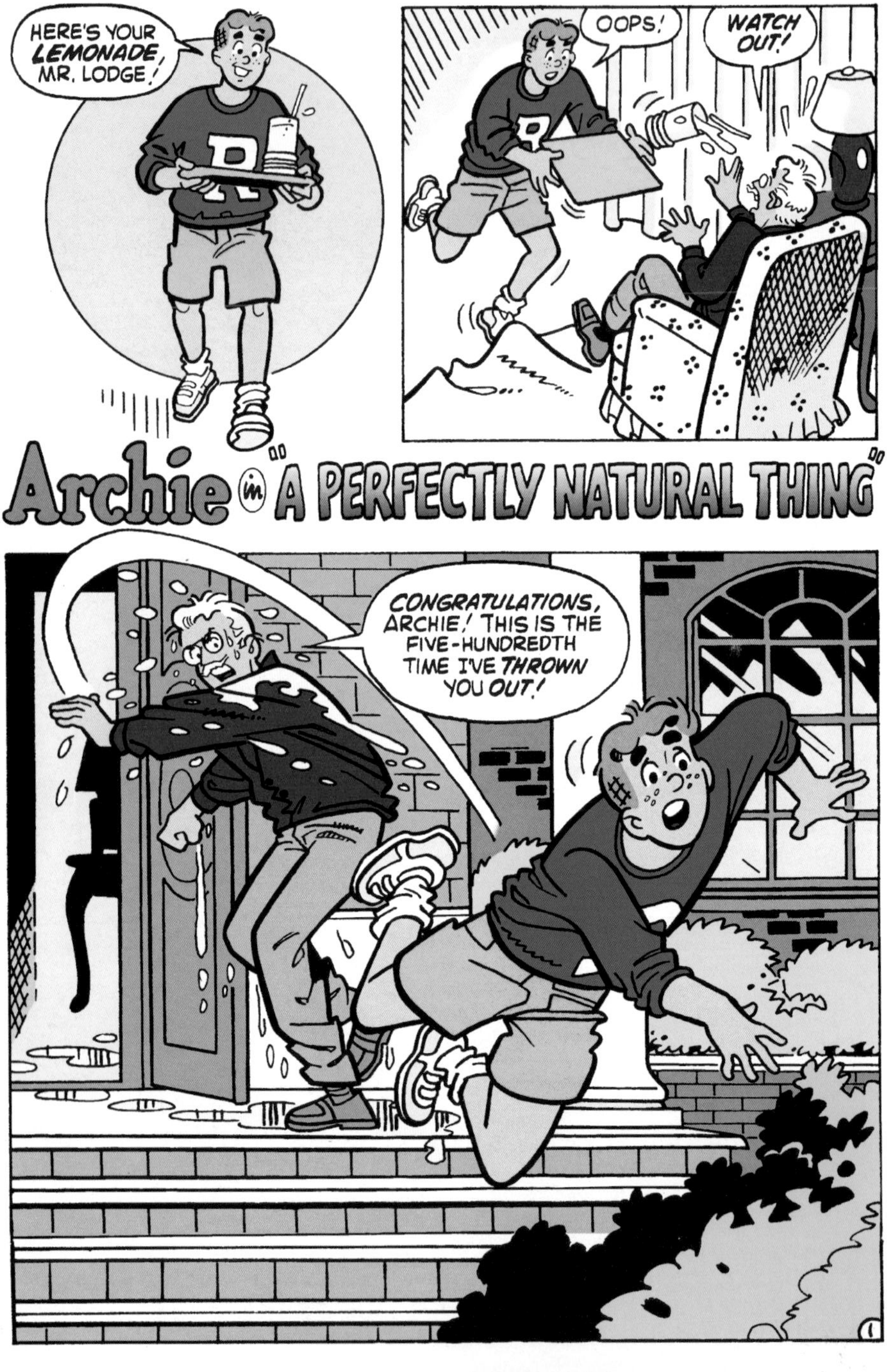
HERE'S YOUR LEMONADE, MR. LODGE!
OOPS!
WATCH OUT!
Archie in "A PERFECTLY NATURAL THING"
CONGRATULATIONS, ARCHIE! THIS IS THE FIVE-HUNDREDTH TIME I'VE THROWN YOU OUT!
1

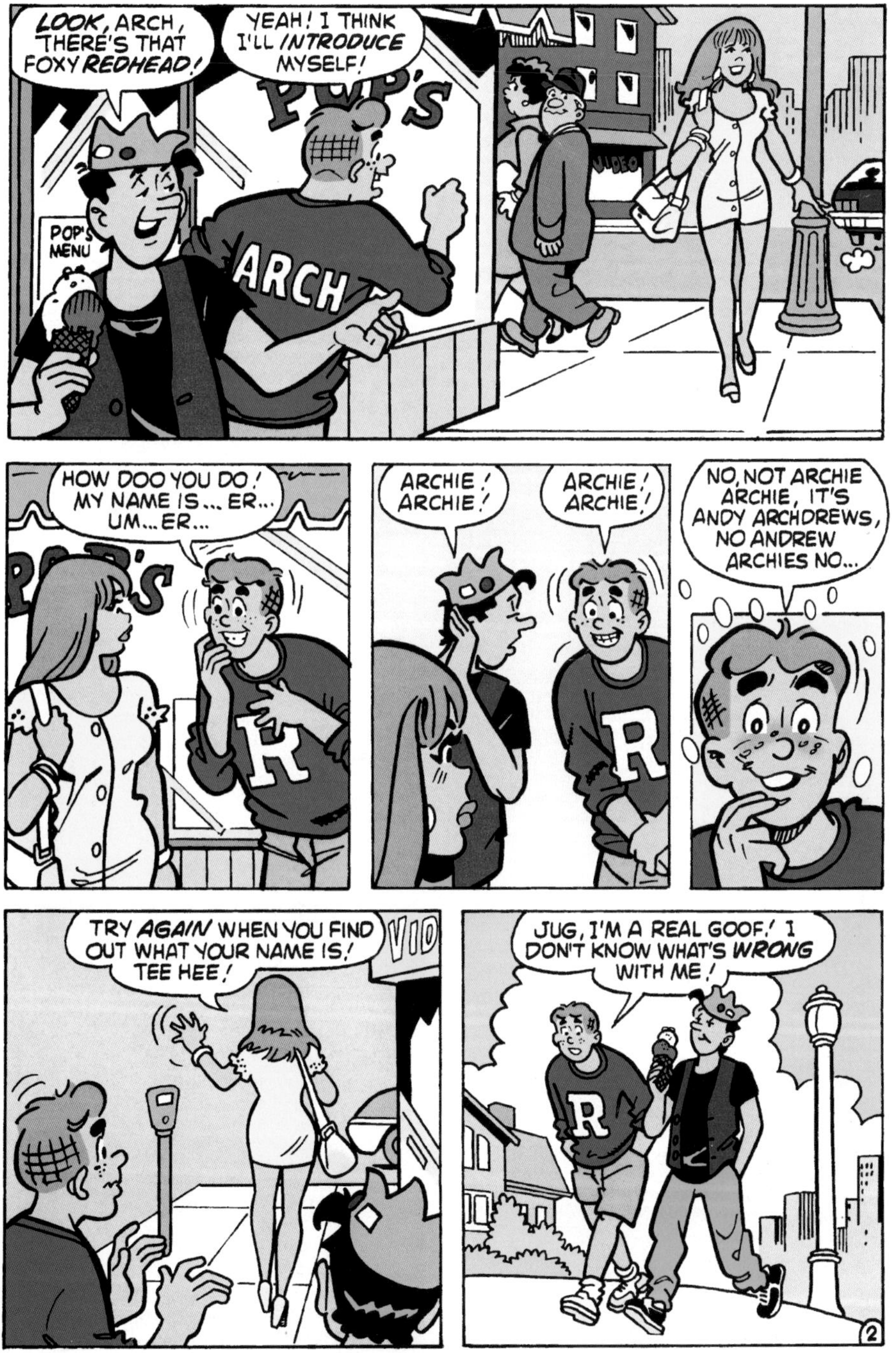
LOOK, ARCH, THERE'S THAT FOXY REDHEAD!
YEAH! I THINK I'LL INTRODUCE MYSELF!
POP'S
POP'S MENU
ARCH
VIDEO
HOW DOO YOU DO! MY NAME IS... ER... UM... ER...
ARCHIE! ARCHIE!
ARCHIE! ARCHIE!
NO, NOT ARCHIE ARCHIE, IT'S ANDY ARCHDREWS, NO ANDREW ARCHIES NO...
TRY AGAIN WHEN YOU FIND OUT WHAT YOUR NAME IS! TEE HEE!
VID
JUG, I'M A REAL GOOF! I DON'T KNOW WHAT'S WRONG WITH ME!
2

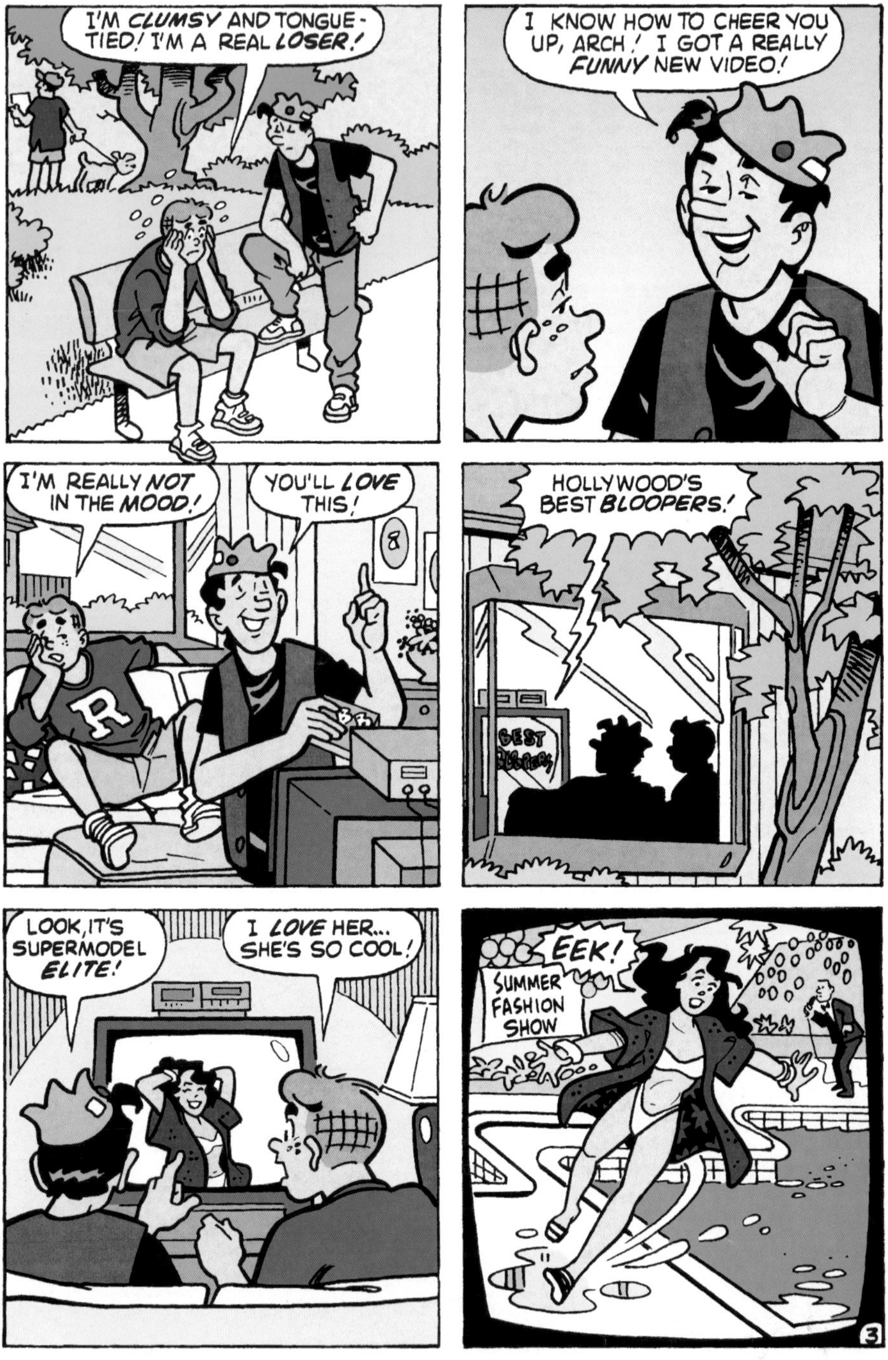
I'M CLUMSY AND TONGUE-TIED! I'M A REAL LOSER!
I KNOW HOW TO CHEER YOU UP, ARCH! I GOT A REALLY FUNNY NEW VIDEO!
I'M REALLY NOT IN THE MOOD!
YOU'LL LOVE THIS!
HOLLYWOOD'S BEST BLOOPERS!
BEST BLOOPERS
LOOK, IT'S SUPERMODEL ELITE!
I LOVE HER... SHE'S SO COOL!
EEK!
SUMMER FASHION SHOW
3

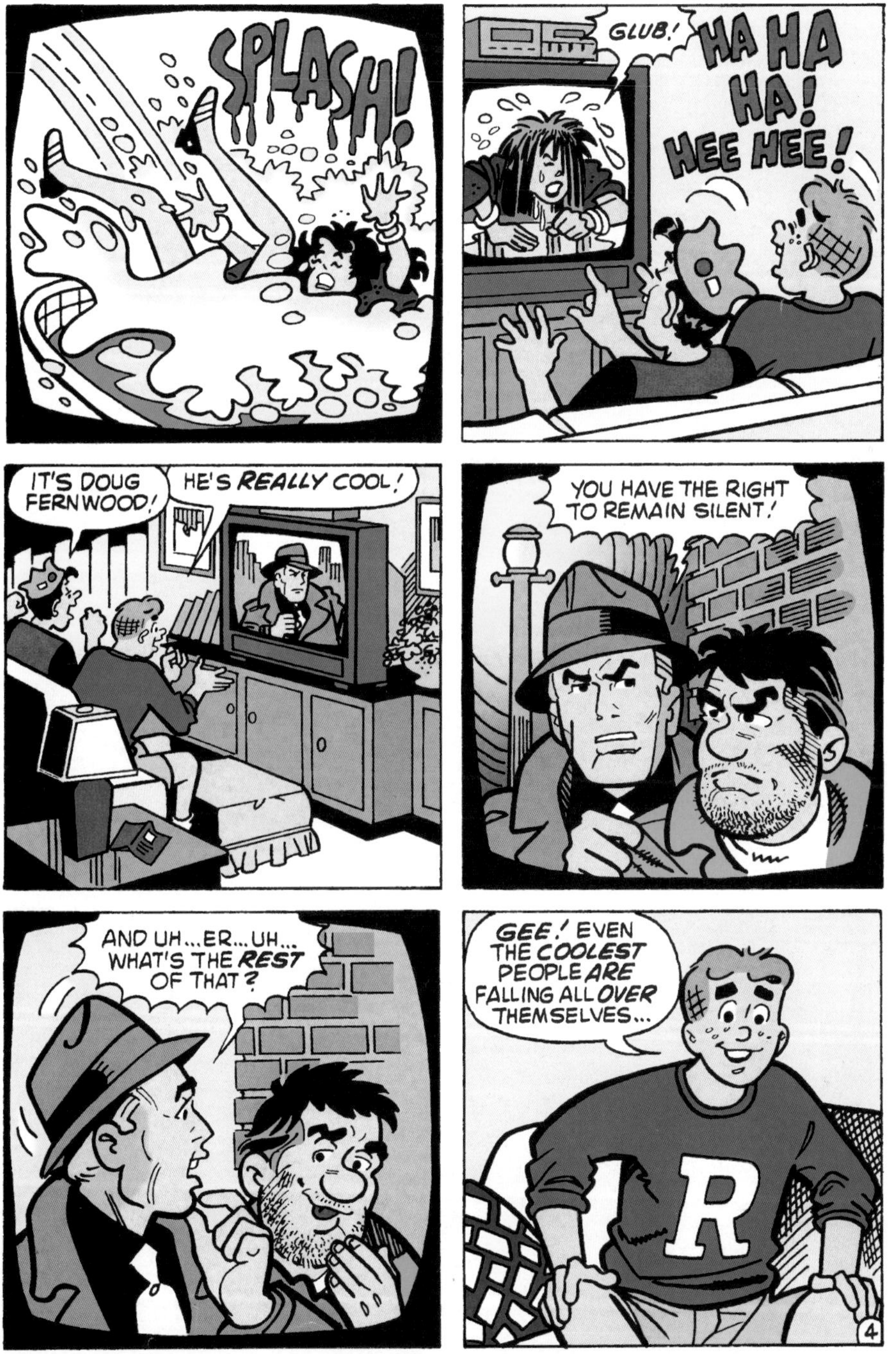
SPLASH!
GLUB!
HA HA HA! HEE HEE!
IT'S DOUG FERNWOOD!
HE'S REALLY COOL!
YOU HAVE THE RIGHT TO REMAIN SILENT!
AND UH...ER...UH... WHAT'S THE REST OF THAT?
GEE! EVEN THE COOLEST PEOPLE ARE FALLING ALL OVER THEMSELVES...
4

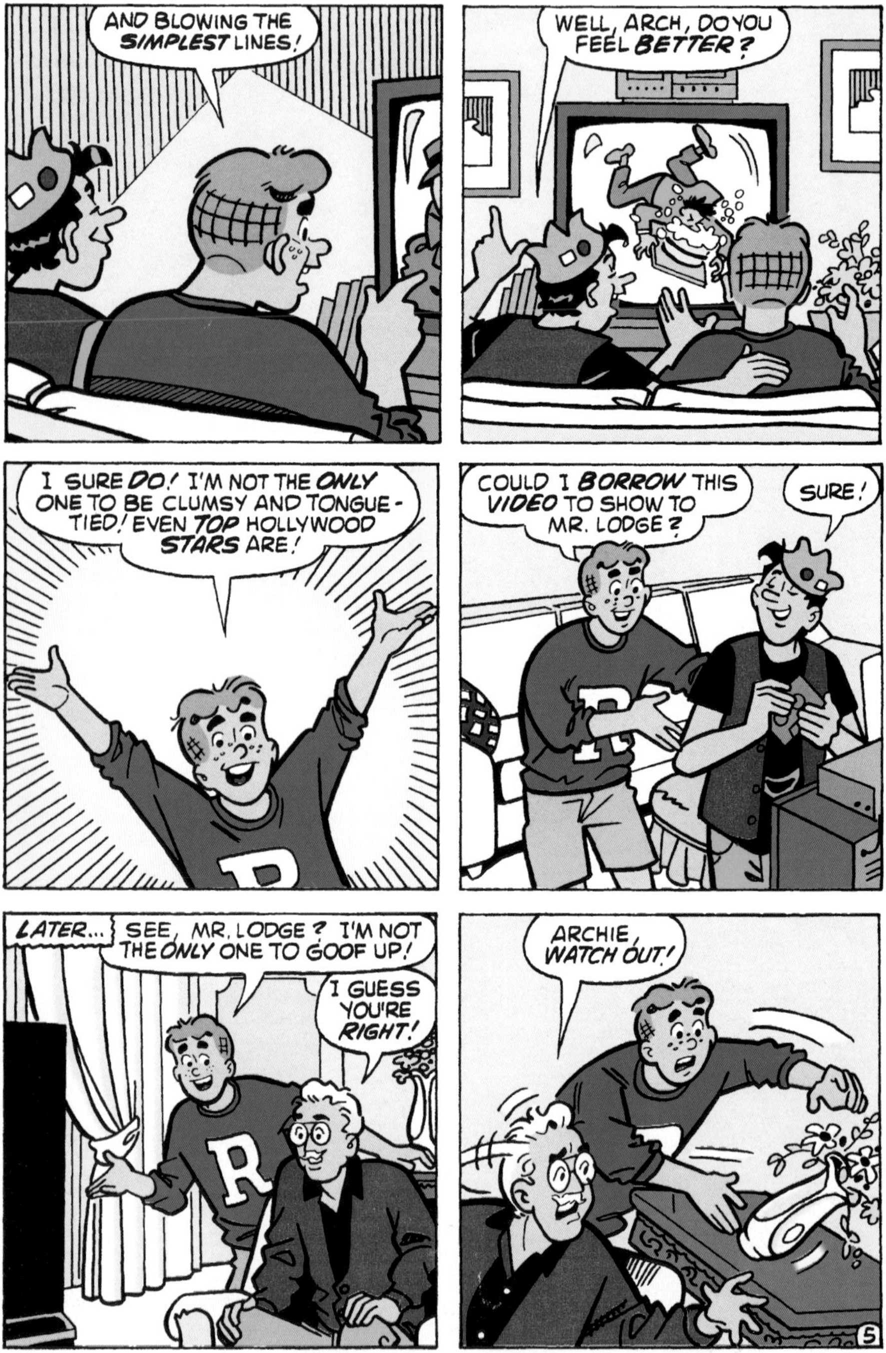
AND BLOWING THE SIMPLEST LINES!
WELL, ARCH, DO YOU FEEL BETTER?
I SURE DO! I'M NOT THE ONLY ONE TO BE CLUMSY AND TONGUE-TIED! EVEN TOP HOLLYWOOD STARS ARE!
COULD I BORROW THIS VIDEO TO SHOW TO MR. LODGE?
SURE!
LATER...
SEE, MR. LODGE? I'M NOT THE ONLY ONE TO GOOF UP!
I GUESS YOU'RE RIGHT!
ARCHIE, WATCH OUT!
5

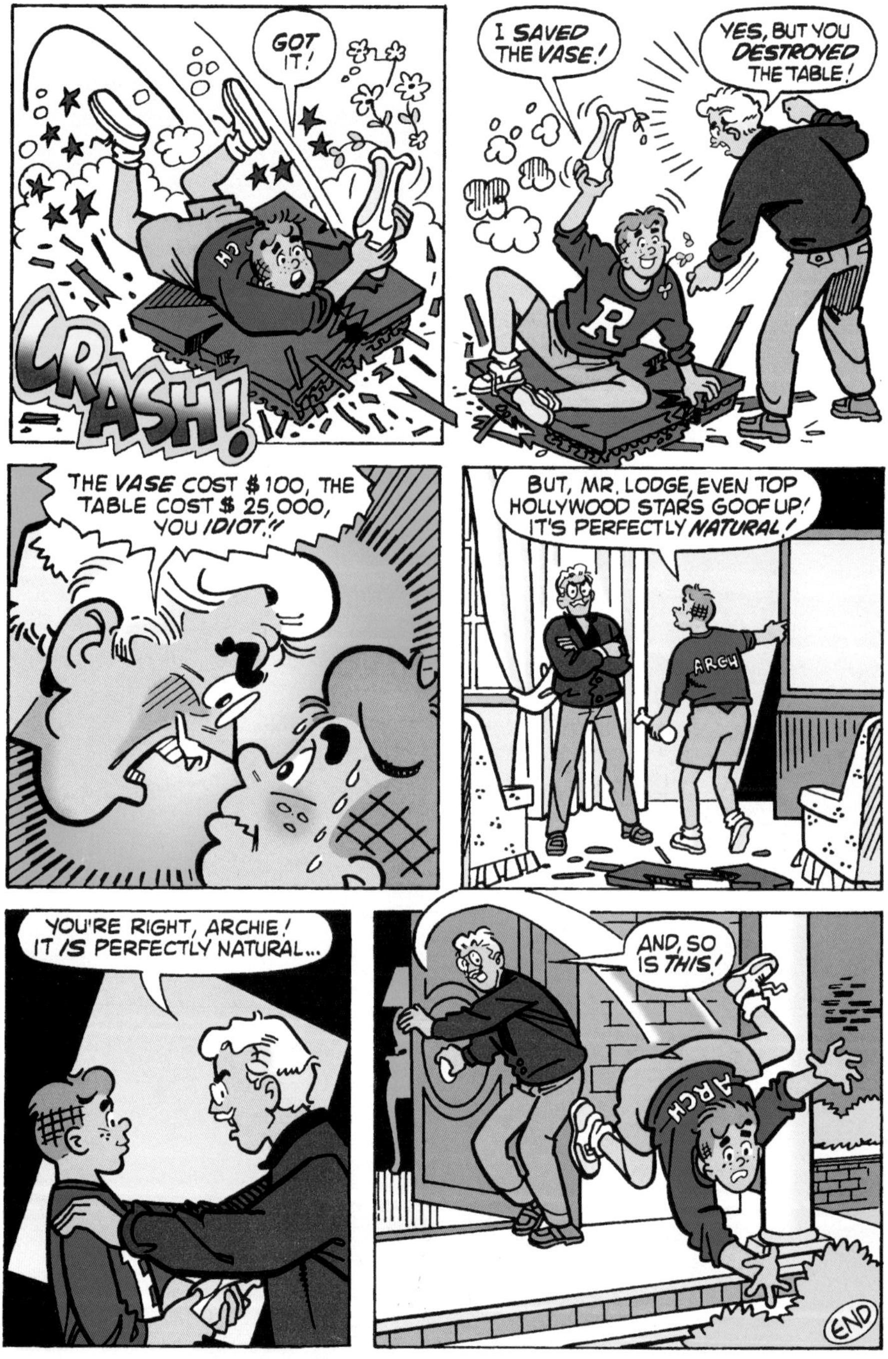
GOT IT!
CRASH!
I SAVED THE VASE!
YES, BUT YOU DESTROYED THE TABLE!
THE VASE COST $100, THE TABLE COST $25,000, YOU IDIOT!!
BUT, MR. LODGE, EVEN TOP HOLLYWOOD STARS GOOF UP! IT'S PERFECTLY NATURAL!
YOU'RE RIGHT, ARCHIE! IT IS PERFECTLY NATURAL...
AND, SO IS THIS!
END

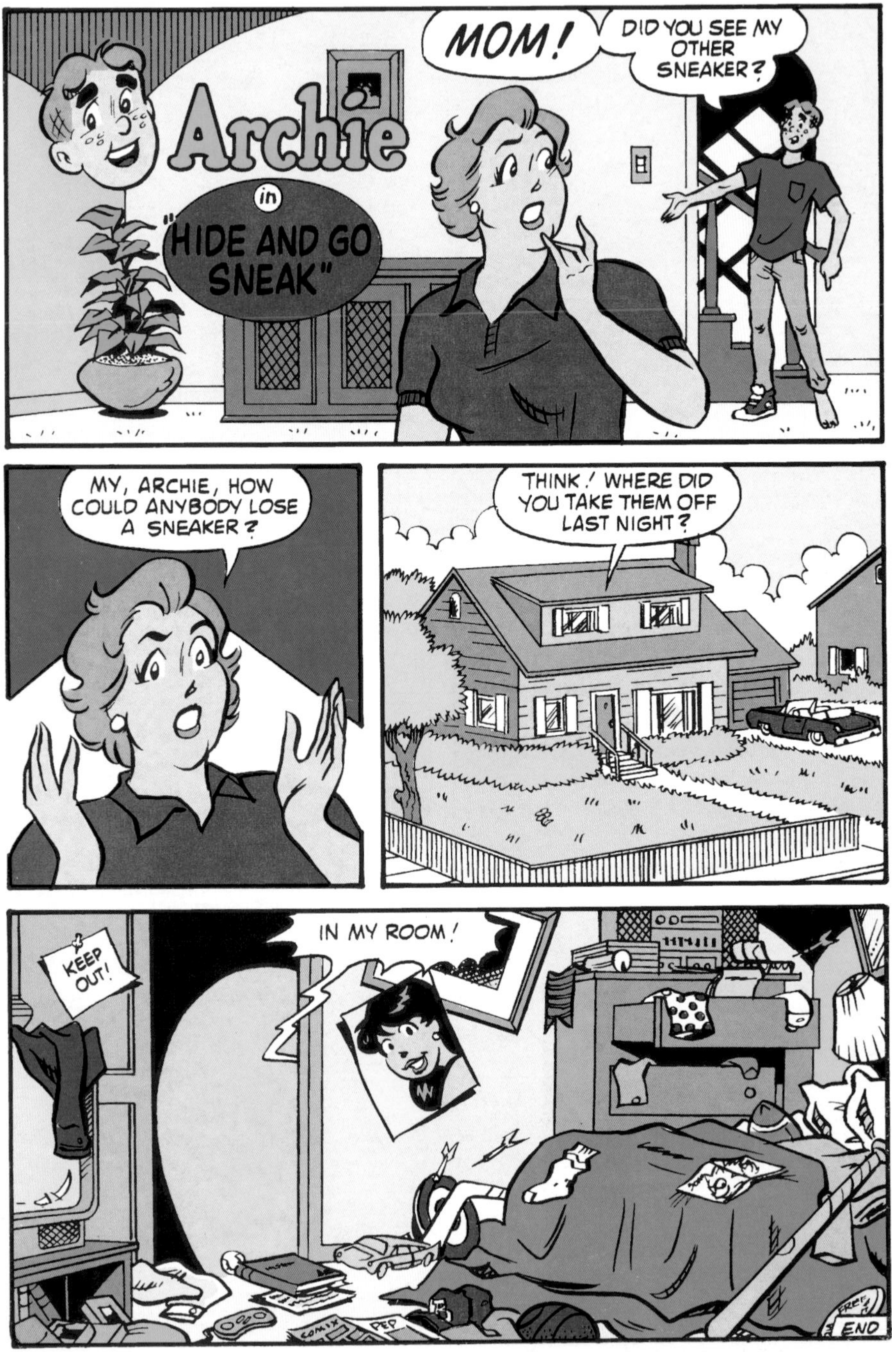
Archie
in
"HIDE AND GO SNEAK"
MOM!
DID YOU SEE MY OTHER SNEAKER?
MY, ARCHIE, HOW COULD ANYBODY LOSE A SNEAKER?
THINK! WHERE DID YOU TAKE THEM OFF LAST NIGHT?
KEEP OUT!
IN MY ROOM!
COMIX
PEP
END